War, Hell and Honor

A Novel of the French and Indian War

Brenton C. Kemmer

HERITAGE BOOKS
2007

HERITAGE BOOKS
AN IMPRINT OF HERITAGE BOOKS, INC.

Books, CDs, and more—Worldwide

For our listing of thousands of titles see our website
at
www.HeritageBooks.com

Published 2007 by
HERITAGE BOOKS, INC.
Publishing Division
65 East Main Street
Westminster, Maryland 21157-5026

Other books by Brenton C. Kemmer:

Redcoats, Yankees, and Allies:
A History of Uniforms, Clothing, and Gear of the British Army in the Lake George-Lake Champlain Corridor, 1755-1760

Freemen, Freeholders and Citizen Soldiers:
An Organizational History of Colonel Jonathan Bagley's Regiment, 1755-1760

The Partisans
Second in a Series of Novels of the French and Indian War (1756)

So, Ye Want to be a Reenactor? A Living History Handbook
Brenton C. Kemmer and Karen L. Kemmer

International Standard Book Number: 978-0-7884-1875-0

To my ancestors, my family,
my descendants yet to be;
and
to my "extended family,"

THE LIVING HISTORIANS

Reasons and Methods

In writing this story I selfishly chose the main character to be a lad from old Massachusetts-Bay. There are several reasons for this. First, my personal ancestry goes back to the 1600's in the colony. Second, I have an extremely large accumulation of primary sources from the soldiers of the era of the French and Indian War, specifically Colonel Bagley's Regiment. And third, I used this story to mentally slip into a different time; to time-travel, as it were.

Years ago I set a list of goals for myself. One of these was to write a novel. With the publication of this story that goal has been achieved. Not only is this novel a story of the "Battle of Lake George," but also it is meant to be a family military saga. Even now I am working on the second of the series.

The main objective of my research for this book was to derive the story from primary sources. In my quest to keep it as accurate as possible I have not changed the historical moments but only intertwined the main characters within actual events surrounding this battle. Also, in keeping historical precedence I have used diaries and letters for dialog as much as possible. I consciously tried not to change the historical atmosphere of 18th century military life, but rather tried to invite you, the reader, back to a different time: a time of values, a time of war, when men volunteered to fight for their feelings, communities, colony and their king and were taken from their structured New England lives and thrust into the hell and devastation of war. A time when a man's honor meant everything and no one could take it away from him. I hope you enjoy *War, Hell and Honor.*

Brenton C. Kemmer

THE DECISION

On this crisp morn in March of 1755, Charles Nurse's life would take a dramatic change.

At six o'clock the freezing fog was just clearing, leaving a crystalline coating on every work of nature and man. Another week was beginning on today's Sabbath as Charles stumbled from his featherbed, slowly walking to the hearth in the small "great room." He squatted near the gray ashes and felt cautiously for hot embers. After placing several pinecones into the ashes and erecting a new log fire, Charles reached for the iron blow tube, and slowly directed his breath through the pipe onto the coals until the cones burst into flames.

Several moments later, warmed by the hearth, he strolled to the window and peered out at the Powow River and his farm. The wooded lot to his east was coated with white remnants of the frozen early morning fog, resembling the white sparkling hair of his grandfather who had passed on just last month. To his west stood his small board and batten barn, weathered gray as his house, with its snow covered roof. Beside it mingled his horse, two cows, and six hogs, rooting in the hay pile he had spread for them the previous eve. Beyond the pens lay the rolling field of random snow, dirt, and greening weeds. The fog made the far edge of the ten-acre field barely visible, revealing glimpses of the stone fence surrounding his farm's boundaries. Near three hundred feet in front of his house, across the wagon road, the small Powow River meandered, clean and dark from its rich bottom soils. The fog was thick enough he could not see the opposite bank of the narrow brook.

As though still in a light sleep, he shook himself to consciousness and mixed some cold meal with fresh water and placed it over the hearth alongside a tin of hot water. Charles then sliced some brown bread, cheese and cold venison, placing it on the wooden tureen on his small trestle table. Then checking his meal on the hearth, Charles filled an old pewter porringer with the warm mush and placed a wedge of chocolate in a pewter mug of hot water. Silently he sat enjoying every spoonful of his morning meal.

Charles walked into the small bedchamber in the back of his small cottage. The little eight-by-eight room had only an old chair, rope-bed, and his grandfather's pine highboy his father had given him when his grandfather died. He traveled the rough pine plank floor to the highboy and started laying out fresh clothing for the Sabbath service and meeting: his new buckle shoes; brown wool breeches; his new flannel, gray waistcoat; and his green frock coat. He started dressing in the preparation for the arrival of his parents, Caleb and Margaret, and his younger brothers, William and Enoch. It was his custom to ride with his family to church on the Sabbath.

When he was nearly dressed and was combing his hair, Charles heard the sound of horses approaching. Quickly he grabbed his coat and went into the great room in time to greet his family. His cottage door swung open as William and Enoch entered, stomping their feet.

"If it's not the two misfits."

Enoch, the youngest, leaped six feet across the room, landing on Charles' back. Enoch was twelve, and though wiry and spry, did not even make Charles stumble. Charles, 22, was near six foot tall and had a well-defined, muscular body from ten years of working on the farm and building boats. He laughed and knocked Enoch to the floor with a gentle rap of the back of his right hand.

William, fifteen, stepped forward and picked up Enoch exclaiming, "Brothers, this would not be a good morning for getting hurt from a fight; Mother being ill is enough of a worry."

"What's that, Mother is ill?" questioned Charles.

"Mother woke with a pain in her head and a terrible cough. Father sent for Goodwife Greenleaf to come and see to her," answered William.

"Was she of the fever or chills?" asked Charles.

Enoch interrupted, "Got any food left from your morning? I haven't eaten anything today."

"Yes, cut yourself some cheese and bread," said Charles.

"Father wants us to go to meeting without them. He said it was important for you to make sure we have our prayers today," said Enoch, his mouth stuffed with cheese.

"I hope Mother doesn't have the fevers; maybe she worked too hard, being just recovered from the pleurisy. I am disappointed though; I wanted Father to be at the meeting after service. Moses Titcomb and Jon Bagley were bringing the congregation's men news about the war from Governor Shirley. I know how Father enjoys these meetings, especially when the old soldiers talk, refreshing his memory of Louisbourg," said Charles.

He slipped on his coat and grabbed his best tricorn off the peg by the door, and he and his brothers went to the barn and saddled his horse. The younger boys retrieved their horses, and off the three rode slowly to the west, toward the junction of the Powow and Merrimac Rivers.

Along their ride the brothers chatted and enjoyed the morning, discussing the melting of the snow, the beginnings of spring, and the possibility of the governor calling up troops for a new campaign. At the river junction the three riders passed the line of wharves and boat-building shops; Lowell's, Bagley's, Merrill's, Clough's, and others. They turned north on the main road of Amesbury flanked by dozens of cottages, Cape Cods, and "saltbox" houses. Most of these clapboard homes were weathered gray but several were painted black, red or white. As the lazy ride progressed, neighbors joined them on the road on horseback, in carts, wagons and on foot. The brothers eventually approached the top of the tiny knoll, and the Congregational meetinghouse came into view.

The house was the community building of Amesbury, utilized for church services and town meetings alike. The brothers' parents had been wed in the church, they had all been baptized within, and their grandfather had just been buried in the churchyard. The building measured about thirty by forty feet, and stood two stories high. The walls were grayed clapboards but the shakes on the roof were new. Several windows lined each side of the church, and two large, thirty-paned windows flanked the imposing double doors made of pine. A symmetrical, unstained, four-foot picket fence surrounded the meetinghouse grounds, and the Union Congregational Cemetery sat softly on the rolling hillock behind the fence. The road was congested with animals, carts, wagons and people as Charles and his brothers slid from their horses and tied them to the hitching post rings outside the front fence.

The congregation was filing through the front doors of the Amesbury meetinghouse as Charles and his brothers brushed the dust and morning moisture from their coats and walked toward the gate in the fence. Reverend John Wells stood by the doors, greeting parishioners as they entered. He was dressed in his black frock coat, waistcoat, and breeches of fine wool with dark gray, plush hose that matched his hair. About his neck he wore his Geneva collar, which was strikingly white.

As the brothers entered the gate, Samuel George greeted them. "Glad to see you on this fine morning."

"Glad to see you, Samuel," answered Charles.

Next, Dr. Putnam, his wife and their children passed and waved, "Hello, neighbor."

"Hello, Amos. Fine morning," replied Charles.

Then John Benjamin, the local blacksmith's assistant, came up and shook Charles' hand. "Where are your father and mother? I thought Caleb was anxious to hear Moses Titcomb's and Squire Bagley's meeting after services today."

"Mother is ill; we're hoping it is not the fever. I was also hoping to go to the meeting with him. Now I have my brothers to watch after," replied Charles in disappointment.

"Why don't Enoch and William go with my wife and daughter after services, and we can pick them up after the meeting? William knows Mary from school," offered Mr. Benjamin.

"But I want to join the army and fight the French!" interrupted William.

"No, Mother and Father would never allow it, and besides, everyone in the Amesbury militia knows you're not sixteen yet. Mr. Benjamin, that sounds like a good idea. I'll see you after services," said Charles.

Then after shaking Reverend Wells' hand, the brothers entered the meetinghouse. When filing in, one's eyes were drawn directly to the raised pulpit in the center of the room. It was mounted near six feet in the air, lofting the minister toward the heavens during sermons. In front, under the pulpit at a long pine table sat the deacons and elders, and on each side of the central aisle were rows of straight-backed, short-seated, wooden pews. As was the custom since the time of their Puritan ancestors, the men were seated in the pews on the right of the pulpit and the women were seated on the left. Further seating distinction was made with the most prominent members of the community sitting in their purchased pews in the front, while others took their places further toward the rear of the meetinghouse. A balcony in the back also held pews for Indians, slaves, indentured servants and the poor. Charles and his brothers took their seats near the middle of the meetinghouse and a hush fell over the congregation as Reverend Wells climbed into his pulpit.

"Let us pray. Oh, Lord Jehovah, thank You for this fine day and the gathering of so many wonderful parishioners. You have shown Your grace on us this week by bringing Spring to us and offering the return of some of our waterfowl. I am asking You, Jehovah, to stop the fevers from affecting more of our town; possibly Your Spring will help us defeat this before it becomes an epidemic." The Reverend paused. "Lord, the French and their heathen allies have been tormenting our Massachusetts borders too long. They have taken their toll on frontier communities such as Deerfield and we pray for Your assistance in our quest to drive the papists and the devil's heathen Indians from Your, Christ Jehovah's, lands! I ask You, oh Lord, to be with us at our meeting following our service. Several men, including our own Jonathan Bagley, are here to bring us new information from our Governor William Shirley. Please, Lord, keep us safe in Your plans, and in our preparations to subdue Your and our enemies, in God's name, Amen."

Then for the next two hours the Reverend Wells expounded on the glory of God and His march to drive the heathen and Catholics from North America. He intertwined doctrine with contemporary examples and utilized his readings to inspire and encourage his congregation for the following meeting. Charles heard only part of the sermon as his mind churned from worry about his mother, the disappointment of not having his father to accompany him to the meeting, and the anxiety of wondering if the meeting was meant to recruit from the militia for the upcoming campaign the townsmen had been talking about.

Suddenly Charles stirred to consciousness as Reverend Wells was finishing the final prayer. Enoch anxiously jumped to his feet, ready to move again, and William and Charles reverently rose. The congregation filed slowly from the meetinghouse, congratulating Reverend Wells on his inspiring sermon. As the brothers exited through the large doors, families were loading wives and children into their wagons and carts. William, Enoch, and Mrs. Benjamin and Mary climbed in the Benjamins' rickety cart and drove away.

As the women and children drove away, the men filed back into the meetinghouse with a hum about them, discussing the possibilities of the meeting. There was great anxiety as they awaited and speculated about the news. Quietly a group of men took their seats at the deacon's table in the front of the meetinghouse. When all were finally seated, Jonathan Bagley stood to address the crowd.

Bagley was a 38-year-old wharf owner who had prospered in Amesbury. He was of medium build, with very dark straight hair and coal colored eyes. His most distinguishing feature was his large hooked nose. Many present knew him and his family, who had resided in the community for years. His father, Orlando, had been one of the town's fathers, and now Jonathan was one of the town's leaders.

"Gentlemen, we have called this meeting not only because of the interest in our community, but also at the orders of Governor William Shirley of our fine colony. Many of you who participated in the Great Louisbourg Expedition served with me, and many of you know Colonel Moses Titcomb from his valiant command of his Bay Colony battery in '45." Bagley pointed his hand graciously at Moses Titcomb, who was seated beside him. He continued, "I would like at this time to reunite and introduce to you the spokesman for this meeting, Colonel Moses Titcomb."

Moses Titcomb rose. "Thank you, Squire Bagley. Governor Shirley has entrusted in me vital information to deliver to you, the men of Amesbury. It has become paramount for the colony of Massachusetts-Bay to unite and force our might upon the French and their Indians. As you could understand from the good Reverend's invigorating sermon, this is not only a war of colonies and countries, but a Holy War as well. In meetings with British forces' representatives, colonial governors, and representatives of the various legislatures, we have made a decision to mount a catastrophic assault against our enemies," he paused, "your enemies, the French and Heathens! I have been sent here directly to enlist as many of you as possible for this campaign.

"The governor has commissioned me colonel of the Essex County Regiment. Mr. Shirley has given me full authorization and blank commissions to designate my officers within this county regiment. It is my hope, and his, that this regiment be formed of the most enthusiastic men in our colony! Seated here with me," he waved his hand in gesture across the table, "are some of our officer corps that I and some of the other communities have selected. Let me introduce my second in command, whom you already know, Lieutenant Colonel Jonathan Bagley, our Major, Mr. Nicholes, and Captains Burk and Webster. It is the hope of your colony, and these men seated here at this table, that you understand the important role you can play for your families by enlisting in this regiment! Captain Burk," he commanded, "read the beating orders issued you for the regiment from Governor Shirley!"

Captain John Burk stood and read:

"One. You are to enlist no person under the age of eighteen years, nor above forty-five years.

"Two. You are to enlist none but able-bodied effective men, free from all bodily ails, and of perfect limbs.

"Three. You are to enlist no Roman-Catholic, nor any under five feet two inches high without their shoes.

"Four. You are to assure such persons as shall enlist, that they shall enter into pay and subsistence upon their first general rendezvous.

"Five. That they shall at the day of their enlistment receive a good blanket and bounty for a good firelock.

"Six. That their pay will be 26 shillings and 8 pence, per month, lawful money, during their service, one month and a day upon being mustered.

"Seven. That they shall be exempt from all impresses for three years next after their discharge.

"Eight. To such of them as shall be provided with sufficient arms at their first muster, they shall be allowed a dollar over and above their wages, and full recompense for such of their arms as shall be inevitably lost or spoiled.

"Nine. You are to enlist no person but such as you can be answerable for that they are fit for service; and whom you have good reason to think will not desert the service.

"Ten. You are before your delivering the blanket allowed, or any other bounty that may be allowed by this government to any person, to cause the second and sixth sections of war to be read to them, and have them also sworn before, and their enlisting attested by, a Justice of the Peace."

"Thank you, Captain." said Colonel Titcomb. "We will now entertain your questions, gentlemen."

Gideon Lowell, ship builder and owner of a wharf, stood and asked, "How many men are being recruited from Massachusetts to attack the French?"

"The governor has directed his regimental colonels to recruit 4,500 men." replied Titcomb.

Timothy Colby stood and asked, "What about the other colonies, are they to hold up their end in this fight, or are we to carry the entire British empire on our backs?"

"According to the figures I received from the governor, Connecticut is to recruit 1,200 men, New York 800, New Hampshire 500, and Rhode Island 400," answered Titcomb.

Thomas Greenleaf, a carpenter, stood and asked loudly, "Are we to serve with the redcoats or are we going to fight in our own army, like at Louisbourg!"

"Mr. Greenleaf," responded Stephen Webster, "we are under the understanding that the men of this colony are to be united in an all provincial army with only advisers from His Majesty's Regiments."

Joseph Nicholes asked, "How long are we enlisting for?"

Colonel Titcomb responded, "You're promising eight months in the service of your King and colony, Sir."

"When is our muster?" asked Samuel George. "Some of us have businesses and crops to plant."

"All Amesbury men must march to Boston to be mustered in on May 28," directed Colonel Titcomb.

There was a lull in the questioning and the men began to talk amongst each other. John Benjamin talked anxiously to the men around him. He could see the possibility of furthering his profession in a colonial regiment and after mustering out, perhaps being able to start his own shop, maybe even toward the west. Charles, on the other hand, was confused and wanted to discuss the possibilities with his family before committing to military service.

Colonel Titcomb and Lieutenant Colonel Bagley rose and Titcomb stated, "Gentlemen of Amesbury, the governor needs your services. He was very specific about wanting men of your community, because of the large numbers of tradesmen, carpenters, and boat builders amongst you. Captain Webster has placed himself at a table at the back of this house. Those of you ready to enlist, please file back to him and we will join you to record the information. In three weeks we will return on your militia muster day, on which day we have given orders to your muster master from the governor, to have the Amesbury Alarm List Company assembled for inspection and further recruitment to take place. Those of you who are not ready at this time, please think hard about enlisting at your muster! Thank you, gentlemen, for your interest and time."

The officers marched to the rear of the meetinghouse and a line of about twenty men formed at the table where the officers started accumulating information from their new recruits. John Benjamin was ready to join but was talked into checking with his wife by several others in his pew. Charles and John walked out of the meeting, both full of excitement, but Charles needed more time to make his decision.

They walked south on the Amesbury road, Charles leading his horse because John was on foot. Two blocks down the road they came to David Blasdell's house, a modest story-and-a-half, red Cape Cod. Behind the house stood an old, gray, run-down hobble with a lean-to attached. The lean-to was the forge shop with a small tool shack. This was Blasdell's blacksmith shop, John's place of employment and residence. Part of his wages included free rent in the small one-roomed house attached to the shop.

Tying up the horse near his brothers', Charles walked with John toward the door. John said quietly, "Let me bring up enlisting; I can talk Sarah into it." John lifted the door latch, opening the door, "Hello, we're home, and do I ever have the news!"

Mrs. Benjamin was bent over the hearth and Enoch was lifting an old iron pot off the trammel for her. William and Mary Elizabeth sat at the crude half-log table; Mary was stitching a sampler. As Charles stepped farther into the room and removed his hat she slowly lifted her eyes to his face and smiled. Charles noticed her radiant smile, her gleaming eyes and her long auburn hair. She was only sixteen, six years his junior, but mature for her age.

"Everyone gather around the table; we have some exciting things to discuss!" said John with enthusiasm. John was almost shaking with excitement. He truly wanted to join the regiment.

"Mother, you know how we have always wanted to have our own blacksmith shop? Could you imagine having our own home with nice furniture, linen curtains, and fine feather beds; being able to have a nice wagon to go to meeting instead of our old ox cart, and new flowered dresses for you and Mary?" started John.

Charles sat in astonishment, trying to understand how John was going to get his family's support. John continued.

"Moses Titcomb and Jonathan Bagley were at the meeting with some sad and good news for us. The government is getting ready to send an army off to fight the French out west. They have been sent here to recruit men from Amesbury. They are looking specifically for tradesmen, carpenters, and boat builders. Every regiment in the army always needs a blacksmith!

"Remember how Blasdell went to Canada ten years ago with the army? He had just started his shop here in Amesbury and he needed money to get things going. I think this could be our big chance!

"I could join this army and serve as a blacksmith and come home this fall with the money to start my own shop. Maybe I could even find cheap land in the west and we could move. We'll be seeing all kinds of lands in the next eight months!"

"I'm not sure if this is a good idea, John," responded Sarah. "How would Mary Elizabeth and I live while you are gone? What about the dangers of the war? Who will take care of you?"

"Charles can take care of me, he's joining," said John.

"Great, I'll join too!" interrupted William.

"We already told you, you are too young, they want men 18 to 45," said Charles sarcastically. He looked at John and said, "I told you I wasn't sure! I want to talk to my family first. I'm not so sure about army life."

John lightly rapped his clenched hand rhythmically on the table, squinted his eyes, and bit his bottom lip. There were a few seconds of silence while John thought. Then he opened his eyes wide and pointed with the index finger of his left hand and said suddenly to Sarah, "You and Mary Elizabeth can come with me! The army will need camp followers to cook, wash clothes, sew, and see to the sick. Armies always travel with followers, even Massachusetts."

"Did they say anything about women at the meeting?" inquired Sarah. "I'm not so sure we should do this, John. Are you sure we can make it? What about Mary Elizabeth?"

"Mary Elizabeth is sixteen; some girls her age are already married. She knows how to take care of a kitchen, sew, and watch over the sick. You have seen to that, Sarah. Let's do it, Mother! I'll just tell them, if they want a blacksmith, you'll have to go, too," said John calmly in a reassuring voice. "Don't worry, I won't leave you and Mary Elizabeth here alone."

John smiled and rose quickly from the table. He strode to the corner of the room, near the woodpile. Removing an old gallon jug from the corner, he proposed, "Charles, let's drink some rum, to our joining the regiment!"

Charles replied, "I will not say if I'm joining yet, but I will drink with you though, to you and your family's success."

John grabbed in one hand three large horn tankards and sloshed rum into them, handing one each to Sarah and Charles, and keeping one himself.

"John, I don't drink," said Sarah in disgust.

So John gulped his and said, "Fine! I'll drink yours, too! To Old Massachusetts-Bay, and our adventures!" John and Charles banged their tankards together and drank.

"Charles, we need to get home. I want to see how Mother is doing," suggested William. He had always been a worry-wort.

Charles stood and said, "Thank you for the company and your hospitality today, but William is right, we need to check on Mother. I also need to talk to my father. I am interested in his suggestions about the meeting. Let's go, boys." He shook John's hand, and Enoch, William and Charles grabbed their hats, walked out the door, and mounted their horses.

As they rounded the corner and headed toward the wharf area William started quizzing Charles about the meeting. "Were there soldiers there in uniforms with their muskets?"

"No," said Charles, "there were several officers, but no uniforms."

"Charles, I really want to join! It would be so much fun marching around and shooting one of those 'Brown Bess' Redcoat muskets, and best of all, if I get one of those uniforms, Mary will pay attention to me," said William excitedly.

Charles had not really been listening, "Mary who?" he asked.

"Mary, John's daughter, who do you think?" said William in exasperation.

"First of all, William, you're not old enough, they won't take you and there is no way Mother and Father are going to lie for you," stated Charles. "I need to think. Keep quiet till we get home, will you," said Charles. It was now early afternoon and the brothers continued their ride past the wharves and down the road going east past the junction of the rivers. The road meandered with the Powow past Charles' small farm to his father's, the next on the road.

As Charles approached the stone fence on the east of his farm he gazed over the fields that led his eyes to a tree line of large oaks nicely manicured with a rail fence enclosing about an acre. From the road the brothers turned onto the trail leading to the fenced area. Centered in this area Charles could see his parent's homestead. In the 1690's, his grandparents had settled here in the fertile river valley. The house was a tall, straight saltbox with narrow clapboards painted a russet red, faded to a pale mauve. The windows were set symmetrically, their wooden sashes stained brown, as was the plank door.

Behind and attached to the house was a fenced garden area about thirty foot square. To the east of the house stood an old, weathered tool shed and the barn that Charles and his brothers had enjoyed so much to play in. The rest of the land as far as the next hillock consisted of fields awaiting the spring cultivation, and beyond the fields lay the woods where Charles and his brothers learned to hunt.

Charles and his brothers rode up to the barn and dismounted. "Brothers, will you tie my horse in the stable with your horses? requested Charles. "I'll go in and check on Mother."

"I'll do it, William," said Enoch sincerely. Go on in with Charles; I know how worried you are."

Charles and William walked across the farm trail around the fence and into the back door, which led into the lean-to of the saltbox. Inside, their father stood by the trestle table, pouring hot tea into a mug. He was a large man, almost six feet tall, and muscular. His hair was brown, but graying. He wore it short and cropped on the sides and back. He was slightly hunchbacked from decades of hard work on the farm and on the wharves.

Caleb turned toward them, focusing his dark, piercing eyes on their faces. "Good, you're home," he said. "I trust service was inspiring today?"

"It was long," said William.

"How did the meeting go, Charles?" Caleb asked in an inquisitive voice.

"First Father, how is Mother—is it the fever?" asked Charles worriedly.

"She's going to be alright. Goody Greenleaf came over and thinks your mother just overdid it. She gave her a tonic to drink to relieve the coughing and help her breathe. I am mixing some more for her now. She has eaten some broth and is resting. Let me add molasses and you can take it up to her," said Caleb reassuringly. He slowly added some rum and molasses and stirred it all together. Then he handed the tonic to Charles. "Don't keep her awake too long, she needs her sleep."

Charles walked into the great room at the front of the house and climbed the steep, narrow, turning stairs. At the top of the stairs he turned to the right and walked into the large bedchamber of his parents.

On his left stood a brick lined fireplace. The rest of the room was pine paneled. There was little furniture: a spinning wheel in the corner by the fireplace, two old chairs—one by the fire and one by the door closet that sat between the windows at the front of the house—a large chest on the opposite side of the room, a three-quarter sized, four-post rope bed against the wall across from the fire, and a blanket chest at the foot of the bed. The green drapes on the bed were partially closed as Charles approached.

"Mother," Charles said softly. "I have your tonic."

"Come over and sit with me, dear, right here on the edge of the bed," she answered weakly.

Charles pulled back the drapes and handed her the mug of steaming tonic. She was lying still with her head propped up on a pillow and bolster. Her light brown hair was mixed with gray, giving it the color of a chestnut horse. Her hair lay long and straight, draping down the pillows and her sides. Around her shoulders she wore a wool shawl, and a white cap covered the top of her head. Her Bible lay open, face down on her breast. She opened her eyes slowly and reached for the mug.

"Thank you, Charles," she said softly. "This will help me." His mother coughed with a gravelly, crackling sound. She brought the mug slowly to her mouth, blew into the mug and began to sip the tonic.

"Your friends were asking about you today," said Charles. "Everyone was praying you didn't have the fevers. Reverend Wells even said a prayer for your recovery. Do you think you'll be alright, Mother?" asked Charles in a soft, sincere voice.

"I think I just need some rest, Charles." She hesitated and sighed, "Goody Greenleaf's tonic and a couple of days' rest should cure me. Don't worry," reassured his mother. "I think your father needs you to talk with him," she said in a worried tone. "He is too worried about me and I think he is also worried about the news he had heard that they were going to bring up at the meeting today. Is it war? I don't want him going—I still remember the last war."

Charles took her hand in his and said, "Mother, don't worry about it. I'll sit down with Father tonight and talk with him. You rest now and we'll talk more tomorrow." Charles stood part way up and leaned forward, kissing her on the forehead. Then he quietly rose and walked out of her room and climbed down the stairs to the great room.

"Come and sit for a moment, Charles," said his father. Caleb was seated in his armchair on the right of the large hearth, and Enoch and

William were setting on the settle in front of him. Charles sat in his mother's rocker. His father was holding his head in his hands. He slowly raised his head and in a calm voice started to speak.

"Boys, I think your mother will be alright, if she gets enough rest. Goody Greenleaf looked her over pretty good and stayed several hours with her. She thinks she just overdid it, working too hard after being ill. Your mother does have a consumption sound in her chest, but Goody Greenleaf's tonic should loosen that. We are going to have to work extra hard and give your mother some time to recuperate. Enoch, I need you to help out with some of the chores of the house and William, you may have to help with some of my farm chores when I need to help Enoch or your mother. I want you all to not worry, just work together and give her some time. Now, let's go out, William and Charles, and we'll get to the chores we neglected yesterday and today. Enoch, you need to get enough water drawn and boiled to start washing our clothes."

Charles asked in a puzzled voice, "What can I do to help?"

"Son, I don't want you worrying, you have an important choice to make. Once you have made it, you will be very busy. I think we should talk after supper. Let's go to work."

Enoch started carrying buckets of water from the well to the kitchen in the lean-to. Caleb went out to the tool shed and worked sharpening and honing the farm tools and his tools for work at the shop tomorrow. Charles and William went to the barn to feed the cattle and sheep, and clean the stalls and put in fresh straw.

Around dusk, gray clouds started rolling in from the northwest and the temperature began to drop. Charles and William left the barn and walked to the house. As they entered through the back door, the warmth from the kitchen hearth drenched their chilled bodies. The room had a soft yellow glow to it and was filled with the smells of roasted meat. Enoch was slicing bread at the table and Caleb was just entering the room. He had just come down from treating his wife with a bowl of hot broth and fresh bread. He had a sincere smile on his face as he greeted his sons.

"Everything ready, Enoch?" he asked.

"Yes, Sir," replied Enoch.

Father walked to the table. "Let's sit and enjoy our feast."

All four took their seats, Father at the head, Enoch and William on a bench against the wall on the left of the table, Charles in a chair at the table's right, and Mother's chair empty at the foot of the table.

Enoch reached forward and grabbed the ladle in the wooden bowl of beans and his father said in a quick voice, "Sons, let us give thanks to Jehovah," and he prayed in a solemn voice, "Lord, allow us to thank You for this fine day. We are so much looking forward to spring and our weather has been so nice lately. You have sent us hope today that my wife and our mother is healing. Thank You, Lord; You know how much she means to us. Lord, I have known battle and understand how we can be Your fists in punishing Your enemies. If You find it necessary to use our family in a Holy War, we await Your command. Finally, Jehovah, thank You for this bounty of food and bring us fair weather and peace for our spring. Amen."

The four started piling beans, dried peas, bread, butter, and thick, juicy, fat pieces of beef on their wooden terrenes. Being their second meal of the Sabbath, they ate heartily.

After their meal, William and Enoch were excused and Charles volunteered to help his father. They retted the table and went into the great room to sit and talk. Charles stoked the fire and his father sat in an old ladderback armchair. He put his feet up on an old pine stool and took his grayed clay pipe off the stand beside his chair. As he packed his pipe with tobacco he asked calmly, "What did Bagley and old Titcomb have to say today? Is it war again? Are we finally going to march north again?"

Charles turned his head toward his father, "Yes." Then, turning back to tend the fire he continued, "They were here to recruit for a regiment under their command. The governor had asked for our men because of their skills."

"Bring me a light, son," Caleb requested.

Charles laid a sliver of wood in the coals. When it had burst into flame he walked slowly with it cupped in his hands and handed it to his father.

"Father, they said it would be a quick war, only eight months."

Caleb slowly puffed the flames from the wood sliver into his pipe bowl. When he had lit his tobacco, he shook out the sliver and looked at his son. Charles had seated himself in the winged settle at the side of the hearth.

In a questioning but excited tone, Charles said to his father, "I'm drawn in two different directions. On one hand, my career at the wharf has been advancing nicely. I believe I can prosper. My farm, though small, helps me, and eventually will help supply most of my household needs. On the other hand, the prospect of excitement and adventure is intriguing. I have heard many old soldiers talk of their glory at Louisbourg. What is it truly like? I must know if I am to make a decision. They promise only short enlistment. I don't want to regret some day not being involved in this fight."

After a short pause Caleb laid down his pipe and in a reassuring tone answered his son. "Your mother and I worked very hard raising you and your brothers. We have always tried to give you chances to make your own choices. I am not sure what you should do. Back in '45 when I was in Titcomb's unit at Louisbourg, we sailed into the port and unleashed our cannon on the fort. Finally we landed and advanced. Everything I remember tends to fade, but I can still recall seeing some of our men being struck down, and the terror I felt. For us it was a short campaign which ended in a year of glory and with many memories of adventure." Caleb paused and looked down. Then after a few seconds he looked back to Charles and in a concerned voice said, "I'm not going to tell you that if you join, you will have the same experiences. If the campaign does not fare well, your experiences may be horrible. I will tell you that if you do join this regiment, you will be commanded by one of the colony's best officers, and his second, Jon Bagley, you know yourself. My advice is to sleep on it and take your time, your decision could affect the rest of your life."

"Thanks for being honest, Father. I agree, I need to take more time. After all, on muster day they are returning for more recruits."

Darkness was starting to set in and Charles rose and said, "Well, it's time I head home and care for my animals. I'm glad Mother is doing better. Don't worry all night about her, and don't worry about my decisions I must make; just rest. I'll see you at the wharf tomorrow. Good night, Father."

Charles slipped on his coat and hat and walked out the back door, entered the barn, mounted his horse, and rode home. All along the way and the rest of the evening he mulled things around in his mind. He knew he had an important decision to make and he dug deeply into his soul in the next several weeks, manipulating the possibilities until he decided which direction he would take.

MUSTER DAY

Charles arose with excitement on muster day, after weeks of anticipation. He ate a quick morning meal, and then went to his barn to care for his animals, knowing he would not have the time later. Muster day was a day-long, community-involved festival. After his chores, Charles went back into his house and changed into his hunting clothes. He donned a brown tricorn, dark red checked shirt, brown and black striped waistcoat, brown jacket, deerskin breeches and leggins, and old shoes. Each man was to fall out on muster with suitable arms and gear or would be issued the same from the militia stores. Charles, upon leaving his house, equipped himself with the long hunting fowler his father had given him four years ago for helping in the fields, an acorn-colored bag containing tools and ammunition for his fowler, a powder horn, haversack, and a tan striped blanket, rolled up and tied, and slung over his back on a tumpline.

Charles jumped on his horse and rode toward town. Once on the main north road leading to town, the path became congested with horses, carts, wagons, and people on foot. He rode up to the village green between the meetinghouse and the hill to its north. Here, nestled in the hollow, was about a ten-acre plot of well-manicured lawn, owned in common by the townsmen. It was mostly level, with beautiful old maples lining its perimeter. The back several acres were wooded, and a small creek meandered south from the hill to the Powow River. Near the road there were fewer trees, and hitching posts lined the way.

Charles rode to the nearest post, slid from his horse, and tied it to the post. His eyes searched the green for his family. Everywhere, like bees hovering around an old tree, townspeople and their families were selecting spots to lay out blankets to sit and watch the day's festivities. Many friends of Charles and his family greeted him as he walked onto the green. His progress was greatly slowed until finally he spotted his parents and brothers arranging their gear, baskets, and blanket under one of the clumps of trees on the south of the green. Charles waved to them and walked toward their well-chosen spot.

After a few minutes of socializing, all the families had settled into their small areas on the green. Then Colonel Bagley walked into the center of the green with the officers of the Amesbury Alarm List Company: John Burk, Samuel George, Jon Bagley Jr., Thomas Pike, Thomas Stevens, Josiah Sergeant, Timothy Barnard, and Caleb, Charles' father. Samuel George, the militia captain, stepped forward and motioned Phillip Sergeant to step forward. He marched out in front of the officers and began beating his drum. With huge strides Sergeant Timothy Colby stepped onto the field, positioned himself in front of Phillip Sergeant, turned about and bellowed, "Amesbury Alarm Company, Fall In!"

Men from all directions about the green grabbed their muskets and bags, and ran toward Colby. Once in position, he and several others began placing the men of the militia into two long ranks. When they were done, forty-five men, including officers, were standing awaiting orders. The women and children about the green congregated in groups along the perimeter cheering their sons, fathers and husbands. Children were yelling and dashing about in excitement. Then suddenly silence befell the green.

From the south side of the green where Reverend Wells and several veterans stood, Colonel Moses Titcomb marched into the green. He was dressed in a red uniform with large cuffs. The coat, waistcoat and high cocked tricorner were gloriously trimmed with sparkling gold braid. Across his right shoulder was a crimson sash and around his neck he wore a gold gorget with the pine tree of New England engraved on it. Fifty yards out he halted, drew his sword and turned about face, and in a gruff voice gave the command, "Captain Taplin, Parade And Fire Your Detachment!"

Captain Taplin, standing at the edge of the green, drew his saber, saluted the colonel with his sword and gave the command, "Detachment, Take Care! To The Front, March!"

Immediately the captain stepped off, followed closely by twenty soldiers in two ranks. They were followed by a drummer and a colour bearer with the pine tree flag of New England. The detachment was methodical in its pace as it slowly advanced toward the center of the green. Titcomb had selected this group from his earlier recruits for the purpose of impressing communities in recruitment. The unit was uniformed smartly from head to foot. They wore black tricorns with white wool trim, red waistcoats, red breeches, gray hose, and dark navy regimentals with red facings. Each man carried a Brown Bess musket, cartridge box, powder horn, haversack, brown cowhide knapsack, and white blanket rolls. They were superbly uniformed. Taplin's uniform was like his men's, except his had bright gold buttons instead of pewter and his waistcoat and tricorn were laced in gold.

As the unit reached the center of the green, the townspeople's mouths were agape and the Alarm List Company stood stunned. Taplin called out, "Take Care! Halt! Rest Your Firelocks! Face To The Right!" and the detachment turned. "Prepare To Fire! Recover Your Firelocks! Cock Your Firelocks! Present! FIRE!"

The twenty men simultaneously discharged their muskets in a unified thudding roar and billowing smoke. This brought cheers and yells from the crowd.

"Recover Your Firelocks! Shoulder Your Firelocks!" ordered Taplin. Then he marched his detachment around the green, performing close order maneuvers to impress the onlookers with their precision.

After several minutes he halted the unit in front of the militia. Colonel Bagley ordered his militia to, "Present Your Firelocks!" In this position the entire militia honored Taplin's detachment with this military salute, and he ordered his men to return the honor. After both units had ordered their firelocks, Moses Titcomb asked for permission to address the militia company. Jonathan Bagley saluted him, and asked him to proceed.

Titcomb faced the militia and started to pace back and forth during his oration. "Gentlemen of Amesbury, I have returned today in hopes that you have had time to consider your circumstances and discuss the colony's need for your enlistment in the Essex County Regiment. The preparations being made are not just for adventure, fortune, and glory, but are also for God. This is a Holy War we are engaging in. A war to rid our continent of the French Catholics and their Devil-worshiping heathens. Governor Shirley has told me that General Braddock has been named commander of the British Army in North America, and at his meeting with the colonial governors, recruiting was so good that he has decided that this regiment will be engaged in a campaign against Fort St. Frederic near Crown Point. I understand the importance to you men to serve together, and Governor Shirley has assured me you will be serving on this campaign only with your own officers. Your army will be all provincial."

As he talked, the militiamen looked back and forth at each other, nodding and expressing affirmative gestures.

"For your enlistment the government has authorized me to pay each of you one pound, four shillings a month. In addition to the eighteen shillings before offered, I have been told to offer you an additional six dollars bounty if you enlist today and bring your own firelock to war. For your travel and subsistence to the general rendezvous, the colony allows you eight shillings a week. You are expected to travel fifteen miles a day. Once at your rendezvous you will receive victuals from the colony. You will receive daily 1 pound of bread, 1 pound of pork, ½ pint of peas or beans, 2 ounces of ginger, 1 pound of flour, 1 pint of Indian meal, 4 ounces of butter, 1 pint of molasses, 1 gill of rum, and weekly 1 pound of sugar. What say you, gentlemen? Are you willing to serve God, the King, and your colony? Step forward, men, in the ranks of your alarm list company and perform to your best, adding to the day's festivity and impressing your wives, sweethearts and children! Thank you."

Bagley stepped forward and ordered Samuel George to parade the militia. As George stepped forward the militiamen began to fidget, aligning themselves and standing more erect, as the internal pride welled up, due to Titcomb's talk, which had so inspired them. Then in concise, clear orders, George issued his commands.

"Take Care! Shoulder Your Firelocks! Form A Line Into A Column Of Six. By The Left, Wheel!"

The men swung to their left and aligned themselves into six columns facing the north. Those not adept were given directions, and several men were placed on the flanks to guide on the march. The officers placed themselves to observe as Timothy Colby positioned himself on the right of the first rank.

"Mr. Colby, Parade The Troops!" commanded Samuel George.

Colby responded quickly by commanding, "Take Care! To The Front, March!"

The militia marched and wheeled about the green, passing first the perimeter, to the cheers of their families. The men marched proudly, not with the skill of Taplin's detachment but, in their own minds, as well as any King's regulars. Many waved and yelled to their families as they passed. Then finally they passed the observing officers in review, trying their best to keep their ranks as straight as possible and stay in step.

"Take Care! Halt!" came George's command.

"Mr. George," commanded Bagley, "Dismiss the company. Have them enjoy the midday with their families and friends and reassemble at two o'clock to receive new recruits in our Essex County Regiment."

"Take Care! You heard Jon Bagley, men! Be ready to reform at two. Dismissed!" commanded Colby.

The men gave a cheer and with excitement walked to their families and friends. The women were laying out blankets and opening baskets, preparing meals on the lawn of the green. Charles' family was excited; his brothers were jabbering nonstop as he approached. Several families, the Lowells, Greenleafs, Benjamins and the Nurses, had all grouped together under a clump of maples. Charles was stripping off his gear as John Benjamin and Caleb walked up.

"The company looked good today, son," praised Caleb.

"It really felt exciting on the green today, like we really had a purpose," replied Charles.

"I can't wait till next year, I'm going to find a way to be there," said William.

"Some day my son, some day," reassured Caleb.

"Now it's our turn to show off. Caleb, you and the men get over here and inspect our meal," politely ordered Margaret.

"Yes gentlemen, let us take in and enjoy all of this wonderful lunch," coaxed Caleb. The men and boys crowded around the blankets and retrieved terrenes from the women, filling them with cold boiled ham, rice, bread and butter, pie, and mugs of punch. Each family, upon being seated, said a blessing and began to enjoy the food.

After the meal, the men relaxed under the trees, the children played games on the green and the women retted up the meal. Gidion Lowell, the eldest brother owning the Lowell boat shop where Caleb and Charles worked, asked,

"Caleb, are you sure you aren't going to be able to enlist with us? You would be a good officer for us and Bagley would get you a commission."

"No, I'm not enlisting. There is just too much at stake for me. Besides, I am too old. Leave war to you younger men. Our family will be well represented, no need I go as well," answered Caleb.

"I talked to Sarah about me going to kill those Frenchmen and the only way we figured it will work is if she and Mary Elizabeth can serve as followers with us. An army always needs women to nurse, cook, and care for the men," offered John. For the next hour the families wandered around the green catching up on gossip and news. The children continued to play, small groups of men relaxed, and groups of women worked on sewing and group quilting.

Just before two o'clock the men began to don their gear once more, and the families began to congregate for the afternoon formation. The company was called out and formed and the Reverend Wells was asked to lead the community and militia in prayer.

"Lord Jehovah, You have blessed us with a beautiful spring day for our muster. Our men have performed well and shown they are always ready to serve You. We now stand before You in reverence, many ready to start a new adventure in their march to drive the French, Your enemies, from our continent. For years now we have been plagued by the raids of Indians and French from the north. The governor has seen it fitting to raise this regiment, and developed its core from our community. Jehovah, as more of our young men step forward and join You today, be with them always as they act as Your right hand in this Holy War. We understand some of these fine boys will be slain in Your name, but please if I may ask You, bring the majority back to us, as they are our neighbors, sons and fathers. Remember them always in Your plans, Jehovah. Praise to You, O Lord, Amen."

Moses Titcomb again stepped forward and addressed the Amesbury Company. "Gentlemen, you have heard what the government will offer you. The Reverend Wells blessed this expedition. You have been assured that you will be serving with your own kind in a regiment of your own officers. Many of you who were at Louisbourg in '45 can attest to what we will accomplish. You have had time to consult your souls and families. Now I ask you to step forward and accept an eight-month service with us for your King. Gentlemen, we are going north, and will drive the enemy before us! Those willing, say 'Aye!'"

The company began to cheer and a chorus of "Aye!" chimed through the soldiery.

"Now men," said Samuel George, "when dismissed, those who are enlisting, form a line by that table and sign the enlistment papers. You will receive a month's advance and part of your bounty money." He pointed to a table to the east as he spoke. "Gentlemen, God Save The King! Take Care! You Are Dismissed!"

About a third of the company stepped to the table to enlist. Officers began writing each man's information in the regimental book, and each man in order signed by his name and received his money. Charles had made up his mind weeks earlier, and now he took his place in the line. The men all were excited and congratulated each other repeatedly.

John Benjamin was several men in front of Charles. When he was asked for his information he explained that his wife and daughter must sign as followers if he was to enlist. "I am a skilled man. I can beat iron for the colonel and repair all the tools needed. I would like to be blacksmith for the regiment."

The officer looked up at Titcomb. "Sir, I already have an armourer. You say you are skilled? You have a shop here?"

"No, Sir, I work for Mr. Blasdell," replied John.

"I can offer you the chance to be my armourer's assistant and you may enlist your women as well. We may be in the need of laundresses and nurses."

"Thank you, Sir, I'll sign," said John enthusiastically.

When Charles reached the front of the line, Captain Burk asked, "Name?"

"Charles Nurse."

"Residence?"

"Amesbury, Sir."

"Age?"

"Twenty-two."

"Do you have your own firelock?"

"Yes, Sir, a fowler."

"Then here is your month's pay and two dollars of your bounty. You are to muster here on May 23 and march to Boston by the 24th. There you must pass muster, you will receive billeting money, the rest of your bounty, and march for Albany with this regiment. Any questions?"

Charles hesitated, "No."

"Sign the book, Goodman Nurse, here," Burk pointed to his name and Charles signed.

Charles walked away from the recruiting table toward his family. As he walked he congratulated and received congratulations from men he passed. His father greeted him with a handshake.

"Son, I know you have made a good choice. You are the next of our family to fight for his God and colony."

The rest of his family, and the other families they had eaten with, all congregated and talked with excitement of the upcoming campaign.

Charles' mother put her arms around him and said, "Charles, you take care of yourself. Be careful and come back to me. The next thing you know, if this war lasts more than a few months, more of my men will join, and I cannot bear that thought."

Close by, the other women were listening and doing the same to their loved ones. Mary Elizabeth tapped Margaret on the back and whispered calmly, “Don’t worry, Goody Nurse, I’ll be there to take care of him.”

As the families’ excitement waned and the afternoon became late, the people of Amesbury collected their belongings and headed home. The prospect of adventure clouded the thoughts of most of the enlistees. The excitement of the day and the short few weeks to prepare to leave would keep everyone busy until departure on May 23.

WE MARCH TO WAR

It was a bright spring morn in May when the volunteers of the Amesbury Alarm List Company formed on the village green, preparing to march for Boston. The fresh smells of tender green plants filled the air and a gentle breeze made it comfortable for the men who must march at least fifteen miles this day. This Friday morn saw the families grouping together, saying their farewells to fathers, husbands, sons and friends. There was an air of excitement and adventure, mixed with mild anxiety. Everyone expected a quick and decisive, European-style battle that would push the enemy from the continent within a few short months.

Amongst the emotions, tears, caressing, and good-byes of the families, the Nurse family had grouped together to say their good-byes to Charles. Caleb stood proudly before his son, adjusting the straps on Charles' equipment.

"Son, the day is finally here for you to leave us and march to your regiment. Your mother and I are proud of your decision to join the other men of Amesbury. We know that you are prepared to fight for God." Caleb hesitated, quit fixing the straps, and looked Charles directly in the eyes. "When I went to Louisbourg my father gave this to me." He handed something to Charles. He placed his hands around Charles' as if to shake his hand. "At those weary, homesick, heart wrenching times, looking at it comforted me." Caleb slid away his hands, revealing his father's silver watch. Charles held it to his face. It was engraved CN. He opened the cover producing the yellowed face of the watch.

"Do us proud, son. Remember, our prayers will be with you," said Caleb in a soft shaking voice.

Charles reached forward, placing his right hand on his father's shoulder. "Thanks, Father. Don't worry about me."

Margaret stepped forward, and she and Charles embraced. She buried her head on his shoulder as tears streamed down her face.

"It will be all right, Mother. Don't do this; I hate to see you cry. I'll be back home by harvest time."

His mother's voice was quiet and shivered with the shaking of her whimpering body. "Please, Charles, be careful. I could never stand to lose one of my boys. Write me often. Your father and I will be sending you letters." She reached into her pocket and pulled out a red, leather covered book, about five by eight inches. "Take this, son. Your father always talks of his adventures at Louisbourg. He kept a journal of his observations, which he reflects upon when he needs reminding of his experiences. You need to keep this journal for your remembrances. Write in it often, what you see and do, and record your thoughts and feelings; your sons someday will want to know. Charles..." Her voice started to crackle.

Caleb reached over and took her by the shoulders and drew her close to him. "Now, Margaret, don't sadden the boy. He should be in good spirits to leave."

William and Enoch were standing behind Charles. He turned around and shook William's hand. "Thanks for watching over my place while I'm gone. Just make sure the place doesn't fall down. Don't worry about the fields; next year I can put them in. A year's rest for the soil will be good for it. Watch the animals, though. They should get along with Father's. Keep any wool or milk you can sell for helping."

Charles stuck his hand out for Enoch and he jumped forward and Charles hugged him. "You need to do me a big favor, Enoch."

"What's that?" sighed Enoch.

"Help Father with the chores and help him take care of Mother. There will be fewer of us men here this summer and you'll have to work extra hard. I'll be home near the end of summer. Will you take my horse out on a ride every week for me?"

"Sure," answered Enoch, sniffing back his tears.

"Just make sure you water him and wipe him down afterwards."

Suddenly the company drummer started beating, and men started yelling orders to assemble. Charles had time for one last caress, handshake, and kiss from his family, and men started forming on the green. Several men were forming the recruits into a line. Sounds abounded on the green: families were weeping and calling to their loved ones, the drum was beating, men were giving orders, recruits were talking to each other with excitement; one man was even being followed into the line by his barking, yipping dog.

Shortly after all the men were formed, Jon Bagley stepped forward and ordered Timothy Colby to march the men to Boston, instructing him to try and make Wenom by dark and Boston by the next day.

"Mr. Colby, you are to take up lodging at Benjamin Johnson's barn in Wenom tonight and make Boston by tomorrow. You are to see to your men's and followers' needs, causing no commotion along your route. I will be following on horseback. Report to the officer in charge in Boston, join your regiment and await the colonel's orders. You are free to march!"

Colby saluted Bagley, who returned his gesture, and the troop was formed into a column of twos and marched onto the road. A small group of camp followers, both women and children, formed up behind the troops. They did not appear as eager, but were ready to serve nonetheless. They plodded along in the rear of the column.

Yells, cries, and cheers rose from the column and the families alike. The men were not professionals and were unaware of the etiquette of maintaining a quiet march. The families crowded the roadsides as the men marched along, and they continued to follow until several miles from the river.

The rest of the day the volunteers marched with their heads high and excitement in their hearts. They were heading to rendezvous with their generation's chosen army of New England. Their destiny was to succeed in valor, as did the army of '45. That evening they arrived at Johnson's barn. Most of the men got little or no sleep, not from the conditions of sleeping on straw in the barn, but because of the all-night conversations.

The next morning the men rose early and quickly ate a cold breakfast of bread and cheese. They started immediately for Boston. All along the road they passed group after group of fellow volunteers marching or preparing to march for Boston, where they all would meet later that day, form regiments, receive orders, and march forward to drive the French from North America in their Holy War.

Late in the day, Charles' unit of volunteers halted several miles from Boston. The men had spread out on the march and no longer appeared like a military unit. Colby had the men sit and relax while they awaited the rest of the volunteers to catch up. The two-day march had very little effect on the men physically because of their high morale. After about a half an hour all the volunteers and followers had caught up. The unit was given a fifteen-minute break to refresh the stragglers and Tim Colby reformed the unit to march.

"Men of Amesbury, we need to keep together now as we approach Boston. There will be hundreds of men in the city and we must not split up in all the confusion. More importantly, we want to show the other men of Massachusetts-Bay and our officers how ready we are to serve! Take Care, Men! Shoulder Your Firelocks! To The Front, March!"

With refreshed enthusiasm the unit marched for Boston. As they neared the city Colby commanded, "Drummer Sergeant, Beat Your Drum!" The cadence started and the men attempted to march in step.

Farms became more numerous, eventually adjoining each other continuously as they lined the road from the north. A graceful fence flanked both sides of the road, intermingling stone walls and rail fences. The steeples of the town's churches, meetinghouses, and halls appeared beyond the narrow neck of land leading into Boston. Many of the men had been to Boston before, but the few who had never ventured south were taken in awe of the town's grand appearance.

The recruits entered the center of town via Salisbury Street, which was lined on both sides with the houses of Bostonians. The citizens covered the cobblestone streets. People were walking, congregating at doorways and conversing, children were scurrying, and men and women were burdened carrying packages, bundles and baskets. Carts, wagons, carriages and men on horseback were everywhere. The deeper into Boston they marched, the more shops appeared on the streets, until on their right stood Faneuil Hall. This was the central marketplace of the metropolis. The hall was two stories tall, built of brick, as many of its surrounding buildings were. The first floor was covered with awnings, as were the rest of the multi-story buildings, forming a grand outdoor market behind Faneuil Hall to the east. The hall was immense, with sixty windows, each larger than a man. Atop the roof perched a gilded weathervane in the form of a grasshopper lying on its back—an appropriate furnishing for such a grand building.

Onward the column marched, as the townspeople of Boston cheered. The recruits continued along Salisbury Street, passing the three-story State House on their left in the next block. This lavish, symmetric building loomed over the square and had a balcony on the second floor. A gilded lion and horse flanked the third story, symbolizing the honor of the king. A fine, three-tiered cupola topped the magnificent structure. As the soldiery rounded the corner on their left, they swung onto Common Street. On the left, its spires reaching toward the heavens, stood King's Chapel and its burying grounds. Behind it was the meetinghouse.

With mouths agape, the men plodded forward. Approaching a rolling green, the soldiers could see a woodlot in the distance. The green was encircled by beautiful homes and mansions, while trees and fences surrounded the green itself. This was their destination, Boston Common.

As they swung their column onto the green, the men were in awe of not only the beauty of the Common, but the number of men, soldiers of the colony, pausing for their march to rendezvous. The men were encamped with no uniformity, utilizing blankets and tarpaulins brought from home for makeshift tents. Thousands were sprawled out in camps, meandering in all corners of the green, and companies drilled and marched about, trying to bring a semblance of military discipline. Colby halted the column as a mounted soldier careened down on them.

"What unit are ye?" he yelled.

"Moses Titcomb's Essex County Regiment, Sir," replied Colby.

"Have your men march yonder to the frog pond. You'll see Titcomb and his regiment camped there."

"Thank you."

Colby and his men marched across the green toward the pond in astonishment at the chaos that surrounded them. Then, just over a knoll to the north of the pond, they caught notice of their regimental officers, Glazier, Taplin, Burk, Webster, Mooers, Sergeant Whipple, Pike, and men from Amesbury who enlisted early: George, Greenleaf, Merrell, Smith, and Woodbury. And centered within the men, Moses Titcomb.

"Sir, Lieutenant Timothy Colby reporting with the detachment of recruits from Amesbury."

"Lieutenant," replied Titcomb, "see to a spot for your men over there," he pointed to an opening. "Have them use whatever they can find for makeshift shelters, feed them, and after they are comfortable report back to Captain John Burk. You will be in his company."

"Yes, Sir," replied Colby as he saluted the colonel and turned about, giving orders to his men as they marched forward.

The men of the colony were dispersed in random groupings about the green. About fifty yards forward they halted in an opening and Colby gave his orders. "Men, this will be our home for a few days. Take some of your blankets and anything else you have suitable and make shelters. Eat your meals and relax. Your orders are not to wander into the city, but stay here on the commons. Dismissed."

Most of the men collapsed on the ground. After a short rest, they organized themselves and set up for the evening. Charles and John collected several fallen tree limbs and made a lean-to from one of their blankets, for themselves and John's family. Mary and her mother collected wood from the distant woodlot and started a fire to cook their meal. John fell asleep but Charles walked through the camps, astounded at the array of men and camps nestled on the common.

For the next four days, time was spent marching, drilling, and learning how to be soldiers. The militia musters had done little to prepare them for this expedition. First the men were marched around the green. Special care was taken to insure a perfect 30-inch stride. This would ensure 2 miles an hour and keep the army together, resulting in no stragglers.

Then the men who did not bring muskets were given sticks, and the monotonous, repetitive training of the manual exercise was begun. Day after day, the men repeated the drill with the ideal goal of it becoming second nature.

By the end of each day the men would congregate and share their stories and tales, trying to outdo one another. After the evening meal, the men were assembled and inspected, and the regimental chaplain would give an inspiring sermon. Each evening before sleep, Charles took out the journal his mother had given him and scribed his daily routine.

On the evening of the 28th, Lieutenant Colby was making the rounds of his company and he stopped, taking notice of Charles writing in his journal. "Nurse," bellowed Colby.

"Yes, Sir."

"I have noticed you writing every eve. Let me see your book."

Charles handed him his journal. "My mother gave it to me when I left. Told me to record my journey for future reflections and my children someday."

"Quite a good hand, Nurse. The captain is looking for a clerk to record our expedition. Since you're already doing that, would you consider making an official record for the captain? You would not be relieved from your normal duties, but there is extra pay. What say ye?"

"Yes, Sir! I can do that."

"Then report to the captain on the morrow and he will instruct you as to your duties. Good night."

In the morning, Charles reported to Captain Burk. He was given another journal book and instructed to attend all officers' meetings, record what was said, and to record all expeditions, statistics, equipages, travel, and other pertinent information.

After returning to his unit, Charles rushed to collect his belongings. The men were forming into companies for the march to rendezvous, Albany. Charles joined the ranks just as the field officers of the Essex Regiment rode off into Boston.

"Men," addressed Burk, "we are to prepare for our march to Albany. This is our designated place of rendezvous for the entire army. The field officers will join us there after meetings with General Braddock and the governors. We are expecting the march to take near two weeks. Sergeants, I expect you to keep your units together and at all times keep the men's behavior appropriate and God-fearing.

"Take Care! Bring Your Men To Shoulder! Slow March! To The Front, March!"

Slowly the column marched down Common Street to the southwest, then turned northeast and onward toward Cambridge.

The first several days were a relatively easy march over the flat lands of eastern and central Massachusetts. The days varied from 12 to 35 miles of march, bivouacking in Cambridge, Sudbury, Southborough, Brookfield and Springfield. All along the way the men slept in barns, taverns, common houses and fields. Then the march not only became tedious but more challenging, for they had reached the mountains. They marched on the sixth day through West Springfield and over the Connecticut River. Then day after day they marched higher into the hills, past Sheffield and Kinderhook and finally north into Albany on June 8.

At noon the men marched into the fortified town on the Hudson River. It was as pretty as an oil painting on canvas. They marched through its great streets lined with lush grass. On both sides of the streets stood quaint Dutch homes, mostly made of stone or brick. The style of these dwellings was narrow and high; many with stair-step type gables. Each home was detached from one another with its own well, garden, green, and large shade trees. Before each home was a large porch with seats. In the middle of Albany were her market, town hall, guardhouse, and two churches. The Old Dutch church was brick with long narrow windows, with a white cupola holding a bell resting atop the roof. St. Peter's Church, as well, was brick, but it was a gambrel-shaped structure with a brick steeple and a domed top, and was crested with a cross. At the end of town stood the old fort that was to protect this colony from the French to the north.

The unit halted before its gates and the captain moved forward to ask his duties. He was escorted into the fort and the soldiers were ordered to remain in ranks, but to take their ease. The men gawked at the surrounding town, chatting with relief that their march was finished. The followers walked between the ranks offering water from their buckets and the men refreshed themselves momentarily with the stale water.

Captain Burk, after several minutes, walked out the fort gates and issued orders for the column to advance out the city's Schenectady gates. They marched out of the town and a short distance to the "Flats," as the meadow just north of the town was called. Here the soldiers were ordered to make camp, for this was to be their home for several weeks until the entire army had collected for the advance north.

"Gentlemen," ordered Burk, "these flats will be our area for encampment. Unfortunately, we have made it here ahead of our baggage trains and stores. The quarter guard will report to the old barracks at the fort for duty. Officers, you are to report to the adjutant at the fort for your housing, and sergeants, see to it your men are made as comfortable as possible here on the meadow. Keep your men together. I expect an officer's call in two hours at the head of our camp. You may dismiss your troops." The officers and NCOs saluted Captain Burk, turned toward their men, issued orders, and dismissed them to set up the camps, as they were.

The next morning they were issued tools and ordered on work details. For weeks the men did nothing but caulk batteaus, build more boats, repair and make new cannon carriages, make repairs on the fort at Albany, and drill. To make things more unbearable, the stores of equipment, clothing, and gear did not arrive. Many of the men had to survive in makeshift shelters for weeks, not to mention cooking their meals without kettles! Slowly, though, the rest of the army trickled into Albany, first the Bay Colony men, then in mid-June the Connecticut troops, then the rest of the Yorkers, and finally the Rhode Islanders. By July most of the army except the New Hampshire levies were at rendezvous. Massachusetts men were camped on the flats north of town and the other colonial troops were camped at Greenbush, about two miles south of town.

On July 7 General William Johnson arrived in town. A messenger galloped into camp with a letter inviting the field officers to meet with Johnson tomorrow. Under orders, Charles was to accompany the officers of his company to the meeting and record information. They arrived at the stately Dutch dwelling of Landlord Lattridge's, where Johnson was to quarter. Upon entering, Charles and the other scribes placed themselves against the walls in the rear of the front chamber. All the furniture had been removed from this room and six tables with green tablecloths had been placed in the center with four to six chairs at each.

General Johnson welcomed all the officers as they entered and took their seats. The officers took a moment and introduced themselves. There was Lieutenant Colonel Bagley and Major Nicholes from Charles' regiment, also from his colony Colonels Williams, Pomeroy, Ruggles, and Gilbert; from Connecticut there were Colonels Goodrich and Whiting; Colonel Cole from Rhode Island and another dozen officers he did not have time to pen to paper. Colonel Ephraim Williams was forty-one years old from Stockbridge, Massachusetts. He was tall, over six feet, and portly. He had been a major on the 1745 Louisbourg expedition, served as a member of the General Court, and was a deputy sheriff. His second-in-command was Lieutenant Colonel Seth Pomeroy. He was forty-five and from Northampton. He, as well, had been a major at Louisbourg. In civilian life Pomeroy was a blacksmith. Colonel Timothy Ruggles was from Hardwick. He had graduated from Harvard in 1732. Ruggles was a lawyer, tavern owner and landowner. Nathan Whiting commanded a Connecticut regiment. He was thirty-one and from New Haven. He had graduated from Yale in 1743 and served as an ensign at Louisbourg.

General Johnson, on the other hand, was forty. He was an Irish immigrant who had made friends with the Iroquois and accumulated large tracts of the Mohawk Valley. Johnson was nearly six feet tall, of medium build, with dark hair, and with eyes that varied in intensity from gray to blue. Until this expedition, he had had no military experience. Some say he had never even seen a battle! But here he was, appointed commander of the Crown Point expedition. Obviously a political move.

Johnson began to address his field command. "Gentlemen, welcome. I would like you to meet Major General Phineas Lyman. He is to be my second-in-command." Lyman stood and bowed. He was five-foot nine, with brown hair and eyes, and was well groomed. Lyman was a well educated man, having graduated from Yale. He had been a tutor at Yale, and most recently a lawyer. Johnson continued, "I would also like you to meet Captain William Eyre of the 44th Regiment of Foot. He will be in charge of our artillery, engineering, and will set up our quartermaster's department." Eyre had been a veteran of Culloden in 1746, had been an engineer at Flanders, and had been appointed to Johnson's expedition by Braddock himself. "I believe most of the rest of you know each other."

"Sirs, our orders are as follows. We are to construct a fort that will command Fort St. Frederic. It is to be erected on the high ground three hundred yards west of Fort St. Frederic. If attacked, as we expect to be, we will appear to be the injured party, rather than the aggressor. Here is our proposed line of march."

Johnson motioned to Eyre, who produced a map of the Hudson River, Lake St. Sacrament, and Lake of the Iroquois. Pointing at the route, Johnson continued, "We will send forward an advanced party of about 1,200 to cut and repair the road from hence," he pointed with his finger, "to Fort Lydius, here at the Great Carrying Place. After the arrival of this party, we will bring forth the remainder of our army in two divisions and enhance the Carrying Place into a fortress. Next we will advance to Lake St. Sacrament and build a second fort to utilize as our forward supply depot for our final push to Fort St. Frederick. Captain Eyre, I expect you to work on the engineering of these fortifications so we are ready to move forward immediately. Gentlemen, I expect you to finish the training of your troops and have the batteaus and wagons completed for the army's movement. I believe we can expect to move forward in days. Any questions?"

"Sir," questioned Pomeroy, "our men, as well as most of the New Englanders, have not yet received our stores. We have no tents, equipment, kettles, or medical supplies for an expedition. How can we be expected to advance?"

"This is correct, General Johnson," supported Bagley, "I have but one company, Captain Burk's, who has received powder, bullet, and flints. None of my regiment is fully equipped for a campaign, Sir."

Johnson hesitated, and then replied, "Gentlemen, I fully understand your dilemmas. I have contacted your governments and will send off immediately another dispatch following this meeting about the urgency for your stores. Meanwhile, you must do with what you can, relief is on the way."

Johnson reached forward, and, taking a bottle and glass from his table, lifted them and said, "A toast! Fill your glasses, Sirs." He paused and filled his. "To our success in this grand provincial expedition! To the King, your colonies, and to God! Lead your men to valor, glory, and honor! HUZZAH!" And they all lifted their glasses and drank. "Gentlemen, please dine with me in the next chamber before retiring to your troops. Thank you." The corps of officers slowly exited the room and enjoyed an evening of wine, punch, food, and entertainment. Many of the evening's moments were undoubtedly filled as well with conversations encircling the impending campaign. The clerks and scribes were sent back to camp.

Charles did not mind returning to camp, though, as he had received his first letter from home. Everything was well at home, as he found out, reading over his parents' letter half a dozen times before retiring.

The fourth day of rain—quite damp, Charles noted in his journal.

Their makeshift tent leaked like a sieve. The only thing that kept most of the bedding dry was a tarpaulin Charles had bartered from a Dutchman. John and Charles traded several hours' work on his barn, and Sarah and Mary traded several days of candle and soap making to the Dutchman's wife. This had been a tedious month of building, repairing, caulking, and drill. Today they got some inkling of whether the drill was to pay off.

At ten o'clock the Bay men, over a thousand of them, were mustered, to be viewed by the general. The officers strutted about, waving their swords, and the sergeants barked orders to the corporals to get the men in line. After getting the soldiers in ranks six deep, they scurried down their rows, making sure all were straight and attentive. Then, from the right, a distant beat of a drum and a slow march tapped out. Charles was near the far right of the first rank and could see in the distance the regimental colours of their field officers in a massed presentation. Slowly they came toward the formation and the captains gave commands to their troops to take care. The soldiers had practiced daily and upon this command stood erect and held themselves proudly. As the procession moved closer Charles could tell it was not just the colours, but the field officers and General Johnson leading the way. When they passed in front of his company, Captain Burk commanded, "Present Your Firelocks!" The officers returned the salute and marched on to the end of the Massachusetts troops. Before dismissing the troops, Captain Burk told them General Johnson was pleased with their formation and to keep up the training.

Again today, Thursday, it was still rainy!

Around eleven they were made aware that William Shirley, Massachusetts governor and commanding general of the entire army, would be arriving in Albany within the hour. Charles' regiment was mustered and marched to the town where the combined armies of Massachusetts, Connecticut, Rhode Island, and New York men were formed up along the streets of the cantonment in his honor. Then they heard muffled drums in the distance. The officers gave last minute orders to the sergeants. Charles' company had been drawn up in front of the barracks area near the front gates to the fort. At this vantage point he was able to see the advancement of Shirley's procession. In the front marched his colours and music under a guard. Following these were the governor himself and several officers on horseback, and behind the officers marched several companies of soldiers.

From behind the army the fort's cannons began to roar in a salute to their arrival. The fort's gates opened and out marched General Johnson and his field officers with their colours behind them. General Shirley's procession halted just before General Johnson and the officers. Johnson and his fellow officers snapped a salute, and Governor Shirley and his officers returned it with vigor.

"Greetings, Your Excellency," offered Johnson.

"Thank you, General," replied Shirley with dignity. The governor dismounted and conversed with Johnson.

Shirley was an elder statesman. Coming to Boston in the 1730's, he established himself as a prominent lawyer and served in many political positions in the colony. In 1741 he became governor. He had also headed the successful capture of Louisbourg, leading the all-provincial campaign. Now in his sixties, Shirley presented the figure of a warrior, statesman and gentleman. Removing his hat, he returned a bow to Johnson, bending his near six-foot body. His long red uniform was crisp and slightly adorned in fine gold braid. The lines on his face revealed a mapping of experience, sincerity and care. To add to his stature of dignity he wore a shoulder-length white powdered campaigning wig.

"General, I have the army formed for you, Sir. They have been preparing and their officers continue to make ready our expeditions," stated Johnson. General Shirley was to personally lead a separate campaign against Fort Niagara to the west.

"Thank you, General Johnson," replied Shirley. "My compliments to your officers and men. Let us retire to our quarters and prepare for meetings."

"Sir, if I may," interrupted Johnson. "The officers wish to drink to your health, Sir. Bring forward the refreshments."

A group of soldiers carried out a campaign table and several trays with bottles of wine and glasses. The soldiers poured the wine and Johnson, the field officers, and Shirley raised their glasses to toast. "To your health, General Shirley, to our successful campaigns, and to the King!"

Shirley nodded to his officers, said thank you, and they drank their toast. Johnson turned and ordered the officers to dismiss their troops, and Generals Shirley and Johnson and their officers entered the fort. The army was dismissed to their soggy camps for another day.

After suffering through several more days of rainy weather it got dry, but hot, very hot!

Then, a week after Governor Shirley had arrived, Colonel Titcomb came in, and with him eight wagons of stores for his regiment. They pulled through the encampment and drew up before the regiment. The men charged them in hopes of their long-awaited needs being met. The regiment had been going without or making do for so long one could feel the tension at the officers' meetings when the subject of supplies was brought up. Those few units who had received stores had been required to share or to purchase what they could.

The soldiers were dispersed back to camp and formed up by their officers. Then Captain Burk stepped forward and gave orders to place the men into messes of six men and then to send representatives to the wagons where Commissary Taylor would distribute equipment and gear to each mess. Charles was grouped in with John, Samuel George, Thomas Greenleaf, Joseph Nicholes and Gideon Woodwell. According to regulations, followers of any in the mess were as well messmates. Consequently, Sarah and Mary continued with John and Charles. About one o'clock, Gideon, Thomas, and Charles returned to the wagons for their mess stores. The men were delighted as they were issued a tent, poles, pegs, blankets, and a kettle! Charles and the other two returned to their messmates who could hardly wait to set up their new home. Sarah and Mary were thrilled to get the kettle and started preparing a stew of salted beef, rice, and peas.

Around two o'clock, their corporal, Nathaniel Lowe, told Charles' mess to report back to the wagons. They were unsure of the reason, but they left immediately. Upon their arrival, William Taylor ordered them to strip off their waistcoats and coats. They did, reluctantly, and he produced a regimental coat from a crate. The six men were stunned;

their long awaited uniforms had arrived! Each of them tried on their red wool waistcoats, red breeches, and dark navy regimentals. They were unlined, without buttons, with red lapels and cuffs. Several men approached each of them and with pins temporarily tacked the coats to fit better. Then they left them and the next morning they were issued the tailored uniforms! Along with them, each man in the mess was issued a soldier's hat, shoes, stockings, shirt, knapsack, a tumpline for his blanket, powder horn, bullet bag, haversack, hatchet, and a Brown Bess musket! God, they were proud! They pranced through the streets of not just their regiment, but what felt like the entire British army, looking dapper and fine, dressed like soldiers!

For several days there was a buzz around the camps. It was suspected that either the enemy had advanced or the army finally was to be moving north. Something had to change quickly, for they became more bored by the hour! With some time free from duty, Charles sat down to pen a letter home.

Dearest parents,

I greet you with the news that all remains well in our army. None have perished and no battles have been fought. As of yet we have not taken a step north of Albany, but I expect to daily. I truly hope we will march. If we don't see a change soon I am afraid that our grand campaign will fail or boredom will destroy us. Many of us have become tired of building, and grumbling increases daily. Yesterday, we did receive uniforms and our long awaited stores. John, Sarah, and Mary send their greetings. They have helped make it bearable for me, especially the women. It is nice to have their personalities enhancing our camps. They are much different than the followers of some of the other colonies, but I do not feel it is appropriate to describe what I have witnessed. With God's guidance we will soon move forward and I will be home to share the harvest with you.

Write soon, Charles.

Charles placed the letter in the dispatch pouch at the adjutant's tent of his regiment and retired for the eve.

Saturday, Charles awoke to the voices of the corporals issuing orders. "Men of the regiment, fall in to receive orders. Fall In!" They crawled from their tent and stumbled into line. "Men, we are to get ready to move. Pack your gear and equipment. Wagons will be formed for you to pack your tents. After packing your gear reform. Nurse, you are to report to the fort and be prepared to copy orders for the captain. Dismissed."

The men and followers immediately began packing. Mary said she would stow Charles' gear for him. As he left for the fort he passed several wagons being loaded with ammunition, cannon stores, batteaus, and other stores. As he entered the fort Charles was directed to the aid-de-camp's office. The door was open, a guard asked his business and he directed Charles to enter. He did so and Captain Burk motioned for him to step to the rear. Several minutes later General Johnson entered.

"Gentlemen, our time has come. We will be moving forward today. The army will be divided into three divisions to advance. General Lyman, you are to lead the first division. These are the orders for you and your officers. You are to take into your charge two brass field pieces, their carriages and stores, which will be delivered to you by the commissary of the artillery, and to march with all the officers and men effective of the regiment under your command, with the batteaus, ammunition, stores, etc., to the Flats where the Massachusetts troops are encamped. There you are to take under your command, the regiment commanded by Colonel Ruggles, also the officers and effective men of Colonel Williams' company, of Lieutenant Colonel Pomeroy's company, of Captain Hawley's, Captain Porter's, and Captain Burk's companies.

"You are then to proceed with your command to the house of Colonel Lydius, near the Carrying Place, where you are to erect log magazines covered with bark sufficient to contain and secure from the weather, the ammunition, provisions, etc., belonging to the army under my command. I must recommend to you such a situation for these magazines as may best secure them from any attempts of the enemy. This you will also be very attentive to, in the encampment of your troops, which must be so laid out as to cover the magazines."

"From the Flats to Colonel Lydius', you are to open the road, twenty-five to thirty feet wide, where it will possibly admit of it, to have the trees, logs and all obstructions cleared away, the stumps trimmed close, bridges well repaired where necessary, and good ones made where wanted, on the whole as good a road made for carriages as possible, and besides the officers, who are over the workmen, you will please to take a review yourself. As you are well apprized of the sudden and lurking attacks of the enemy, I make no doubt but you will so dispose your troops and keep up such a discipline amongst them, as will secure the whole body from any reproachful insults from the scouting parties of the enemy."

"I shall speedily send out, and shall be constantly keeping out, reconnoitering parties of Indians about Crown Point and the surrounding country. Some white person, as an officer, will always be with them, though there should be but three or four Indians. I shall distinguish our friendly Indians with a red fillet round their heads and, should a single one by any accident fall in your way, I shall direct him to call out, "Warraghiyagey," which is my Indian name. You will take care that a few Indians do not draw you into an injudicious pursuit and that no man, upon pain of death, dare pursue the enemy without proper orders from his commanding officer. Any questions, Mr. Lyman, or your officers?"

The men in the room looked around at each other for a few seconds. "No, Sir, we understand," replied Lyman.

"Then carry out my orders. You are dismissed." The officers returned salutes and exited the office.

When Charles got back to where his camp was, all that was left were some wagons, and his company was formed and ready to march. He quickly joined his rank and saw Lyman and his artillery and the Connecticut regiment marching toward the flats. Soon the entire column was formed and they marched, slowly, ever so slowly. As they approached afternoon, rain began to fall and the road narrowed. A party of about twenty was sent forward to scout and 250 of their 1200 men were sent forward to widen the road to thirty feet. Trees and brush had overgrown the route, for it had not been used for large troop movements for several years. Their advance followed the west bank of the Hudson.

For two days the soldiers alternated work teams on the road. They advanced over the junction of the Hudson and the Mohawk Rivers, until on Tuesday they arrived at Half Moon. Here the troops rested for several hours trying to keep out of the day's rain. A dispatch rider came in around ten o'clock with a letter. It was an express from General Johnson. General Braddock had fallen in ambush on his expedition! All were shocked! What would they do? Was it true? In the letter General Johnson swore all to secrecy. General Lyman, as well, told his officers and clerks who heard the letter not to repeat a word of this to the men, but somehow rumors spread.

The next day they made it to Stillwater. Here the soldiers again had to rest. This work was terrible; the hardest Charles had ever attempted!

The road, they now found, in many places was only fifteen feet wide! Now the troops marched toward Saratoga, several days of hard work. It was so wearing on them that it took three days to get to Saratoga, and they rested again to continue. Here, north of the settlement the army was to cross the river and head up the eastern bank to the Carrying Place. At the portage north of Saratoga they had a rough going. The terrain was rugged; everything had to be unloaded from the carts. The boats were pulled over shallows by ropes and carried around rapids then reloaded. What strenuous and tedious labor this was! The weather was the only good aspect of late. The earlier days of rain and heat had brought out the insects to hamper them. They could not even open their eyes or breathe without swallowing any of these critters.

An express rider came in this eve and the General called together his officers. The captain sent for me. The General received a letter confirming Braddock's death and defeat; they are stunned, but no longer must keep it secret. General Johnson also informed Mr. Lyman as to other proceedings he is to advance toward, and elaborated on the importance of the wagon road and bridges. At the end of his letter he also added in reply to a letter from General Lyman, "that as to bad women following or being harbored in our camp, I shall discountenance it to the utmost of my power. As to men's wives, while they behave decently, they are suffered in all camps and thought necessary to wash and mend.

The next day, Charles did receive good orders! He and his mess were to march back to Albany and deliver dispatches, then move forward again with the next division and the rest of their regiment. This was easy duty compared to late!

They were given orders and a dispatch letter to deliver to General Johnson before leaving the next morning. With the attitude, the soldiers were starting to change. Morale was falling, tempers were short, and the men felt compromised leaving Sarah and Mary, but their orders were to return, just the six of them, quickly, and deliver the dispatches. Just before dawn they said quick good-byes and started marching back to Albany. The six moved at great speed compared to the advance. All along the route were gangs of men still working on the damned road. On the fourth day they arrived at Albany and took the dispatches to the general. While awaiting the general to dismiss them he asked, "In the letter, General Lyman recommends that we transport the remainder of our army's stores by wagons rather than batteaus?"

"Yes, Sir, it was very rough going. The rocks, rapids, and falls along the Hudson make a strenuous and I believe much longer movement," replied Charles.

"Very well men, return to your regiment." The messmates did so and spent a restful night reunited with their friends.

Early the next morning Charles was summoned to record the marching orders at Peter Maxwell's office, General Johnson's adjutant.

"Colonel Titcomb," addressed General Johnson, "by ten you are to advance with the second division to the Carrying Place. You are to take with you the rest of the stores, ammunitions, and artillery for the army. You are to load the batteaus on wagons and, as well, under General Lyman's recommendations you are to use wagons to transport all your stores. You are to transport in artillery, two 8-inch mortars, one 13-inch mortar, six 6-pounders, six 18-pounders, two 32-pounders, and all their stores, carriages, and ammunitions. I am of the understanding that the road north is ready for your departure. Any questions?"

"No, Sir, I am ready to move north. Advancing in wagons is an excellent choice as most of my batteaus are leaky and unfit for duty. This will allow me to see to their serviceability at the Carrying Place."

"Good luck, Sir," ordered Johnson. "I shall follow with the third division by the middle of the month."

After the officers received their orders, the men returned to their regiment. Since Charles and his mates had been up and down the road to the Carrying Place they were placed on the advanced party of Colonel Titcomb's column. The march was slow, but nothing like the torturous march cutting their way through the woods with the first division. Finally, after nearly a week, they arrived at the Carrying Place.

They could see a turn ahead in the river and then suddenly a voice called out from the thicket on their left.

"Halt! Who approaches?"

Quickly the lieutenant in their party raised his hand and halted them, turned around and sent a runner to the main party behind them, and replied to the voice, "Lieutenant William Taylor of Colonel Titcomb's Massachusetts Regiment."

"Advance!" replied the voice.

The advanced party walked forward slowly at the ready. Up stood three men. They had reached the advanced guard of General Lyman.

"Are you with the second division?"

"Yes we are," answered the lieutenant.

"I am Captain Payson of Lyman's Regiment. I'll send one of my corporals to lead you into the camp. Sorry for the delay, go ahead." The Connecticut corporal took the lead as they pushed forward.

As they rounded the next curve in the Hudson they crossed over a small creek. Nestled on the bank of the Hudson to the left was General Lyman's tented camp. In the center stood an old two-story, log blockhouse-type structure set within an old rickety stockade. This was Lydius' trade house. At first glance it was noticeable that Lyman's men had cleared more of an opening, built some temporary breastworks, and pitched their tents.

As Charles and the party came into the encampment there was little uniformity, although within each company most tents had been set up in some resemblance of straight lines. It was nearly time for the evening roast beef (as military dinner was called) and many groups of men were clustered around their fires preparing their meals. As the party was forming up and General Lyman was conversing with Colonel Titcomb, a party of six men came into the camp from the north. None of them were in uniform and looked like they had been in the woods for weeks.

The man in charge of this small party came immediately up to the general and saluted him. The general returned his salute. Charles could hear him ask, "Captain Babcock, what did you and your Rhode Islanders find on your scout?"

"Sir, we traveled north into the wet lands, I presume near the east side of Lake St. Sacrament. We saw nothing of an enemy. There was good sign of game though."

"Very good, Captain, see to your men."

"Colonel Titcomb, we are glad to see you. Did you have a difficult advance from Albany?"

"No, General, it was quite event-free. We saw no enemy parties and the road was quite sufficient," replied Titcomb.

"Obviously your men are tired from their long march. Dismiss them, Sir. Have your officers report to Colonel Williams and he, as officer of the day, will see to our encampment areas for your division. After dinner would you report to my tent to discuss our plans until General Johnson arrives?" asked General Lyman.

"Yes, Sir, thank you," replied Titcomb. The two exchanged salutes and the division was dismissed to set up their encampment. Charles and his mates were dismissed and, after inquiring about Captain Burk's company's encampment, headed toward the northwest corner of the camp. As they neared the area they were directed to, they could see the other company members huddled around their fires. Then they spotted Sarah and Mary at theirs.

"John! You're back!" yelled Sarah. They hurried to each other and embraced.

"Of course we're back, and we're hungry too," replied John.

Mary left the fire as well and hurried to her father.

"It's so nice to have you all back with us. Things have really been different this week since arriving here," expressed Sarah. "Come over and get rid of those packs, and Mary and I will fix you a fine stew," commanded Sarah.

They all walked to the tent and took off their gear and collapsed on the ground around their mess fire. "Oh, it's good to set down and know you can relax a couple hours and not have to get up and march tomorrow," said Charles with a sigh.

"Was it a hard march?" asked Mary.

"No, not as bad as it was when we had to clear the road, but we've been marching for weeks now. It's time to give our feet a rest."

"There hasn't been much rest around here," replied Sarah as she started to add food to the kettle. "Most of the men have been either building or on guard duty."

"I'll take guard duty any day," said Thomas Greenleaf. "I'm done marching for this campaign."

Within about a half an hour the two women had a stew finished and the messmates devoured it happily. Then a corporal came by and ordered half of each mess to report for guard duty. Samuel George, Thomas, and Gideon Woodwell took this duty and the rest of the men just sat back and relaxed. All around them the rest of Titcomb's Regiment were setting up their tents and preparing their food. This gave time for Sarah to catch them up on what had been going on.

"Most of the men have spent the majority of their time cutting timber, setting up some resemblance of safety around this place, and standing guard. Every day the general sends out scouts to the north but no sign of an enemy has been found. This is good news, for everything has not been peaceful around here," said Sarah. "We can not believe some of the actions of these so called men from some of the other colonies! And our New Englanders have not always been innocent."

"What kind of problems have there been in camp?" asked Charles.

"I think most are just tired of all the backbreaking work. They have been drinking and gaming and there have even been several men shot by their fellow soldiers who randomly fire anytime, anywhere they choose. This morning a soldier called Bickerstaff was whipped and drummed out of camp with a rope around his neck. They took him to Albany. They gave orders to jail him until the campaign is over. He had been using the foulest language and last night had tried to force a woman from one of the other camps to commit unspeakable acts. This was not the first time I had heard he had tried this."

"No wonder you were so glad to see us," said John.

"And I was very glad to see you, Charles," added Mary.

"I promised your mother I'd watch over you, and I intend to."

Shortly after sunset the conversations waned, and the tired travelers settled into their tent and slept.

WILL WE EVER GET TO FIGHT?

The next morning the army awoke to a very fair and pleasant day. After the morning meal and inspection, several groups of men were sent out to scout for enemy parties, other groups were assigned guard duty, and the rest were placed on work details. About thirty men, including Charles, went into the surrounding woods to cut timber. They were issued axes, shovels, picks and saws. Once they found a good site, ten men with muskets covered the work by acting as the cutting party's guards, while the rest started cutting. Once a tree was felled, one team of men would cut the tree into sections while another team trimmed off all the branches and limbs. Then a team of oxen was chained to the sections and dragged them off to camp. The soldiers did this all day. For a week they did the same monotonous things: cut timber, set guard duty, or build storehouses and picketed walls. The storehouses were made in an L shape, seventy feet long on one side, forty on the other, and fifteen feet wide. The roof was a simple lean-to. Two portholes were cut in the walls, from which to fire weapons if necessary. The stockade was about half an acre around. John had been assigned to make the hinges and other hardware for these buildings. He was happy; this was the work he was best suited for.

On Monday Charles and several friends went hunting and fishing. This was a relaxing pleasure! They killed two deer and caught thirty large fish. What a wonderful feast they supplied! This was well earned, for they were all growing weary with the continual work and the endless waiting to advance to take the enemy's forts to the north.

In the evening, Mary and Charles took a walk through the camps after dinner.

"That was a wonderful feast," said Charles, with a sigh of contentment. "I have not eaten that well since I left home."

"The fat doe you brought in was young and tender," replied Mary, with a flirtatious air.

As they wandered down the company streets of Massachusetts they greeted many soldiers they knew or had met. They decided to venture into the streets of the other troops as well. As they left Connecticut's camp and entered the Yorkers', it was like entering a different world. There was noise coming from many of the camps; yelling, swearing and fighting. Charles hurried Mary along to a quieter end of the camp. Then, from the flicker of candlelight between some tents, the strolling couple reeled in shock at the appalling sight of naked flesh! Two whores and a half-clothed, bare-chested Yorker were groping at each other in a trio of lewd debauchery! Immediately Charles and Mary turned about and scurried from the camp, passing the Rhode Island picket guard where several officers and soldiers were engaged in gaming and loud drinking. One in this group yelled, "Got yourself some pleasure for tonight there, friend? How about sharing a little?" Charles was shocked and Mary was instantly scandalized. Coming from old New England stock, they were revolted at such an outburst.

As they hurried back to their camp, Charles apologized. "I am so very sorry, Mary. I had no idea that sort of thing could have been going on or I would have never taken you from this camp!"

"Don't worry, Charles, it wasn't your fault. It is difficult to walk through these camps and not run into immorality. It has been a constant reminder of how far away we are from home. I have even seen the whores that follow the New York and Rhode Island troops in the New England camps," confided Mary in an ashamed voice. Cutting their walk short, they returned to their own camp and retired for the evening.

The next day the army was in preparation for General Johnson's arrival. About four in the afternoon the drums of the camp began beating to arms. All soldiers immediately dropped everything they were doing and hurried to their assigned formations. Burk's company formed near the middle of Colonel Titcomb's Regiment, with their backs to the stockade of the storehouses and facing the west, toward the river. Within minutes the army had been formed and word was being passed that the general was arriving, and to prepare to honor him. The army was quickly reformed, placing the Bay Colony Regiments on the right side of the main road leading into the camp to the storehouses and Lydius' house. The Connecticut, Rhode Island, and New York Regiments were formed on the left of the road. All were faced into the road and brought to attention. Two of the six-pound field pieces were placed at the head of both columns and loaded to fire a salute.

Soon they could hear the drums of Johnson and the third division. First entering the road was a company of Yorkers who undoubtedly had acted as Johnson's advanced guard, followed by Johnson, his field officers, and several Indians. After this marched the remainder of the army's troops from Massachusetts, Connecticut, and Rhode Island. Then with great dignity and pomp entered another forty savages. The two six-pounders were fired and both the right and left columns of Lyman's men snapped to salute the general by presenting their arms. At the head of the street, General Lyman greeted General Johnson with a smart salute. Polite military welcomes were exchanged between Johnson, Lyman, and the field officers.

"Welcome, General, to Fort Nicholson. Your command has been assembled and awaits your orders, Sir. They are anxious to do battle, Sir," addressed General Lyman as he doffed his tricorn in a gracious salute.

"Thank you, General Lyman. This is a grand assemblage of fighting men. I am pleased to hear they are anxious, for the time to fulfill our destiny is drawing nigh" replied Johnson.

"We await your orders, Sir," stated Lyman.

"General, I would like to have these regiments that just arrived encamped and my marquee and the tents of our army's field command set up on the island across the river. As to the rest of our army, have an extra gill of rum rationed out in celebration of our united force, and then prepare for an inspection in the morning. After the inspection I would appreciate a tour of the area, followed by my first council of war. It shall take place at my tent."

"Very well, Sir, I will see to it," replied Lyman. He then turned to the field officers and ordered, "Gentlemen, you have heard the general's orders. I expect all preparations to be taken care of immediately. Relocate your quarters to the island with the general's. Any questions, gentlemen?" Lyman paused, "Fine, then issue your commands and dismiss your regiments." The officers of the field command and the generals returned salutes, and commands were issued down the regimental chains of command. In no time the tents of the newly arrived soldiers were set up and Johnson's and the commanders' marquees and wall tents were erected into a command headquarters on the island.

There was gossip of an Indian ceremony about to take place. Being curious, many of the men wanted to observe. A large fire had been kindled and an entire ox had been placed over it to roast in honor of the savages. Samuel, John, Mary, Sarah and Charles arrived to a crowd of onlookers. They were able to maneuver their way behind some of the officers who had placed themselves very close to the spectacle. The obscenity of the savages' dress was very new to many in the audience. Most of the natives were nearly naked, wearing only an apron or short skirt over their loins. The only other garments they wore were moccasins on their feet. Their bodies as well as their faces were painted many colors: blue, yellow, red, black, green and white. Some of them had tattoos on their faces and bodies and some had the most peculiar mutilated earlobes; some stretching to their shoulders. Many had only a tuft of hair near the top of their heads, but some had shaved their heads in a line from their ears forward and painted their foreheads red. Those with tufts of hair adorned them with feathers, beads, and paint; twisting the mass all together in a colorful arrangement. They hung jewelry about their necks and wrists, and some even wore jewels and feathers in their nostrils.

The natives entered the fire pit area silently, skulking mysteriously and driving many a white man from his wits. "Samuel, look at that one, he's staring right at you!" said John excitedly, poking Samuel in the arm.

"Don't scare people, John, it's bad enough simply having to witness this barbarity," scolded Sarah.

The majority of the soldiers sat or stood in awe of the spectacle in front of them. Just in front of Charles and his friends, some of the officers were making comments as well. Suddenly there were yells from within the crowd of natives and many of them began to run and dance around the circle the soldiers had created around the fire. Many in the crowd jumped with fright at the beginning of the noise and Sarah and Mary almost took off running.

Mary yelled, "Charles! Keep them away from me!"

"Relax, Mary, it's only a ceremony. Relax," Charles said in a reassuring and sensitive voice.

Suddenly, the noise and movement stopped, and into the center walked an older Indian. "It's King Hendrick," whispered one of the officers to another in front of Samuel. Hendrick was a Mohican who was born in Westfield, Massachusetts. He was over seventy-five years old and was General Johnson's major liaison with the Mohawks. His native name was Theyanogiun. In 1680, when he was only a boy, his family had migrated to the Mohawk Valley and was adopted into the Wolf clan. In 1690, Hendrick converted to Christianity in the Dutch Reform Church and traveled north into New France. Twice Hendrick traveled to England, first in 1710, meeting Queen Anne, and again in

1740, meeting King George, who presented Hendrick with a courtier's costume of blue laced with gold, and a gold-laced tricorn hat. Accompanying Hendrick was thirteen-year-old Keghneghtaga, or Joseph Brandt, the brother of Johnson's Mohawk wife.

Hendrick stood before his tribesmen and gave a short oration in their language, then motioned to several ominous looking braves at the edge of the circle and yelled, "Warraghiyagey!" and waved his arm as if he were collecting something. Quickly two of the braves brought General Johnson into the circle. Removing his tricorn and waistcoat, Johnson handed them to his nephew. Several other savages walked over to Johnson, holding shells filled with paint. One by one, Hendrick took each shell and raised it aloft as if making an offering to the four cardinal directions. Then Hendrick smeared Johnson's face with grease and a yell went up from the Indians who all started moving in place as if keeping rhythmic time. Hendrick, taking one color at a time, applied all the colors of war paint to the general's face, as the soldiers watched, stunned. After that, a smoldering conch shell was brought over, and Hendrick anointed Johnson with the smoke from head to foot. Hendrick chanted a short oration, and the savages, led by Johnson and Hendrick, began dancing, jumping, and parading about the fire with their weapons drawn. After several minutes General Johnson, who looked more savage than white, raised both arms to the sky and yelled in their tongue a chant, stopping all the sounds and motions. Then in English, Johnson yelled, "I Warraghiyagey, Johnson, brother of the Mohawk, will lead you in battle! Your King Theyanogiun, Hendrick, my brother, leads you to victory! Our father, King George, calls us here to drive the French from our valley of the Mohawks. Take heed, I will show you victory!" Then in a shocking single movement Johnson drew his sword from his side, raised it above his head and drove it downward in a violent arch, slicing the air and lobbing off a large chunk of the ox over the fire. Lifting it over his head and raising a goblet of wine handed him by Brandt, he yelled, "Take notice my children, my brothers, I take the first flesh and blood in our victory!" Then Johnson bit a piece of the ox and drank from the goblet. Immediately the savages started devouring the ox and wine from a keg at the edge of the circle.

The soldiers were horrified. Very few could utter any words. Then Charles could hear several officers in front of him, one saying, "It will be much greater pleasure if I can see them fight against the French with as much eagerness as they have drunk their wine and eaten their roasted ox." In a state of mental paralysis, the colonists returned to their camps, undoubtedly filling their further discussions and dreams with what their puritan morality viewed as obscenities acted out by Johnson and his savages.

Early the next morning, Charles was summoned to record information from a council of war. Quickly retrieving his quill, ink pot, and journal, Charles walked across the makeshift bridge over the Hudson and approached the large marquee holding General Johnson's office. Outside the tent stood two armed sentries and a lieutenant of the New York Regiment. After identifying himself, Charles was allowed to enter, and took his place in the rear behind the Massachusetts field officers. Present were Generals Johnson and Lyman as well as the majority of the colonels, lieutenant colonels, and majors of Massachusetts, Connecticut, New York, and Rhode Island. General Johnson called the meeting to order.

"Gentlemen, in talking to several of you about our situation and the morale of our troops, I feel we need to discuss some issues in order to be successful in our campaign. I, from my tour of our encampment this morning, have drawn some of my own conclusions as well. At this time I will entertain questions or statements from you."

General Lyman rose and asked to address the officers. "Fellow officers of this command family. We are brought here as the united right arm of God. As we know, we are to help drive the French, God's enemies, from North America. I personally feel that this body, if advanced quickly, will be successful. I also believe that if we hesitate we may pay severe penalties."

Next, Lieutenant Colonel Edward Cole of Rhode Island stood to address the corps. "Gentlemen, it is as well my belief that we are ready for an engagement but I am very concerned about our numbers. I feel we should augment our army with an additional 5,000 men from our colonies."

Colonel Cockcroft of New York interrupted, "Sir, I agree that we need to increase our numbers, but I think, considering we have not had any engagements with the enemy—not even a small scouting party sighted—that our colonies would be unwilling to vote higher levies to fight ghosts."

"Unfortunately gentlemen, I am of the understanding that Rhode Island has supplied all the men she can spare," offered Colonel Cole.

Colonel Ruggles of Massachusetts next spoke, "I recommend sending to the Massachusetts General Court for additional support."

"I agree we should contact our colonial court for reinforcement, but I believe Massachusetts-Bay cannot support all of North America by herself. What of New York and Connecticut?" asked Lieutenant Colonel Pomeroy of Massachusetts.

Colonel Goodrich of Connecticut stood and said abruptly, "You need not worry about Connecticut, we have many men of honor who will gladly answer our call for reinforcement!"

"And I can vouch for more New York levies," responded Johnson.

Colonel Whiting stood looking at a paper he had jotted some figures on, "Realistically, gentlemen, I believe our colonies could supply 1,500 more men for this expedition without opening all colonial borders to the enemy. I recommend raising 400 men from Massachusetts, Connecticut and New York, and 300 from Rhode Island."

"Sir," interrupted Cole, "I do not believe Rhode Island will raise more troops. Before leaving and in correspondence from my colony, they have expressed repeatedly no more Rhode Islanders will be raised for this campaign. I am sorry, gentlemen."

"I believe Massachusetts could augment up to 500 men from their levies. I felt in the last General Court meeting I attended before leaving that the body was prepared to fully support this campaign," offered Colonel Williams.

"As well I believe Connecticut can raise 500 instead of 400 gentlemen," said Lyman.

"Gentlemen, I feel we need to limit our call for reinforcements to 1,400. I feel it may be too much of a strain on New York to call up another hundred men since the campaign is being fought in our colony. We are being imposed upon enough at this time," said Johnson, concerned. Then he paused, rubbed his forehead, and pointed to Peter Wraxall "Take this down, Mr. Wraxall. Gentlemen, I propose that letters be sent immediately to the colonial legislatures of Massachusetts, Connecticut, and New York for 1,400 men to support our army in this campaign. What is our next concern, gentlemen?"

Ephraim Williams stood and addressed the officers in a sincere tone of saddened disgust, "We are a wicked, profane army, more especially New York troops and Rhode Island—nothing to be heard among a great part of us but the language of hell! I am truly concerned about our army's morality. My belief is that part of this deplorable behavior stems from the bad women following our troops."

"Mr. Williams, to a degree I believe some of our followers may cause problems, but, I will need more time to look into the behavior of our soldiers and camp followers. As to the behaviors of our army, I have seen and been privy to many recent reports of petty offences in our camps."

"General, in defense of recent behaviors, I have received from my company officers concerns and grievances about the boredom and strain of road, boat, and fort building. The heat and insects have been hampering this work as well," offered Colonel Ruggles.

General Johnson continued, "If we do not take charge of these situations in our camps, it will be impossible to beat the French, when we are beating ourselves! Drunkenness, swearing, breaking the Sabbath, and unauthorized firing of muskets just break the surface." Johnson continued while rapping the forefinger of his left hand on the table before him as he lectured, "Even my officers have lowered themselves to debauchery! Mr. Ruggles, do you not recall the lieutenant from your colony who was convicted for inciting his men to mutiny? And what about your Connecticut captain, Mr. Lyman, who was confined for selling rum to the Indians? At times the insatiable thirst of rum by our natives takes up the majority of my days. Furthermore, the continual complaints of ye officers leads me to an opinion that New Englanders are a low, weak people. It became apparent many officers of this army would rather join their men than restrain them!" The New Englanders sat stunned!

Moses Titcomb rose from the accompanying silence and stated in a calm, methodical voice, "General, it is my recommendation that you personally observe this fine army more before you judge so severely. Remember, this is not the first provincial army to succeed against our enemy, the French. Also, Sir, please keep in mind, without our entire unity we cannot succeed in God's glory! I, and the rest of the New England officers, am of the opinion that part of our army's problem stems from the idea that we New Englanders have signed on to fight, and the quicker we are brought to bear on the French the better our morale will survive. We are ready to follow you to St. Frederic, but don't delay."

"Very well men, return to your soldiers and prepare them to advance. In a short time our preparations will be done, and in days we will push forward. I formally request your indulgence to holding your men to their military duties. I retract my premature conclusions and will continue to re-evaluate my opinions. Gentlemen, you are dismissed," ordered Johnson.

Around evening, the fort's sentries were alerted that a party was approaching from the south. They quickly learned that it was part of the New Hampshire Regiment that the army had been waiting for. It was under the command of Colonel Joseph Blanchard and Lieutenant Colonel Willard. In a hastily called officers' meeting, Blanchard was upset that Johnson had not left supplies for the New Hampshire Regiment. Blanchard's men had marched from western New Hampshire southwest to Albany with little supply and reached Albany finding no food or stores for their near-starving troops. Johnson immediately ordered Blanchard back to Albany with orders to cut all red tape and to get the food for his men. Blanchard left Willard in charge and hurried south that evening with a small escort.

On Sunday, all but the guard attended services, as usual, then part of the men were assigned work details. Charles and his messmates had spent a relaxing morn when their side of the camp was alarmed by yells for the surgeon and the running of men toward the northern gun emplacements. Charles, Thomas, and Gideon took off running toward the yells as well. When they arrived they were in a crowd of soldiers from Massachusetts. Peering around an end Charles saw the reason for the commotion. While attempting to move one of the heavy 32-pound siege guns into position, it had become unsecured and had rolled over the leg of Big Winchell, one of Ephraim Williams' men. Winchell was an ox of a man, standing six foot three and weighing near three hundred pounds. It was quite common to seek his assistance on this type of close-quarters, strenuous work. He lay there with the most hideous look of torture on his face with six men trying with all their might to move the cannon from his leg. Quickly, drag ropes were hooked to the carriage and four men grabbed each rope and released Winchell. Thomas Williams, the colonel's brother and surgeon of his regiment knelt down beside Winchell and daubed the excess blood that spurted from the leg exposing the bright white jagged broken thigh bone which protruded through the ripped flesh. Dr. Williams quickly pulled a piece of fabric from his pocket and lashed it around the leg just as his two assistants Perez Marsh and Billy Williams arrived with a stretcher. Winchell was lifted on the stretcher by eight men and strenuously carried off to the surgeon's tent. Charles and his friends were shaken up, as were most of the soldiers who witnessed the accident.

After returning to camp, their mid-day meal was ready. Charles took only a small portion of his rice and a slice of bread. He strolled to the edge of camp and sat down with a heavy sigh, resting his back against a stack of crates. He had had about all he could stand of this military experience. Setting his food aside, he pulled some paper, a quill, and his inkpot from his pocket and started to write a letter home. He did not have much time to write when he felt a soft touch on his right shoulder. It was Mary.

"What are you doing, Charles?" asked Mary in a soft voice. "You barely took any food; are you sick?" Mary sat down close beside Charles.

"I thought I would write a letter to my parents."

"Charles, you can tell me what is bothering you."

"Mary, I don't think it would be fair to burden you with my feelings."

"Is it my age, Charles? I am very interested in your feelings. Don't let our ages keep you away from me, I am going to be seventeen in two weeks."

"I know, but that is only part of it."

"Was it the accident?" asked Mary.

"It is much more than that. I have virtually reached the end of my rope with this soldier's life! I don't know how you and your mother can take it! First, we get to Albany and have no supplies. Then, we have to cut a road all the way to this place and daily we are building roads, boats, or this fort. I signed on to fight the French, God's enemies, but the most fighting we have seen is fighting to keep enough supplies, and the constant battle with the flies and mosquitoes! If that isn't enough, the morality of these camps is deplorable. I truly wish you and your mother did not have to witness the drunkenness, swearing, gaming, and bad women. Either I must soon go to battle or return home before I can no longer distinguish these behaviors as wrong! Please Mary, don't think wrong of me, I hate this situation."

Mary took his hand in hers and whispered, "I understand, Charles. Don't worry. Write to your parents and remember I am here with you."

Charles was confused by her concern for him and her statements. To him she had been the daughter of a friend. He remembered his brother's interest in her as well. For the first time though, Charles saw her more as the young woman she was, and took great comfort and pleasure in the warmth from her caressing hands.

Just at that moment, an Indian scouting party came into camp. Their news raised a commotion; for they brought reconnaissance that several hundred enemy natives had attacked supply wagons coming from Albany. They also stated there were hundreds of Indians waiting in ambush. Johnson immediately called together his officers and had three parties organized. First, 400 soldiers were sent to relieve the supply wagons. Since Massachusetts had the largest contingent, Lieutenant William Taylor of Titcomb's Regiment took 40 men for the second party. His party consisted of 15 of his own, 10 of the Yorkers, 15 from Connecticut, and 5 Rhode Islanders. Taylor also was given three of Johnson's Mohawks to guide them. The lieutenant's party was ordered toward Fort Anne, an old blockhouse used in the previous war, and South Bay, between the Carrying Place and Old Fort Anne.

Captain Burk led the third party. He commanded twelve men from his company including Charles, Sergeant Colby, Gideon Woodwell, Samuel George, Nathaniel Hunt, Ebenezer Davis, John Cooper, Theodore Hoyt, William Noyce, Ebenezer Buck and Abraham Young. Johnson also sent three Mohawks with this party. Burk's party was to scout north to Lake St. Sacrament. They were ordered to carry a shirt and pair of stockings rolled up in their blankets on a tumpline. Then they were called to muster and were issued two pounds of bread, two pints of peas, and two pounds of beef that had been boiled. This they placed in their rough linen haversacks. Into their tin flasks and wooden bottles they poured three gills of rum to mix in their water. Charles was ready to march.

From the edge of the formation Johnson, Hendrick, Titcomb, and Burk were discussing the orders. Then Captain Burk saluted the other officers and marched over to his detachment. "Alright men, we are to head up the Indian trail along the west side of the drowned lands and South Bay to Lake St. Sacrament. I want us to stay together with silence on the march. We are marching into enemy territory, so be alert at all times. You were selected because you have hunting experience, so move as if you are hunting a deer. Sergeant Colby, take the Mohawks and take the point. Once we get out of the stockade, men, spread out, but keep close enough to see me. My orders will be by hand, not voice. Move forward," ordered Burk.

Burk's scout exited the safety of the stockade, and the sergeant and Mohawks ran to the cover of the woods. The rest spread out and walked into the woods. Moving quickly, the Mohawks led the party onto a narrow path resembling a lane in a farm field. The trail ran fairly straight northward. Huge trunks were spaced apart, creating vast openings under the trees. In most areas the path zigzagged around fallen trees or limbs but occasionally they hurdled fallen trunks nearly three feet in diameter. On the left the flankers constantly had the river in sight. Near the area where the Hudson turns west the trail forked, one trail following the river, the other turning northwest.

The fair day's sun trickled through the trees, warming and lighting the route. All through the march Burk kept the Mohawks in front, as well as a man on each of the flanks and two behind so no enemy could sneak up on them.

Gradually the march became more rugged and Charles could see huge mountain tops several miles ahead. Near noon the soldiers forded a small brook, and about a half-hour later they were stopped by a Mohawk who informed them that the party was about halfway to Lake St. Sacrament. Here they stopped and, after posting several guards, refreshed themselves. Within about fifteen minutes they set off again. At this point in the march the trail narrowed, bringing Charles to mind of a deer trail. The vegetation now changed as well to a lush conifer forest. The canopy of green needles blocked out most of the sunlight, occasionally opening with small exposures to the heavens. These huge pines gave Charles the feeling of walking through miles of church spires. The travel became easier for the lack of undergrowth in many spots, caused by the sparse light on the forest floor. To Charles, the softness of the earth caused by the depth of fallen needles under his feet felt like walking on a feather bed. On this part of their trek the men traversed around any fallen trunks, as many reached diameters of a man's height.

Around two o'clock they forded another brook and headed into what they thought to be a cleft between several noble mountains. Many of them remarked how glad they were, *not* to be climbing these mountains. They passed over three small creeks barely more than a trickle.

Near five o'clock, the party marched into a swampy area with two small rises on each flank. Motioned on by their advanced guard, they caught their first glimpse of a beautiful lake. They angled their march to the small knoll on their right, and staying within the cover of the pines, reclined amongst the trunks and surveyed the lake's perimeter.

From Charles' vantage point the deep blue waters before him appeared to be a large rectangular bay, ringed by lush, tree-covered mountains. Within this vast forested area, it was inconceivable how he could run across an enemy party. The French and their natives, on the other hand, could have been on the tops of any of the surrounding mountains, observing his every move.

After reassuring themselves of their relative safety, the men ate a cold meal from their haversacks and placed their evening guards near the perimeter of the woods. The Mohawks were sent to the top of the mountain to the east to get the best look at the area. As darkness fell over the party, those who were not on guard made deep, fragrant beds of pine needles and boughs, and, without fires, slept until their guard time approached.

Around two in the morning, Nathaniel Hunt nudged Charles to consciousness. He rose, put on his shoes, and taking up his musket, bags, and hat, pulled himself to his feet. In a voice hardly recognizable from the softness of his whisper, Hunt said, "Everything has been very quiet. It's so dark I don't think I've seen, bat, deer, or goblin. Do you have a time piece?"

Charles answered softly, "I have my father's, and a fine trustworthy one it is."

"See you in the morning," whispered Nathaniel.

Charles, in a sleepy stagger, walked to the tree at the edge of the woods near the water and the wetlands where he was to post. He stood there, keeping himself awake for a short time, then gave in to his sore feet and sat down, resting against a large tree. Charles felt himself nodding off and shook himself quietly. Try as he might, he could not stay awake. Suddenly, he awoke with a start, but found nothing that would have awakened him.

He stood up and remained awake for an hour, but then he started to nod off again. Before he totally fell asleep, he heard to his left a rustle in the weeds of the wetlands. His heart began to race uncontrollably. He had been in this situation before when hunting, but this time it seemed different. He raised his firelock to his shoulder, cocked it, and waited. Out stepped a small doe, coming to the lake to drink. Charles relaxed and quietly sighed. Then suddenly from behind him cracked a twig, not like a deer, but like a man!

Charles froze. He swung his eyes to the left, but he did not dare move his head. Slowly Charles raised his musket, inch by inch, until he had it at his shoulder. His head and neck were ready to explode on every pumping of his heart. Every muscle in his body became tense, even his eyelids, as he squinted to peer deeper into the darkness. Twenty feet in front of Charles, near the very edge of the swamp stood a large alder. Charles' eyes caught the motion of what he thought had been a branch. Slowly the branch edged down and forward. Charles began to breathe quickly. He was worried whatever or whoever it was could hear him breathe, so he tried to hold his breath. With another slight movement, the silhouette of an Indian's head edged out between the branch and the tree! Was it an enemy Indian or one of their Mohawks; could he take the chance and not fire? Then softly from behind the silhouette Charles heard a familiar voice.

"Oran ia O wise, (Black Ice) what did you see from the top of the mountain?" It was the captain's voice, speaking to one of their Mohawks.

"We saw nothing but deer," answered the Indian.

Charles slumped, almost going limp from the relaxation of all the muscles in his body. The Mohawk had scared out the deer as he was returning to the detachment. Charles had no problem staying awake the rest of his watch.

FINAL PREPARATIONS

By dawn Captain Burk had pulled in his guards and after directing his forward scouts, rear guard, and flankers, started their march back to Fort Nicholson. They progressed quickly, seeing no sign of any enemy. With the fair weather the party easily reached the fort before dusk. Shortly after arriving, the captain reported to General Johnson, and at six o'clock the general called together his field officers for a council of war. Charles was summoned to take clerical records. When he arrived at the field command headquarters General Johnson was just preparing to begin. He was giving final directions to Peter Wraxall, who was acting as secretary for the council. Present were Major General Lyman, Colonels Timothy Ruggles, Moses Titcomb, Ephraim Williams, Elizur Goodrich, Christopher Harris, William Cockcroft; Lieutenant Colonels Jonathan Bagley, Seth Pomeroy, John Pitkin, Nathan Whiting, Edward Cole; and Captain William Eyre.

"Gentlemen, I have now received reports from the three parties sent out yesterday. First of all, as we know now, the attack on the wagons was a false alarm; no attack took place, and no party of Indians was spotted. The second party, led by Captain Taylor, saw only an old campsite, but no fresh sign of any enemy movement toward Old Fort Anne. Captain Burk's party just arrived back with a report of no enemy sighted between here and Lake St. Sacrament.

"What say ye, gentlemen? Would it be safe and expedient to send one-half of the artillery and train with a first division to march and cut a road to South Bay and there erect a place of strength and build magazines?"

"I recommend we take our artillery. It is a crucial part of our forward advancement," stated Eyre.

"I disagree with Mr. Eyre," said Whiting. "We must not risk the loss of our artillery until a proper road has been constructed to move it. Our speed of advancement, or retreat, may be crucial."

Titcomb interrupted, "It is my belief that any large party moving forward with the mission of fortification must take artillery with them!"

No one else offered any opinion, so Johnson called for a vote. "How many of you are for sending half of our artillery, say yea; those against, nay." Seven of the thirteen officers said yea. "Mr. Wraxall, record that it was resolved to send half our artillery with a road building party north," ordered Johnson.

"The next item of concern is the number of men judged safe and sufficient a party to cut a road to South Bay, and if that road is found practical, or if another route be better."

"Colonels Ruggles and Williams and I were discussing the idea of advancing to Old Fort Anne," replied Cockcroft. "It was our opinion that this old trail would not prove to be the chosen route of campaigns for our army or the enemy."

"This is true, General," added General Lyman. "It has been years since this eastern avenue has taken precedence over the western."

"I agree, gentlemen, that our best choice may be to advance up Lake St. Sacrament toward the heart of the French forts," reassured Johnson. "Let us give thought to our route for our next council. Is 1,000 an acceptable number of men for this expedition?" asked Johnson.

"I recommend 2,000," replied Lyman.

"I recommend, gentlemen, that we say 1,500 at present and if need be, re-evaluate the force at another council," offered Titcomb.

Several answered this statement with affirmatives and Johnson called for a vote. Nine to three voted to send 1,500 men toward the next water.

"Who shall command this first division, gentlemen?"

Several called out, "Lyman!"

"Is it the major general, gentlemen?" Unanimously, they voted yea. "Record General Lyman as the most proper officer to lead this party, Mr. Wraxall," ordered Johnson.

"General, Sir," offered Lyman as he stood to address the council, "If I am to lead this first division, and in my capacity as your second in command, I must insist on cleansing our army of the bad women that follow our soldiery! By allowing these women of the devil to consume our morals we are propagating sure defeat! I fully understand the need of good women as our cooks, seamstresses, washer women, and nurses, but I am appalled with the overwhelming character of the Yorker and Rhode Island followers."

Edward Cole rose in dispute, "General, these women are essential to the success of our expedition. Without them I feel the wind will be struck from our sails and men will not have the gumption to progress.

These ladies are not all bad women, and I, for one, take offense to your comments!"

"I, Sir, take offense to your use of the term ladies in representing these sluts! They shall have us all in Hell before we are victorious! And as to the wind in our sails, I am afraid of your wind dashing us against the rocks!"

After these outbursts the vast majority of the New Englanders grumbled loudly for ridding the bad women from the army. The New York and Rhode Island officers on the other hand expressed their opinions on keeping their mistresses. They were at a standstill as General Lyman stood in great emotion and stated, "I demand all the women be sent back to Albany at the earliest convenience! General Johnson, bring it to a vote!"

Johnson rose slowly, "'Tis a vote you want, how many in favor of sending away the women? How many against?" The New Englanders, with the greatest numbers, won, eight to four. "Mr. Wraxall, record it!" said Johnson in a perturbed tone.

"The final issue, gentlemen, involves the construction of a fortification here at the Great Carrying Place. I have asked Captain Eyre to draw up plans for presentation at this meeting. Captain Eyre, if you would," said Johnson.

Eyre stood up and lifted a canvas from a map he had placed on the center table. Pointing to the various components on the map he described his plan. "This work is to be so situated as not to be nearer than 600 yards to any eminence higher than that which it stands upon; all within that distance, is either on a level with it, or lower. It is designed to contain a garrison of 400 men. There is one magazine for powder, and the necessary barracks and storehouses are now being built. The approximate overall measurements on the north and east walls are 110 feet, and on the south and west, 100 feet. On the north and east sides I recommend a dry moat 14 feet wide and 8 feet deep. The earth from the moat is to be thrown up toward the fort with pickets atop, inclining outward. The west side of the fort is guarded by a natural barrier, the Hudson River, and only requires a stockaded curtain, as does the south, which is guarded naturally by the creek. There should be only three bastions needed of approximately 25 by 60 feet in the northwest, northeast, and southeast. I have planned three gates. One gate is to be on the river side, near the southwest; it is to be the postern gate. A small gate is to be placed in the center of the north wall with a small exterior palisade to protect it. The third gate is an underground passage in the northeast to be used in the event of an emergency. For buildings within the palisades, we will improve the magazine General Lyman built when first arriving here. It will remain one story but will receive a new roof of shingles atop heavy timbers. Lydius' house on the east of the compound will be enlarged to 35 by 20 feet. This will be officers' quarters and storehouse. On the west of the compound, another structure of the same size will be built as a barracks and storehouse. Eight of our cannon will be mounted strategically on the ramparts. Six of the cannon will be on the bastions; two on each. The other two cannon are to be placed one at each gate. Finally, the flagstaff shall be erected at the north gate." Eyre paused, "These, gentlemen, are the plans as General Johnson directed to be drawn from information submitted by you, his military family. Of course, there will be modifications, and, as time progresses, expansions or strengthening may be wanted. Thank you, gentlemen."

"Very well, then," stated Johnson. "General Lyman will be moving forward shortly with a first division to build a better road to the north. Our next meeting will decide which course to choose. This division will take half our artillery, leaving the rest to protect the new fort designed by Captain Eyre and built by the men left here. And as to the women of our camp, they are to be sent back to Albany at the next opportune moment. Gentlemen, prepare your regimental officers with the details from our council; you are dismissed."

At 10:30 in the morning Charles was ordered off a work detail of digging a trench with 300 others around their storehouse. He was ordered to report to Colonel Titcomb's tent to take records for his regiment on a court martial hearing. Colonel Titcomb was presiding as president of the court martial and was seated at a desk flanked by fellow officers of the court. Across from the colonel sat Peter Wraxall, Johnson's aid-de-camp, who was serving as judge advocate. Charles was seated behind Titcomb. Titcomb stood and addressed the court.

"At this time I shall open these proceedings of a regimental court for the colony of Massachusetts-Bay. I will be presiding under orders from General William Johnson and fully authorized by the sanction of Governor and General William Shirley of the said colony. Let it be recorded that at eleven o'clock this twentieth day of August, 1755, I, Colonel Moses Titcomb, president, of ye court, open this meeting by the reading of its members. Present are Peter Wraxall, judge advocate; Colonel William Cockcroft; Lieutenant Colonel Cole; Major Nicholes;

Captains Whipple and Moore of Titcomb's Regiment, Angel and Francis of Harris' Regiment, Hall and Mathews of Cockcroft's Regiment; Lieutenants Parker of Titcomb's, Thoden of Harris', and Hunter of Cockcroft's. Mr. Whiting, record all members of court present. My adjutant, Mr. Whiting, will be acting as the court's secretary. Mr. Whiting, if you would, Sir, read the Articles of War against disturbing the court." Whiting did so and then was ordered to read the general's warrant, the judge advocate's commission, and he administered oaths to the officers of the court.

Titcomb then addressed the court guard. "Bring in the prisoner." From a tent adjacent to the seated court, the guard retrieved the prisoner, who was marched and stood in front of the president. Peter Wraxall rose and stood beside him. Addressing the prisoner, Titcomb ordered, "Give the court your name, rank, and regiment."

"Lieutenant Esa Noble of Pomeroy's company, Colonel Ephraim Williams' Regiment, Sir," replied Noble.

"You are charged with supporting and inciting a mutinous disposition in certain soldiers belonging to the aforesaid company and speaking words tending to mutiny," stated Titcomb. "What is your plea, Lieutenant?"

"Not guilty, Sir."

Evidence was presented in support of both sides, but at the end of the court martial the members found Lieutenant Noble guilty.

"In finding you guilty, Lieutenant, as this is the first offence of this nature on this campaign, it is the recommendation of this military court to sentence you to make a public acknowledgement of your crime with a promise of future good behavior at the head of each regiment. If you refuse you are to be immediately cashiered. Do you agree to the punishment?"

"Yes, Sir, I agree," responded Noble in disgust.

"Then record, Mr. Whiting, that on August 24, 1755, Lieutenant Noble of Company B, of Colonel Ephraim Williams' Regiment, will publicly acknowledge his guilt and promise no future mutinous behavior. This he shall declare at the head of every regiment within this garrison. Release the prisoner."

Then rising one final time, Titcomb stated, "As the presiding officer of this military court, I, Colonel Moses Titcomb, declare this court dissolved. Gentlemen, you are dismissed."

Shortly after returning to camp, Charles was ordered by a subaltern to join in a group of men from his unit cutting timber. He quickly changed into his work smock and headed with several others and an escort of three men to the east of the fort. They marched about a half a mile to where the cutting party was hard at work. At first he was told to start felling trees with one of the men he came in with. They both were issued felling axes and walked into a grove of tall, straight pines. They started cutting a notch in the first tree about knee height, chopping alternately until they had cut a deep V halfway through the side of the trunk. Then moving around to the opposite side of the four-foot diameter tree they cut straight into the back side of the V. The trunk began to snap and crackle. They stopped and looked up, and ever so slowly the tree began to lean toward the direction of the notch. Then as the trunk picked up momentum they stepped aside. With a great force the tree broke branches on neighboring trees as it pushed and parted its way downward to the forest floor where it arrived in a series of crashing thuds. Charles and the other man continued this same process for three more hours. When the tree was down another team of soldiers would trim off branches and a third would cut the trunks into sections. The final stage was for a teamster and his oxen to hook on and drag the logs back to the fort.

As the heat of the afternoon increased, Charles' and his partner's pace slowed. Sweat poured from them and they looked as though they had been in a downpour. The flies and other bugs swirled about them like vultures circling a dead carcass. Finally, the sergeant in charge of their party called them in. They helped hook up the final ox teams and the entire party formed up, ox teams and ax men in column and guards in the front, rear, and on the flanks, and marched back to camp.

They arrived at camp just before the evening roast beef. They were ordered to turn in their tools and were dismissed. Charles went quickly to his barrack, he was tired and very hungry. He hoped that the food was ready. He was delighted when he filled his tureen from the mess kettle. Samuel George had been allowed to go out on a hunting party and had taken a young, fat doe. Charles set his plate aside to cool. Adding the hot meal of venison, rice, and onions to his already overheated body was unthinkable. His entire mess sat in a collapsed stupor slowly eating their food. Near the end of the meal Sarah walked around serving up Indian meal mixed with sugar and cinnamon. This was a true delight!

After this well-earned meal the men lounged on the ground awaiting the coolness of the coming evening. It was so uncomfortable with the humidity drenching their bodies. Around seven o'clock half of the men were called for picket duty. The others were still relaxing. John and Sarah decided to take a walk and try and cool off, but the others couldn't even budge. Mary was nowhere in sight. Finally, around eight o'clock Charles could sit no longer. Standing, he said, "I'm going down to the river for a swim, I can't take this heat any longer. Anyone else want to go?'

"Have you forgotten the drowning a couple of days ago?" asked Gideon.

"I might meet you there if I can get the gumption," offered William.

"Don't forget, the general forbade swimming," warned Abraham.

"I intend to walk down-river a little, almost to the south pickets. It's almost dark and no one will be able to see me. It's about time I wash my clothes, it's been a few weeks," said Charles as he turned and headed out of the postern gate.

He walked along the bank over the creek on the south of the fort and continued on. In one spot there were a half dozen soldiers swimming who were harassing several followers doing laundry along the bank. They were making enough noise Charles thought he should go further south to a quieter spot so as not to be caught. About a hundred yards farther he approached an area where the river indented on the east bank, creating a small bay. The water slowed here and caused the sand and silt to create a clean, clear bottom. Several large trees hung over the inlet, sheltering this hidden spot. The moon had just started to rise and added a crimson hue to the water, forming long shadows from the bank. Charles quietly sat on the edge of the large rock on the bank and started to remove his shoes and hose. The humidity made his clothing stick to his body and added to the labor of removing them from his already exhausted torso. He rolled his clothing into a bundle, tucked it under his arm, and took several steps toward a trunk that was resting one-fourth of the way across the bay. Here he wanted to swim. Standing knee-deep in only his shirt, Charles sat his bundle on the trunk and reached to slip the long shirt over his head. He froze, ducked, and peered into the darkness. He had heard a muffled splash and noticed the movement of ripples radiating from a shadow, twenty feet the other side of the log. Charles dared not move. Was it an animal, another swimmer, an Indian, or the enemy?

He forced himself to not move, not even breathe. He must not be noticed. Then slowly from between the leaf-filled branches of the trees streamed the golden rays of the moon. At first it lengthened the shadows from the rippling area and then slowly a golden bath of moonlight drenched a figure; first the head, shoulders, then torso; it was a woman!

Slowly, she scooped hands full of water and sprinkled them over her shoulders. The droplets cascaded over her round golden breasts. Periodically, drops fell from her nipples while the rest of the water streamed down her firm stomach and around the curvatures of her hips, down her thighs, pooling around her knees and forming the soft ripples in the river.

Charles was stunned. He could do nothing but crouch in the cool water, peering over the tree trunk. The woman continued to quench her skin with the hands full of water which sparkled in the golden shafts of moonlight. Charles was both embarrassed and aroused but not ashamed enough of the predicament to move or quit staring. After several moments of visual arousal Charles' foot slipped off a rock it had rested on under the water and created a quiet plunking sound in the water.

Hearing the noise, the woman slowly turned her head. Long wavy curls, blackened from the darkness, swung slowly over her right shoulder to her back, exposing her silhouette in a golden glow. Then with one more degree of turning her identity was revealed! It was Mary!

No longer could Charles continue to ravage the silhouette in the moonlit darkness. It was not a nameless figure of a camp follower. Before him stood John's daughter, a friend, someone who had recently consoled him. A young woman that until this moment he had not thought of in this way. Now, even if for only a few seconds, he had lusted in his heart and flesh for her. Never again could he look at her in the same way.

Almost as silently as an otter, Charles retrieved his bundle of clothes and climbed out of the water and melted into the woods. His movements went unnoticed by Mary, who went back to her watery relaxation. Charles quickly redressed and rapidly traced his footsteps back toward the fort. As he approached the fort his breath had quickened from his excitement and rapid retreat, and the smoke of the fires hanging motionless in the air nearly gagged him. He was in a totally confused state as he entered the barracks building and climbed to the second story. There was no wind and the majority of the men were not inside. Charles perched himself on the window sill, hoping for a breeze. He was hotter now than when he had left and the frustrations he now began to feel were almost overwhelming. He could not morally allow thought of what he had witnessed, but deep within, Charles yearned to return to the river and make his presence known to the moonlit silhouette. Minutes later Charles saw Mary enter the postern gate and stroll to her father's shack under the southeast bastion. Charles, unable to sleep that evening, was grateful she had not been noticed by any others indulging in the river. He spent the night in a constant battle of morality inside himself over his enlightened view of Mary.

For days Charles could hardly look Mary in the eye, while at the same time he struggled to keep from staring. On Friday he was ordered to record proceedings at a council of war. Johnson called the meeting to order, and in great concern addressed the military family.

"We have received important reconnaissance. Four of my Mohawks returned with stirring news. They report to me that the road from the St. Lawrence River south to Lake Champlain is full of wagons and French soldiers heading south. They believe they ran across a superior force to ours."

Ephraim Williams stood, "Gentlemen, if the enemy is marching with a superior force, we must immediately send for reinforcements."

"I agree," offered General Lyman.

"I feel we are all in agreement; that we should contact the colonial governors for reinforcement. I will write a letter of request to your governors and attach letters from you, their commanders, of the urgency of the response," stated Johnson.

"It is important now that we decide upon which route we will advance, for it is time to move on our enemy now. In talking to the majority of you since our last council, the route following the west of South Bay to Lake St. Sacrament seems to be your choice. Is anyone against this route?" asked Johnson. No one raised opposition, but General Lyman expressed a concern. "It is good that we agree on a single route, but, I must insist that our army, especially that part to be left here, keep out constant parties toward South Bay and Old Fort Anne in case the enemy decides to take that route. We must be constantly kept in good intelligence of the enemy's movements so as to reinforce each other."

"This is true, and shall be part of the orders to the officer left in command here," reassured Johnson. "We must immediately move forward with gangs of ax men to hew out a suitable road to the lake. The road should proceed up the east side of the Hudson, north to the great bend, then west to the falls, and finally slightly northwest to the lake, a distance of about fourteen miles. Mr. Lyman, you are in charge of a 2,000-man division and artillery advancing on the 26th. You are to have formal guard arrangements with stops every half-hour to ensure that the column stays together. Strict military discipline is to be enforced. Your command has not been used to a regular military routine and this will establish and preserve that relative subordination without which every military undertaking will be shameful and very probably fatal." These were Johnson's orders.

"Yes, Sir, I will prepare for this advance," replied Titcomb.

"The formality of this council is also ceremonial, gentlemen. In honor of Edward Augustus, Duke of York and Albany, I name this fortification here at the Great Carrying Place Fort Edward, after the grandson of King George II, second prince of the blood of that name. Now gentlemen, I dissolve this council of war. Prepare your troops for immediate road building details and the advance of our men and artillery to the lake. You are dismissed."

Charles hurried back to the barracks. "Finally, we're going to move on the French! Our time is near," said Charles excitedly.

"I've dreaded the coming of this day," said Sarah.

"What did the officers decide, Charles?" asked John.

"We are to send out ax men today, and Tuesday 2,000 of us march to the lake."

"Let's cook a special meal tonight, Mother. We can get some vegetables and berries from the sutlers to make a pie," said Mary. The women hurried off to the sutlers' tents as the messmates continued their excited conversation.

After the meal John praised his women. "That was the best meal I have ate since leaving home."

"I am so full," said Gideon, rubbing his belly.

Abraham said, "Thank you, ladies, for this fine feast."

"Gossip from the sutlers has it that we followers are to be sent away tomorrow. John, why don't we take a walk? Mary, come with us. Charles, will you walk, too?" asked Sarah.

The four strolled away from the mess fires and down the company streets. John and Sarah held hands with affection as they strolled. Mary and Charles walked behind them.

Charles was visibly uncomfortable. Try as she might, Mary couldn't get Charles even to carry on a conversation. The four walked around the stockade and to the creek on its south side. Here the women sat on an old log and the men stood at the water's edge lobbing and skipping stones.

"Charles, what is your problem tonight?" asked John.

"Father, don't embarrass him, he obviously has something really bothering him," responded Mary.

"Why don't we leave them to talk, John," said Sarah.

"No, we'll go with you," said Charles quickly.

"Yes, Charles, John and I are tired. Stay and keep Mary company," said Sarah as she and John walked away.

"Come and sit by me, Charles, and enjoy the creek and the quiet."

"No, I'd rather walk."

"Alright."

So they walked along the river toward the north guard, turned around, and walked back toward the fort.

"Let's go up on the palisade and look around," said Charles.

They walked into the postern gate, and just to the left climbed the stairs to the top of the palisade. From this vantage point they could see the Hudson, and on the other side of the bank the white tents of the field command seemed to glow in the dusk. Around the command tents they could see soldiers walking from tent to tent, lighting lanterns outside each one. Then, from below, outside the fort wall marched the evening guard. They marched north to replace the guard just beyond the camp's perimeter.

Mary suddenly jumped as a flash and deep thudding boom sounded from a cannon in the northeast bastion. This sounded the order for all to be within the encampment.

"I'm still not used to that," said Mary, her hand at her heart.

They stood quietly for about five minutes, then Mary couldn't take the silence any longer. "Is there something that I have done to make you shun me, Charles?"

"No Mary, I'm just anxious for our advance," said Charles. This was as easy of an excuse as he could come up with, rather than admitting to his hidden feelings from the evening swim. "I have been mulling over things my father and others have told me about their experiences in battle. I have also been thinking about what your mother said about the women being sent off. I truly hope it is so. This is no longer a proper place for the ladies. The unknown perils of Lake St. Sacrament are too dangerous to take any but ready soldiers. I am afraid our enemy is already advancing there as well," preached Charles.

"If we are meant to return to Albany, we will pray and await for the army to call us back to the north. Our concerns will create great anxiety but our thoughts will not leave you. Here, take this and carry it with you." Mary handed Charles a lock of her auburn hair. "I cut it for you this afternoon when Mother and I heard about the rumor. The ribbon that ties it represents the tie between us," Mary said softly as she placed the lock in Charles' hand.

"I'll carry it with my father's watch," said Charles, slipping it into his waistcoat. For the next hour they stood silently on the palisade, Mary dreading tomorrow, and Charles toiling internally about his true feelings toward her.

Early Saturday, an order went through all the army to form twenty men from each colony to act as an escort party for the followers of the army. The escort was to consist of a field officer, subaltern, four sergeants, four corporals, and 100 men. The followers were to be formed at nine o'clock and one wagon was to be supplied to transport their belongings. The rest of the army was to be formed at the head of their regiments.

Sarah and Mary, like most of the other women who were in the army, were lowered to tears of emotion this morning as they prepared for their departure. John was trying to console them as they packed their meager belongings. The wagon assigned to the followers was drawn up and loading was started. Many of the soldiers did not have their women at the front with them, so were performing military duties as normal. Despite this lack of connection, most of the men realized their loss, but on the other hand knew this was the only real way to do away with the bad women of the camps. With extremely sad emotions John led his wife and daughter across the parade ground and out the postern gate. Charles no longer was able to hide all of his feelings for Mary and walked with her. About halfway across the parade he slipped his hand around Mary's and softly squeezed it as they walked. The terror in her face at this moment changed to almost delight as she warmly accepted his emotions. As they got to the wagon, John tossed a canvas bag onto the pile and turned to Sarah with his last words before departure. Charles also lobbed a large haversack into the wagon with Mary's belongings, and then turning around, found himself face to face with her.

She reached out and took both his hands in hers and said, "You must watch after my father. Being an armourer he probably won't see any fighting, but with his over-enthusiasm you never know what he might do."

Charles replied, "I will watch him. I am glad, in a way, that you and your mother are being taken back to Albany. This is not the place for you, and the Yorker and Rhode Island women are destroying our ranks." Charles lowered his head and softened his voice, "I have not been totally honest with you. You have been on my mind much, no longer as John's daughter, but as the beautiful woman I am getting to know and care so much for. I cannot deal any longer with the thoughts, comments, and looks you receive from the other soldiers in these camps. I am uncomfortable with my new feelings for you as well, and am not sure how to deal with them."

She looked up directly into Charles' eyes, blinked several times, and smiled; then Charles, trying to change the subject, continued. "Finally, we are moving to fight. You know how much I have wanted this time to come. We are going to advance and drive our enemies before us. It was good thinking by our officers to send the women away. War will not be a place for them. I'm sure it won't last but a few weeks anyway. Then we will march back to Albany and pick you up on our way home in victory!"

"Yes, I know this is what you have waited for, but I wish I was staying with you," Mary answered softly. Then she leaned forward, stood on her tiptoes, and kissed Charles. He could not hold back any longer and wrapped his arms around her in a warm embrace. But he could not allow himself to hold her long and let go as he again stumbled with his feelings.

Then from the front of the wagon, a command was yelled out. "Escort party, followers of New England, form in front of the wagon, Yorkers and Rhode Islanders behind. Gentlemen of the army, form with your regiments!" The followers and the guard took their places in the formation and the men who had escorted them returned to their units. John and Charles took their places on the western palisade and waited. In a few moments the column started to march and a cheer rose from the New Englanders, "Huzzah!" The regiments stood fast until the entire column was out of sight and then they were dismissed to their duties. For some like John this was a sorrowful moment, but for many it was a release to finally pursue their destiny!

On Tuesday, the army awoke to the insistence of the regimental drums. This was to be the day to advance. For the past several days all preparations had been made and today the army was beginning their last-minute preparations. General Johnson had decided to lead this first division himself. The division consisted of 1,500 New Englanders and 40 Indians. About half of Charles' regiment was to move with this division, including his company. Those departing were busied loading last-minute ammunitions, rations, tools, tents, and equipment onto wagons. The gangs of ax men sent forward after the last council had cleared a new wagon road most of the way to the lake. It was expected that this plus the reconnaissance of no enemy in the vicinity would make for an uneventful march.

The anxiety of the troops reached an almost explosive level as they began to form regiments on the road outside the postern gate. The forty Mohawks were to lead the division, followed by a company of Whiting's Connecticut men. The right flank was to be covered by Captain Burk's company and the left by Captain Webster's, both of Titcomb's Regiment. The rear guard was covered by Captain Payson's company of Lyman's Regiment. The order of march for the main column was to be Massachusetts, followed by Connecticut, then New York, and Rhode Island, followed by the artillery. The 150 wagons and carts were to be in the intervals between the regiments. It was a truly colorful spectacle of uniforms of blue, red, green, and a rainbow of facing colors, especially with the Rhode Islanders in their civilian clothes and the Connecticut men in their militia uniforms.

As the units were being formed, Johnson met one last time with his field officers for instructions on the march and for Lyman's garrison remaining at Fort Edward. "As we advance, gentlemen, I want the ranks kept together, stopping about every half-hour so no one falls behind. I believe by keeping together in this manner, if we are attacked we will prevail. Guard and flank companies, keep alert at such a distance as to be able to warn us, but still be able to fall back into the main body if you are hit. If we come under attack I expect the artillery to be formed in the center of the main body or the most advantageous spot. Mr. Whiting, make sure your company, our front guard, keeps an eye on my Mohawks. They will alert you to any forthcoming enemy. Colonel Lyman, I am leaving you in command of Fort Edward." Johnson handed him a written copy of the following orders. "All former standing orders are to be observed throughout the camp, a scouting party sent every day for two or three miles around. That immediately upon the marching of this division under my command you are to order Colonel Titcomb to remove the encampment of the remainder of his regiment and that one compact camp be formed of the whole. Till you receive marching orders from me, the works now being thrown up are to be carried on. The batteaus to be collected together and secured and sentries placed over them. Upon the arrival of the New Hampshire Regiment, provisions be issued to them conformable to the opinion of the last council. At that time Colonel Blanchard is to take charge of the garrison of 500 New York and New Hampshire men and you are to march immediately with the remainder of the army in a second division to the lake. I have left some Indian officers and sachems to receive and come forward with the Indians I hourly expect. Take all possible care to prevent any rum being given or sold them or any traffic carried on by any of the troops. Finally, if any dispatches should come for me, you will please to forward them. These are my orders, return and prepare to move. Dismissed."

It was nearing four in the afternoon as the officers returned to their regiments. Johnson mounted his horse and rode to the front of the main column and ordered Whiting to advance the column. Then he turned around, rode back, and placed himself in front of the Yorkers and saluted Colonel Lyman, saying, "General, be on your guard. I will see you at the lake in several days." Lyman returned the salute. As the columns advanced, the officers began to echo the commands, "Take Care! To The Front, March!"

The first division began to move forward slowly. Lyman's garrison had been formed between the road and palisade. As each regiment passed with their flags flying, the officers of the column and Lyman's garrison exchanged salutes. Lyman turned, and motioning with his right hand, ordered the fort's artillery to be fired. Great thunderous booms echoed from the bastions as smoke billowed into the air. Then as if challenging the warriors' chants of the ancient Romans, the army began yelling, "Huzzah, Huzzah, Huzzah!"

Once leaving the opening surrounding Fort Edward, the column marched straight down the freshly cut road. This thirty-foot-wide path easily allowed the division to march in a column of six abreast, still leaving room for officers or mounted couriers to traverse along the nearly 1,000-foot-long column. As the main party trudged forward, the flank companies from Massachusetts had it rougher. They were within the woods, advancing at an equal pace to the main body, constantly watching for signs of the enemy. As Captain Burk's company moved through the forest on the right, every man was careful as he quietly placed each foot softly on the ground. Many of this company had been on scouts before and some were skilled hunters. They were extremely stealthy climbing over or maneuvering around the natural obstacles of the forest, each man constantly scanning the wilderness horizon for the enemy.

As Burk's men moved they did not stay in column but rather staggered themselves in twos or threes about thirty feet apart. For hours the army advanced in this manner. The road they marched generally followed the Hudson, slowly arching from north to west. About five miles out, Charles' unit slowed down the column, as they needed to move more carefully. Their flank was skirting South Bay, an area of semi-cleared drowned lands to the north. Cautiously they continued. About every half-hour of the march the army halted to allow stragglers to catch up. This made for an easy march, but a long march.

Around four hours into the march, the army was halted just above the falls on the Hudson. Here they decided to spend the night. The commanders were called together and a decision was made to erect temporary shelters for the evening. One-third of the army was to always stay on guard, divided 100 to each direction north, south, east, and west, and to be posted about 100 yards from the camp. The final 100 were to lay on their arms as the picket guards. The remainder of the army was allowed to prepare food and shelter for the night. Charles and his mess did as most; stepping several yards into the edge of the forest, they started cutting hemlock and pine boughs. Then, lashing one pole between two trees, they leaned the boughs across the pole, forming a crude A-framed shelter. The final preparation was to pile hemlock boughs about two feet deep inside the shelter, lay two blankets over the boughs, and share the remaining blankets amongst the messmates. This proved to be a tolerable sleep.

About eight in the morning the regiments reformed as the day before, and continued toward the lake. One-third were sent forward to finish clearing the road. Near an hour into the march they crossed a small creek and about an hour later a larger brook. The Mohawks said that this brook lay about halfway to the lake. Then around noon, the army halted for lunch near another small creek. The units posted guards and then found comfortable spots close to the road to sit, relax, and eat. General Johnson called together his field commanders in a small oak opening near the east side of the road. Here under a huge tree his servants had placed a camp table and several chairs and stools. As the commanders arrived they were treated to a delicious meal. For an hour they sat under the trees, talking and eating. They were enjoying cold and roasted venison, lemon punch and wine, bread, and cheese.

At approximately one o'clock, Johnson's division formed on the road again and advanced into a heavily forested area. For the next four hours the advance was slowed due to many stumps still in the freshly cut road and the unsecured terrain. From this spot forward, mountains flanked both sides of the road in the distance. As the army crept forward they traversed three more small creeks and then at about four o'clock in the afternoon the army halted. They had reached the lake. Johnson immediately called together his officers and they placed guards and sent 500 ax men to clearing an area to camp on the rough ground at the water's edge. In the rear was the glorious deep blue lake, in the front was the pine forest they had just marched through, to the right was the marsh land of alders and maples where Charles had posted guard on the earlier scout, and on the left stood a low hill. The Indians were sent out to scout and hunt for fresh meat.

As an area became cleared, regiments were relieved to set up the camps amongst the stumps. There was an attempt to align the encampment regimentally, but the terrain made it impossible. Johnson had his tents erected near the left or northeast, towards the water side of the camp. Titcomb's Regiment was ordered to set tents on the far right of the encampment in the west.

Just before dusk Johnson ordered the regiments to be formed and his officers called together. Near the waterfront Johnson addressed his army.

"Men, we have advanced here to this important lake, Lake St. Sacrament. It is from here that we will rise and attack our enemies, the French and their allies. This staging area will allow our army to transport our artillery north and drive toward the heart of New France. This lake, called Lake St. Sacrament by the French, I have now named Lake George, not only in honor of his Majesty, but to ascertain his dominion here. Gentlemen, finish preparing your encampments, and prepare to destroy your enemy. We have now arrived!"

TERROR

The army of Yankees awoke to a fair, but windy day. Friday was to be their first full day camped at Lake George. Work parties were immediately detached to continue the preparation of the land on which they encamped. Other details were ordered to clear the forest on the camp's perimeters so an enemy would not be able to charge from cover.

Around ten o'clock one company of each regiment was ordered to form on the road in front of the camp. Captain Burk's company was sent from Titcomb's unit. These companies were ordered to be in full battle dress. The detachment was to be commanded by Ephraim Williams.

"Take Care!" commanded the captains when Williams marched to the detachment.

Colonel Williams walked to the front of the men and ordered the company commanders to advance to receive orders.

"Gentlemen, I have been ordered to train the army to form and fire in three ranks. This is a form of firing that we are planning to implement and use when we assault the enemy. Place your companies into three ranks and await my instructions."

The captains gave orders to their subalterns and the men were placed into three ranks facing the colonel. Then Colonel Williams ordered Captain Hawley of his regiment to march forward his detachment. This was a group of twelve men from his company who previously had been trained at Fort Edward on this new firing exercise. The men formed facing the larger detachment and Captain Hawley called the commands to the dozen who rudimentally performed the drill. After watching this example Colonel Williams ordered his company commanders to instruct their men on this new procedure. After about forty-five minutes the colonel called all to attention.

"Take Care!" All the men and officers instantly stopped what they were doing, faced front, and shouldered their firelocks. "This time we will actually be loading and firing. Take Care!" The colonel and company commanders placed themselves in the rear of the detachment. "Cock Your Firelocks!"

The first rank dropped to their right knee; the second rank placed their left foot between the feet of the man before them, which placed him off center to the first rank's right; the third rank took a half step to the right placing him in the interval between the ranks in front of them.

"Present!" All three ranks took aim. A slight hesitation and, "FIRE!" resulting in a thunderous boom and cloud of smoke. Two more times this was repeated by the detachment.

"Company commanders, this is to be our standard procedure. Continue this exercise until it becomes second nature in your units. Dismissed." The units faced left and marched back to camp.

Early that afternoon, the wagons were sent back to Fort Edward to transport more stores to the lake. Around two o'clock a small group of natives arrived, creating a small ruckus in the camp. Then at three o'clock the general called a council. Charles was summoned.

"My fellow officers, there are several tasks we must ensure are accomplished. First, the troops must continue the clearing and preparing of the lands of our encampment, and a firing area must be cleared between the camps and the forest. Second, I want carpenters of your regiments to start working on storehouses and magazines for our supplies. These men must also be employed building boats to transport us up the lake. I have also received plans for a flat-bottomed boat, called a radeau, for our artillery. John Dies of New York has sent me instructions. Select your most skilled boat builders and ship carpenters. This radeau should be forty feet in length and is to be moved by twenty short oars. The sides should be tall enough to form a breastwork. Our field pieces and men must be able to fire from portholes cut in the walls.

"The final item, gentlemen, is the training of the men. They all are to be trained in the exercise of loading and firing in three ranks. We feel that this will be far more effective than the normal two-rank firings. This training was started at Fort Edward and will continue here daily. It is imperative that this army prepares itself, for I fear the enemy is on the move. My orders are that daily guards be posted, work details continue on the encampment and the building projects, and one third of the army be exercised in the new firing. Any questions? You are dismissed to instruct your units."

The next morning the general's orders were implemented. Charles and his messmates, being skilled carpenters, were ordered to work on the storehouses. They completed clearing the land, leveling and laying a foundation while awaiting timbers from a woodcutting party.

Shortly before noon, a runner arrived in camp with a message from the rear guard on the road from Fort Edward. Indians were approaching the camp—many of them—several tribes. The messenger assured the men in the camp that the Indians were friendly. General Johnson asked several of his commanders to be with him to greet them. The work parties were called in and the regiments were formed in front of their camps. About a half-hour later, gunfire and yelling echoed from the edge of the woods near the road. Johnson then ordered one of the field pieces fired twice in a salute. The general and several Indians and colonial ambassadors left the camp and marched out to meet the advancing party. In the clearing the two parties exchanged niceties, then entered the camp together. Hendrick had arrived with the wanted natives. Disappointing to Johnson, these one hundred and eighty Indians augmented his native force at the lake to near two hundred. After a short time, the men of the camp returned to their duties.

On Sabbath Day, 150 wagons laden with stores and additional artillery arrived while the men were at services. Much of the rest of the day was spent unloading this train of supplies.

Late in the afternoon word was brought in from a scouting party that had run across the remnant of a five-man scout from Lyman's Regiment. With them they had two survivors. Around noon the scouts had been out several miles to the southeast near a small creek. They stopped to drink and refresh themselves and before they could remove their knapsacks and blankets a party of savages jumped upon them. Two of the scouts were killed instantly and a third was dragged off after being knocked in the head. An Indian jumped on the back of a fourth and was about to dispatch him with a club when the fifth Connecticut man swung around and shot the Indian off the other's back. The two immediately ran in the opposite direction, eventually running into their ally scout who brought them in. Terror swept through the camp this evening as the story was told and retold before the New England campfires. This had been the first loss to the enemy!

With the monotony of clearing the land, building the fort, posting the guard and practicing drill, the soldiers' morale was waning. Now, after the first reported deaths, tension was high. About ten o'clock on Monday, September 1, Captain Jones' company of Colonel Ruggles' Regiment had just come off guard duty and were ordered to draw tools for a woodcutting detail. The men thought this unfair. They were tired of delaying their assault on the French, no longer wanted to be on work details and not exempt from other duties, and because of the deaths from yesterday, refused to report for duty. Several officers tried verbally to persuade them that they would soon be marching north. This was to no avail, and, led by one of Jones' subordinates, the protesters slung their packs, clubbed their muskets and marched off down the road to the south. They had become fed up with this campaign and let it be known to the entire army.

This created mass panic in the camp, and several other units threatened to desert as well. Fortunately, officers were successful in containing other companies. The field officers and General Johnson were alerted, and a detachment of about thirty men was sent out after Jones' company.

About an hour passed and in marched the two returning parties. Jones' men had been promised no punishment if they returned immediately, and were persuaded that they would be moved out soon to attack the French. Furthermore, they were told that there were no large parties of the enemy near the lake and that the work about the camp was safe. After the army relaxed the general called the regiments together and assured them they would be advancing and to continue temporarily until all preparations were complete to ensure success. This, plus the fair treatment of Jones' men, reassured the army for the time being.

For the next several days things progressed smoothly at the lake and Fort Edward. Wagons arrived daily at Lake George and troops as well were advanced to reinforce. On Wednesday the rest of Lyman's and Titcomb's men marched in with supplies and enough natives to bring the total in camp to 300. Lyman himself had followed orders and left Fort Edward in command of Colonel Blanchard. The New Hampshire regiment and part of the New York regiment were in Blanchard's command.

Thursday was exciting, for Johnson pulled all the Indians together and held a conference in their honor. Most of the army's officers were in attendance, arranged almost ceremonially in what appeared to be a gallery; their camp chairs and stools all being placed in the parade. Johnson, his field officers, Hendrick and the other sachems were at the head of the parade; the provincials in chairs, the natives on animal robes. All were dressed in their finery. The colonial officers donned brightly colored uniforms, gold and silver braid, sashes and gorgets. The sachems were painted, and had donned their ceremonial feathered bonnets, jewelry, and finest trimmed blankets. Johnson and Hendrick both mixed white and Indian garments as if symbolically trying to tie the two cultures together. In the center of the parade a large fire had been lit and around the rest of the opening sat and stood soldiers of the four colonies and Indians from various nations. Johnson was first to address the conference. He rose and walked around the fire as he talked.

"My brothers, I welcome you, the Mohawks, the Oneidas, the Stockbridge, and the Mohegans. I, Warraghiyagey, have waited here at this great lake for your arrival. I know that without your warriors I could not defeat our enemies. For years you have known me and known that Hendrick, great king of the Mohawks, has been my brother. As I promised, I have assembled here an army to march north to push our enemy from these lands and to protect the Iroquois Castles. Here with me sit many of our great father's chiefs." He waved his hand at the field officers. "They have pledged, as have you, to destroy the French." Johnson hesitated, dropped his head, and then continued. "I am thankful for your arrival, but I must be honest. I hoped for many more brothers from the Six Nations. I have talked to Hendrick, our brother, about this and he has asked to take this opportunity to explain to all the sachems and white chiefs together why so few have followed Johnson into war." Johnson sat back amongst the sachems and field officers.

Hendrick rose from the robe slowly. He was dressed in his native fashion but wore over it the gold-laced navy courtier's coat given him by King George. He walked to the center of the circle near the fire and turned and addressed his audience. "Some time ago, we of the two Mohawk castles were greatly alarmed, and much concerned, and we take this opportunity of speaking our minds in the presence of many gentlemen concerning our brother, Governor Shirley, who is gone to Oswego; he told us, that though we thought you, our brother Warraghiyagey, had the sole management of Indian affairs, yet that he was over all; that he could pull down and set up." Johnson sat up very straight in his chair; a stern look came over his face as Hendrick continued. "He further told us, that he had always been this great man, and that you, our brother, were but an upstart of yesterday." Johnson's head jerked back in disgust. "These kind of discourses from him caused a great uneasiness and confusion amongst us, and he confirmed these things by a large belt of wampum. He also told us, you think your brother Warraghiyagey has his commission for managing your affairs from the King our father, but you are mistaken, he has his commission and all the moneys for carrying on your affairs from me, and when I please I can take all his powers from him; it was I gave him all the presents and goods to fit out the Indians with. He promised money, weapons and goods for all that would follow him. He said he wanted twenty young warriors from our castle as you promised him. He was two days pressing and working upon my brother Abraham to go with him as a minister for the Indians. He promised pay and said you would pay not. But brother, notwithstanding all these temptations and speeches, we that are come and now here, were determined to remain steadfast to you, and had it not been for Governor Shirley's money and speeches you would have seen all the Six Nations here. Brother, we have taken this opportunity to give you this relation, that the gentlemen here present may know and testify what we have said, and hear the reasons why no more Indians have joined the army." Hendrick stood and looked at Johnson silently for a moment, then pointed to him with his outstretched arm.

Johnson rose again and spoke. "My brother, I welcome your honesty. I am hurt by Governor Shirley's comments to you, my brothers of the Iroquois castles. I will pay, and not from Shirley, but from the King. I have oxen, rum, and presents for you that King George has sent to me to give you for your assistance in driving our enemies from this land. I honor you with this conference and welcome comments from the other sachems."

For several hours the orations continued from various sachems and field officers. The culmination of the conference ended with a feast, after which Johnson and his officers of his Indian department gave presents to the sachems.

After the attack of the party on August 31, Johnson increased the number of scouting parties, both white and Indian. Saturday, September 5, several scouts went out, including one that consisted of fifty men plus four Indians and Old Hendrick.

Workmen continued to clear land this day, concentrating on the area selected for the fort. Several of the officers and Mr. Eyre laid out the fort by driving stakes and roping between them. This took the better part of the day. Then late in the afternoon an awning was raised over what was to be the northeast bastion. Guards were placed around the awning. Charles joined about a hundred soldiers and officers, Masonic brothers, who were allowed to congregate under and around the canvas.

Each brother was wearing his sheepskin apron folded properly. This was all done methodically with the proper words, gestures, and signs. There were the four chairs set at the cardinal directions, and the others who presided. Watching from the side, Charles saw and heard the short ritual and the placing of a cornerstone. The presiding officers of the lodge used square, compass, and trowel to ensure the future of this grand structure they were beginning. Charles had witnessed similar rituals at home in Amesbury as well as at Fort Edward. He had been brought into the order in Amesbury two years earlier, joining his father and grandfather. Although there were subtle differences from what some of the other Masons were used to, all felt comfortable that they had been successful; so mode it be.

The troops awoke on Saturday and started their normal tedious routines. About the time the men were marching to their details the scout from the day before was returning and another was going out. Hendrick reported nothing found. Then the men of the camp went about their routine of guard duty, exercising, clearing land, and building. As the rest of the batteaus were coming up from Fort Edward, work details were started for work on the radeau to transport the artillery. Charles and about fifty other men were assigned this work. Several men he knew and worked with in Amesbury helped. The two Lowells, Gidion and Moses, were each placed in charge of half the workmen. It was a strenuous day of finding and cutting select wood for the boat.

Around midnight the camp was alarmed to the yelling of NCOs and the beating of regimental drums. The officer in charge of the guard called out the picket guard to support the main guard. Men scrambled from tents all over the encampment, stumbling, tripping, falling; trying to throw on their uniforms, grab their weapons and gear, and form within their companies. At the head of every regiment, officers and sergeants were placing men in formation. As soon as a company was formed they were ordered to march to their place of defense around the edges of the encampment. Within five minutes the entire army was formed in defense.

Poised for battle, the men stood shaking off their sleep, trying to recover from their stunned awakening. They stood for nearly an hour; then as quickly as they had been called up they were dismissed, but ordered to stay clothed and fully accoutered, sleeping on their arms. Tensions and anxiety had caused the guard to overreact. Many were terrified that an attack could come at any moment. Few got any sleep.

The next morn was fair and warm. There were a few light showers as the men rose and marched to church call. Many of the men were tired after the false alarm of the night before.

The services had just gotten out when a scout of three Indians ran into camp. The Mohawk in charge of them, Thick Lawrence, was jabbering in Iroquois. Everyone could tell he had devastating news. Lawrence and Hendrick hurried to Johnson's marquee. Hendrick calmed him and listened to his reconnaissance.

Lawrence had been scouting toward South Bay and had run across a large trail of three columns. It was very fresh and was headed toward the Great Carrying Place, Fort Edward. He judged the party to be larger than Johnson's army.

Johnson immediately increased the main guard, called every man to arms, and called a council of war. Hendrick reported the scout's information to the council. Johnson's army could not march with hopes of intercepting the French; they would be too slow. A call for a volunteer went out, to carry a warning to Colonel Blanchard at Fort Edward. One hundred and fifty wagons carrying batteaus had just arrived and Jacob Adams, a wagoner from New York, volunteered. Johnson ordered one of his horses to be saddled and he penned a message to Blanchard. Handing the letter to Adams, Johnson swatted the horse on the flank and Adams galloped straight down the road to Fort Edward.

It was decided to send off additional letters in case Adams failed. Within an hour two couriers and two Indians sprinted out of the clearing down the road to the other fort. The entire camp was in an uproar. Blanchard's garrison may have already been taken. Tensions continued to rise and several of the wagoners deserted, fleeing down the road south with their wagons. The rest of the day very little work was done, the army was held under arms at the ready. By evening all but the guard, which was now half the army, were allowed to retire, but again to sleep with their accouterments and arms.

At midnight the guard escorted several wagoners who had deserted earlier back into the camp. Johnson's messengers who had gone on foot were with them. This time the guard had kept their wits and did not rouse the entire camp. The messengers and wagoners reported they had run into a large enemy party about three-quarters of the way to Fort Edward and turned back. One wagoner said he had heard a shot, and a man he thought to be Adams called out, "Heavens have mercy!" It was also at that time that several of their fellow wagoners were killed or believed captured by the same enemy. No one knew what to do. Johnson, stunned, decided to wait the few hours until dawn to take action.

WAR

General Johnson called a council of war at daybreak. Charles and several other army scribes were called to take notes. The majority of the officers wanted to send 500 men toward Fort Edward to relieve Colonel Blanchard's garrison. Another party of 500 was to be sent toward South Bay to cut off the enemy's retreat. Hendrick strongly disagreed. "By dividing our forces into two parties, our army can easily be beaten. Look at how easily a single stick is broken." He knelt down, picked up a stick and broke it with ease. "Each of these parties of 500 left alone can be easily defeated. They should be together as one." Bending down a second time, Hendrick picked up a handful of sticks, and, bunching them together, strained several times trying to break them. "You see if we remain together, just as these sticks are not broken, we can not be defeated." The officers in the council quickly understood Hendrick and heartily agreed.

"It is agreed then, gentlemen, we will unite the forces, making a single reconnaissance force of 1000 men, who can relieve Fort Edward. Colonel Williams, I would like you to command this column," stated Johnson.

"Your servant, Sir," replied Williams.

"Mr. Whiting, would you march with him with your Connecticut men?" asked Johnson.

"Honored, Sir," replied Whiting.

"I also believe you should take our Indians, Hendrick," said the general.

"I agree, but this party is too small. We must take many more men if we are to succeed. If they are to be killed they are too many. If they are to fight they are too few!" contested Hendrick.

"This is all we can afford. We must not deplete our force here at the lake, in case the enemy attack is meant for here. Mr. Williams and Mr. Whiting, prepare your troops to march immediately. Hendrick, are your Indians ready?" asked Johnson.

"They are," answered the sachem.

"Mr. Eyre, we need a breastwork of sorts if we are to repulse a possible attack. I also need your cannon in a position of eminence," said Johnson.

"Yes, Sir," responded Eyre.

"Survey what we have available for immediate defenses, gentlemen; have a detail start cutting trees and bring the batteaus up from the lake. Turn over some of those damned wagons! You're dismissed, carry on!" ordered Johnson.

As the officers and scribes left the council many walked past the artillery park where the Indians had congregated. Hendrick climbed onto one of the gun carriages and started a long speech to his Indians, persuading them of their duty in helping this army. His voice was strong and commanding; his actions and gestures showed great spirit. Many of the New England officers and scribes stood in awe at his oration, not understanding a single word, but feeling his power as he preached to the Indians in their native tongue.

With the Indians incited to the point of rioting, the two New England commanders, Williams and Whiting, drew their regiments out, formed them into three ranks, and issued their instructions. Much of the off-duty garrison, including Charles, watched the preparing detachment. It was now 8 a.m. and Generals Johnson and Lyman and the other field officers were standing in front of Colonel Williams' Regiment. Johnson was giving the colonel his final orders and he turned to his unit, "Lieutenant Colonel Pomeroy, prepare the regiment to march. Place the column six abreast, colours and music to the front," ordered Williams in a commanding voice.

Pomeroy turned, faced the companies, and commanded, "Take Care! Form Lines Into Columns Of Twos; To The Right, Wheel!" The companies all wheeled, each line into columns of twos, placing each company into marching order, facing down the road six abreast. "Colours! Music! To The Front, Post!" Then Pomeroy and Williams took their places in the front of the entire regiment, saluted the field command, and the colonel ordered, "Take Care! To The Front, March!" With his flags flying and drums beating a slow march, Williams' Regiment began to march slowly down the road.

After Williams' party had left the camp, Johnson and his military family started to prepare a defensible perimeter around the encampment. They distributed every ax in stores to cut trees. Orders were given to form a barricade by turning over hundreds of wagons and batteaus. Then the cut tree trunks were hastily piled about knee high in the intervals between the wagons and batteaus.

While this work was still being done the distant firing of musketry was noticed. Charles and his messmates, busy stacking logs on the right of the line, were becoming tense. The general called together his officers, judging it to be three to five miles off, about where Williams' party was expected to be. The firing continued as the officers listened for the sounds to quit. Many of the soldiers had also quit working on the barricade. Charles and the other men he worked with were squatted down behind the barricade listening long into the distance. Then the brisk winds started to blow the smoke of the firing into the camp. The men's anxiety intensified as the sounds seemed to be getting closer.

The decision was made, and drums started beating. "To Arms, To Arms, To Arms!" rose the yells of the officers and NCOs. Charles and the men in his detachment who had been at work immediately threw down their tools, ran to their tents, and grabbed their muskets and ammunition, then sprinted to their company's formation. When the majority of each company was in line they were marched to their defensive positions about the camp: Charles' regiment was on the far right of all, nearest the swamp. The camp was suddenly set on edge, ready to repulse an attack. The men's senses were bombarded with the sounds of muffled musketry, hundreds of running feet, the rattle of equipment, the bellowing of commands; the sights of rows upon rows of soldiers being formed, ready to fight, others darting here and there, officers directing the final placement of the barricade; and the burning pungent odor of black powder smoke drifting slowly over the camp.

Without warning, from the tree line a handful of men burst into the opening. Several fell into the sand as the rest sped pell-mell toward the barricade. "There they are, the enemy, they're on us!" shouted one of Lyman's men near the center of the line. He jumped to his feet and drew aim with his musket.

"Stop!" yelled Colonel Lyman, "They're our men! Don't shoot!" He immediately leaped in front of his regiment and knocked several musket barrels down while yelling, "Hold your fire!" The terrified men made the opening in seconds and hurdled the barricade, falling in total exhaustion amongst Johnson's formed and ready troops.

"Hide! They're after us! They'll be here any minute!" shouted one of the exhausted men.

"Who's after you, the French?" demanded Lyman in disgust. The man lay on his side, curled up in a ball and gasping for breath. "Pull yourself together, man!" ordered Lyman.

"The Indians, they're cuttin' up our men like cattle at the slaughter!" said the terrified soldier.

"Damn it, get to your feet! Or are you hurt?" asked Lyman.

"No, Sir, we'll perish, they're the devil!" screamed the man. Several of the other men were cowering in front of other officers and several stumbled all the way to the surgeon's tents, feigning illness. The men standing poised at the barricade had diverted their attention to the sporadic stream of men still dribbling into the camp. Stories started to fly as the terrified runners began to spread their tales. One man, Abijah Hedly from Williams' regiment had jumped the barricade near Charles' squad and frantically told what he had been through.

"After a short distance, Williams ordered us to halt. While waiting, the colonel threw out flankers on each side of the road in the dense forest. A drove of deer ran terrified between our column and the flankers, scaring half of us out of our wits. After several minutes Hendrick and his Indians caught up with us. Then Whiting and his men arrived. Hendrick sent his Indians down the road leading the column in single file. Our regiment marched next and Whiting's men followed.

"Just before ten o'clock, I guess, the column was about four miles from Lake George. The colonel was still marching in the front of us and beside him rode Hendrick upon a horse. The Indian was too old and fat to make the march. If it were not for his unbound hair and tattoos, you couldn't tell Hendrick was an Indian. He was dressed head to foot like one of us.

"I could just hear him turn to Williams and say softly, 'I smell Indians.' Both their eyes scanned the flanks. Williams quietly turned and told our lieutenant to warn Pomeroy to be ready for action. It was real strange, all of us in the front companies began to fidget; many of us had seen the colonel's reactions, which startled us. Then the Indians began to skulk as though they were walking through the center of a herd of elk.

"All of a sudden from the left a voice yelled out, 'Whence come you?' It was obviously an Indian.

"We halted without an order and Hendrick yelled out, 'The Mohawks. We are the six confederate Indian nations, the heads and superiors of all Indian nations.'

"Then from the bushes the concealed voice said, 'We are the seven confederate Indian nations of Canada and we come to help our father King of France to fight the Anglay. We have no intention on trespassing on your territories.'

"Hendrick again yelled out, 'We must warn you that we are here to fight Le France and not to enter into a war with our brothers the Cayawaga. We rather offer you to come and join us, or we will give you time to get out of our way so as not to start a war with our brothers. It is the Indians of the Ohio that we have a quarrel with. From whence come you?'

"There was a short pause. I was starting to shake. Then a response, 'Montreal!' For a moment there was total silence, then war whoops, then the forest erupted! The French and Indians had laid an ambush! On our left a pounding thunder of enemy muskets tore through the brush at the top of the ravine, stunning the front of our column and causing it to fold backward like a stiff deck of cards. On the first volley, I saw Hendrick's horse struck and dashed to the ground, pinning him underneath. The rest of the Indians immediately fell to the ground trying to shield themselves. We were riddled like the side of a bear that had been hit by a fowler loaded with buckshot. The Indians jumped up and fired on the enemy as part of them dashed into the woods. Hendrick was trying desperately to release himself from under his horse. By this time we were dead, running or in such a shock, many of us just stood there!

"Then the colonel rallied what was left of us, faced us directly into the smoke belching from the east, and volleyed us into the bushes. Instantly through the smoke leaped hundreds of the enemy, starting a continuous fire from the ravine! The rest of our Indians sprinted through our ranks, some taking to the woods. Hendrick finally freed himself and took off with them. Most of our men ran too! They ran through the ranks of the men behind us, which caused many of them to turn and take flight themselves!"

Those who were around the barricade near Charles who were not unnerved before, certainly were now.

Then in a dreadful, insane voice Hedly said, "There are thousands of them. There were as many Indians after us as mosquitoes on a stagnant pond!"

Catching his breath Hedly continued his terrifying story. "The colonel now seeing how desperate things were, hoped to take the high ground, and, seeing French regulars advancing directly down the road toward us, ordered us to charge up the hill to the west of the road. I think I quit breathing; it felt like my heart even quit! With all possible might the colonel drew his sword and yelled, 'Charge!' Somehow I made my body move and we scrambled up the hill! Just before we reached the top all hell broke loose; they were above us; only about ten feet from us! I saw a cloud of smoke spew from the thicket in front of the colonel and he reeled back with blood and brains spraying from his head! The entire hill was one big musket blast. Everyone seemed to be hit! I flew backwards down to the road from a bullet, here, see." He grasped his wrist showing the listeners. "Then all I can remember is somehow getting to my feet and not stopping until now!"

"Were there any French regulars?" John asked.

"Ya, the road was covered with them, all the way to Albany!"

Then into the center of the barricade was carried another of Williams' men; he had a flowing wound in the right thigh. The two men carrying him handed him to two of Lyman's men, who carried him to the surgeon's table. Several of the officers, including Johnson, seeing his uniform that of an officer, rushed to the surgeon's tent and asked, "What did you see? Where is the colonel? The rest of your regiment?"

"I have no idea," he groaned. "I was several companies back in the column when suddenly the woods were filled with smoke and shot." He stopped and gritted his teeth in pain. "I was struck down immediately and two men picked me up and carried me here." He struggled to catch his breath, then continued. "The companies in front seemed to be trying to return fire. I'm not sure, I, I think," he passed out with a large exhale of air.

Johnson then turned to a drummer boy of about sixteen, "Boy, run to the Rhode Islanders and tell Colonel Cole, General Johnson needs him! Run, boy!"

The boy dropped his drum and ran toward the waterfront where Cole's regiment was being held in reserve. Within minutes Lieutenant Colonel Cole quickly marched up to General Johnson and saluted, "Yes, Sir!" he said.

"Colonel, I want you to take 300 of your men and march immediately toward the firing. You must make haste in order to either relieve Colonel Williams' column or cover their retreat. Go, man! Retrieve your Rhode Islanders and march, Sir!"

Cole turned about and moved his men onto the road and quickly disappeared into the woods. Now the army was waiting in tortured anxiety for what was to happen next; Lyman's Regiment facing the road, three of Captain Eyre's cannon lined across the road, another was placed on the bluff on the left, and the Massachusetts regiments stretched along the barricade toward the right. Five hundred men were drawn from the regiments to act as a small reserve by the water's edge.

Within a few minutes a man was seen crawling across the open field. Several men near the right of the line were sent out to bring him in. They handed him over the barricade near Titcomb's regiment. He had blood pouring from his chest and head. The men near Charles crowded around him.

"Indians!" he gasped. He could barely see through the blood covering his face. "Indians! They killed all of us! I followed my corporal and some of the Indians into the woods to get away. I thought I was going away from the fighting." He placed his hands over his head wound and continued.

"Suddenly I fell. As I started to get up I caught the glimpse of an Indian running past me. It was Hendrick, stumbling as fast as his old legs could carry him. Then I caught a glimpse of other Indians. Hendrick had run directly into the Indian camp of the women and boys! I froze and watched as he tried to change direction and stumbled, falling flat on his face. Almost as quickly as he hit the ground a score of native boys pounced on him striking, stabbing and slashing him with axes, spears, knives, and arrows! It was gruesome; blood and flesh flying everywhere! Then one of the biggest boys, straddled his mutilated body, grabbed Hendrick's hair lock in his hand and scalped him!" The soldiers' body began to shake uncontrollably. Then after a short pause he continued. "Then the boy raised it above his head and, and, yelled a blood-curdling scream!" The soldier began to cry. After a moment he composed himself enough to finish. "I crawled out of their site and took off running again. Then I was shot. A Connecticut man helped me up and brought me most of the way here. Get me to a doctor, hurry!" Several men quickly carried him off.

For another hour the army listened to the distant firing. Closer and closer it came. They were becoming totally unnerved. Charles fidgeted continually; checking his gear, looking at the prime in his musket, counting his ammunition. The waiting was becoming unbearable. Then suddenly the firing stopped, and within several minutes a column of provincials came into the clearing before the camp. It was Whiting's and Cole's men. They marched straight into camp. By this time terror had grown rampant in many of the troops, producing a devastating effect. Many soldiers were leaving their post. Officers from all units began to harangue their men. They ran up and down the lines, first trying to plead with them to steady themselves for the coming French attack. Then they resorted to a pointed verbal confrontation, ordering and eventually threatening. Many returned to the firing lines and the sergeants and corporals prepared them for battle.

With Whiting's and Cole's detachment were the remnants of Williams' regiment. They were dispersed along the defensive line, some of Williams' men were placed near the right.

They quickly began spreading their hideous tales of the past hours. One near Charles' squad told of their retreat. His eyes were wide in terror as he recounted what happened. "At the rear of the our column, Colonel Whiting had his hands full keeping his men calm and cool-headed as our men and the Indians ran through and past them! Part of us joined up with the Connecticut men, the rest never stopped. By the time the enemy had reached our front, we could tell we were greatly outnumbered. Whiting tried desperately to hold us in formation. We fought a continual firing-retreating action! For nearly two miles Whiting maneuvered us, firing one company at a time, then taking turns, falling back toward the lake covered by the other companies.

"At a pond, about two miles from Lake George, Cole's unit joined with us. We were excited that relief had been sent. Thinking the combined parties could slow the enemy, a halt was called and Whiting and Cole began firing our combined unit by platoons. For a moment our fire slowed the French, but Canadians and Indians flanked us. This, with several well-placed volleys from the French regulars, began again to drive us back. The French had many more men than we." He shook his head, and then continued.

"Then Whiting took command of the combined unit and continued his firing and retreating action to about three-quarters of a mile from here. He halted us, placing us three ranks deep, facing the French regulars! There they were, just before us. Standing there in their white coats; it was like they were just staring at us as they kept coming! Whiting allowed them to march into musket range, and we fired three quick volleys, which stopped them! We dropped those Frenchmen like pigeons on a hunt! Taking quick advantage of them being so stunned, Whiting removed us from the field and marched directly here." Then he looked the listeners directly in the eye and said, "You better get ready, it will soon be like hell itself bursting from those woods!" Then he pointed to the edge of the clearing.

A few men still refused to stand in the lines and some officers resorted to drawing their swords and threatened to use them on individuals who left their post. Julles Fonda, a Lieutenant of the New York regiment, went so far as to beat his men back into lines with the flat of his sword. Colonel Lyman, seeing a Connecticut man sneaking to the rear of the ranks, drew his sword and could be heard ordering, "You get back to the breastworks or I'll kill you myself! Damn you!" The man hung his head and returned. By the time Whiting's and Cole's units had taken their places, the majority of the provincial officers had prepared the men and were manning the breastworks awaiting the French.

Suddenly, at the edge of the road Johnson's army saw the white-coated French grenadiers. The regulars marched directly down the new road. Slowly they approached, the sun glistening off their bayonets. At one hundred and fifty yards they halted, dressed their lines, and waited. Many of Johnson's men were shaking with anxiety: French regulars in a frontal European assault; What would they do? Then from all along the woods line rose a terrific war whoop! Charles could feel the hair on his neck and arms stand on end. It must have been every Indian in North America! Several provincials from all along the breastwork ran in fear toward the lake. The woods were full of them, suddenly Canadians and Indians charged down the hill straight for the camp! Charles squeezed his musket, nearly breaking the stock.

"Steady, men," reassured the officers, "Steady. Take Care, Cock Your Firelocks, Present, FIRE!" As the provincials opened fire, many of the enemy dove to the ground to avoid being hit. They sought cover in the bushes, downed treetops and stumps. They started making their way to the right. A continuing fire erupted up and down the provincial line. The Connecticut troops were directly in front of the French regulars and they began to fire volleys at them. Lyman, being behind his troops, sprang to the front and ran down the line of Yankees, putting his own life on the line yelling, "Hold your fire!" and knocking their muskets down. The French were out of range and he did not want his men's muskets fouled before the real battle began.

As if in defiance, the French stood motionless. Then they methodically marched forward, straight down the road. They halted within musket range and began to fire by platoons. Johnson not only answered back with musketry but also fired his cannon, which was mounted on the road directly before them.

Within minutes the roar of cannon and muskets had become general; nothing could be heard but the roar of guns, yelling of commands, and the beating of drums! Officers ran from one end of their units to the other yelling orders. NCOs worked frantically to keep their terror-stricken men fighting through walls of lead from the breastworks. The sounds resembled nature herself, imitating thunder and lightning with great pillars of white-gray smoke billowing forward like huge thunderheads, only to be blown back into the faces and eyes of the defenders by the wind. Eyre's well-placed cannons ripped lanes, streets, and alleys through the regulars' formations, who were forced to take cover along the sides of the road.

Both Generals Johnson and Lyman seemed to be everywhere, getting about, yelling commands, and in general leading their men. At one point Johnson lost his voice and ordered lemons brought to him by his servant. Sucking on them his voice returned. Within moments after the first shots every unit had engaged. There was a constant traffic of wounded being carried or helped to the surgeon's tents and ammunitions being hauled to the units and artillery, men running back and forth in a continual maze of lead bullets whizzing, whirling, and splatting against men and wood!

Johnson, Lyman and several officers and aids stood frantically giving orders near the rear of the Connecticut regiment. Slap! "Ugh," Johnson grabbed his thigh, pain drove into his leg, hot, sharp, like a dozen bee stings. A musket ball found its lodging in his upper thigh. Johnson placed his hand over the hole, looked down and saw blood start to ooze down his breeches.

"Sir, you've been hit! Men, come carry the general to his tent!" shouted Daniel Claus, Johnson's chief interpreter.

"No, continue the fight, pay me no mind. I will not be removed, damn it! Send more ammunitions to those cannons!" Johnson directed. He firmly clapped a handkerchief in his hand and held it pressed to his leg, still directing the defense. Within minutes Johnson limped to his tent with the help of Peter Wraxall. He could no longer stand the pain. Wraxall placed Johnson on his folding cot face down and ordered one of Johnson's guards to retrieve the surgeon. Wraxall sent a second man to get a surgeon, became very frustrated and ran out of the tent yelling for a surgeon and saw the Yorker surgeon running toward the tent. "In here, hurry! It's the general—he's taken a ball," said Wraxall urgently.

"Get me some water and clear that table," ordered the surgeon.

Wraxall yelled to the general's servant for water and he quickly knocked the items from the table. "What took you so long?" asked Wraxall.

"Mr. Wraxall, the poor boy had no idea we had moved our field hospital. The fight was becoming so close that bullets ripped through our tents and were whizzing about our ears. He found us in the storehouse. Now the bullets that find their way through just send splinters flying in our faces. Now give me that brandy and those towels," said the surgeon in a disgusted tone. "Help me put this towel under his leg." The surgeon took out a knife and gently cut open the general's breeches exposing the wound. It was bright red with a four-inch halo of purple bruising. Blood flowed freely from the hole. "Here, place this stick in his mouth," ordered the surgeon. "When the pain is too much, bite on it, General." The surgeon then saturated a cloth with the brandy and wiped it over the metal probe he removed from his medical kit. "Hold still, General." He then poured brandy over the wound, and pinching the wound open, he inserted the probe. Johnson gave a yell, jumped and Wraxall grabbed him by the shoulders and held him down. The doctor probed for several minutes and then, removing the instrument told Johnson, "General, the bullet is still there. If I remove it now you will not be worth a damn for days. That is, if I can remove it at all."

"Can you leave it for a while and stop up the hole so I can get back to the battle?" asked Johnson with clenched teeth. "I can't afford to lie here, the French must be stopped!"

"I'll do what I can, but it must come out today or you may loose the leg," answered the doctor. He again drenched the wound in brandy and, taking a dry bandage, plugged the bullet hole and wrapped the thigh in gauze. "Take a chair out there for the general," ordered the doctor to Johnson's servant.

"No, give me a crutch, I won't be able to see the field of battle sitting down," exclaimed Johnson as he struggled to stand. The surgeon sent the servant to fetch a crutch from the hut and Johnson took it and with the help of Wraxall hobbled back to his command.

General Lyman had assumed command in Johnson's absence and was issuing orders to various runners as Johnson returned. "General, I have strengthened the right, as the fighting seems to be moving from the center," reported Lyman.

"Very well, General. I'll be here as you need, Sir," replied Johnson. Obviously he was in great pain and was not capable of continuing command on the field for very long. He stood on one leg, holding himself up with the crutch, swaying ever so slightly. After several minutes Johnson left General Lyman in command of the field and was helped back to his tent by Wraxall.

Out in front of the Bay Colony troops there was a constant movement of Canadians and Indians. The enemy was getting ready to attempt to flank the breastworks. Colonels Titcomb, Pomeroy and Ruggles were commanding the right flank of the line. "We must tell the general we are being flanked," yelled Ruggles.

"Tell Colonel Bagley to concentrate his firing on that deadfall," Titcomb ordered a messenger.

"I don't know how much more of this my men can take!" said Pomeroy.

"Captain Burk," yelled Titcomb. "Send me a runner!"

"Nurse! Move! Report to the colonel!" ordered Burk.

Charles left the ranks and ran to report to the colonel. "Sir!" said Charles as he recovered his firelock. He was out of breath.

"Make haste to the general. Tell him that we are being flanked and we may need support. Tell him, man! Run!" ordered Titcomb.

Charles dropped his musket to his side, grabbed the straps of his accouterments about his neck and took off on a dead run through the maze of the encampment. He dodged in and out around trees and tents, hurdled logs and carts, zigzagged around men, horses and oxen, and finally arrived at the command quarters designated by Lyman's flags. "General Lyman, Sir, a message, Sir, from Colonel Titcomb!"

"Report, son."

"The colonel believes we are going to be flanked and that we may need some support," gasped Charles.

"Hurry back and tell your colonel to hold that flank. The enemy must not be allowed to overrun this camp! Tell him hold it at all cost! Go!" commanded Lyman.

Charles sprinted back to his unit and told the colonel the general's orders and returned to the breastworks. By this time the men were exhausted. They had been fighting for five hours! The sweat poured down their foreheads, stinging their eyes as it mixed with the gunpowder that blackened their faces and arms.

"Captain Burk!" yelled Titcomb. "Get your company ready for a sally party. My company and yours are going out and stop the heathens before they overrun our right. Hurry!" ordered Titcomb. "Mr. Bagley, you have the regiment. I want a continuous firing of volleys into the enemy."

The men of the two companies quickly took a needed drink, filled their cartridge boxes and wiped the pans and flints of their muskets. "Ready men, CHARGE!" The two companies leaped over the breastwork and charged headlong into the Canadians and Indians.

Several were struck down at the breastwork; most made it into the tree stumps and brush. Charles dove behind some heavy brush with Samuel George and John Cooper. Several Indians were in front of them, running for the cover of the tree line. Samuel's musket roared in Charles' ear and the closest Indian bent forward at the waist and toppled to the ground. Charles threw himself to the ground; a bullet had driven itself into an alder near his head. Peering to his left Charles could see several Canadians and Indians crouching behind a fallen log, firing at them. He rolled into the crotch of a fallen cedar and returned fire.

"Keep down! There are some on our right as well!" shouted George. Just then, Sergeant Campbell, James Reynolds and Isaac Woodbury jumped into the brush with them. The six men returned fire as best they could for several minutes, then fired a volley and sprinted to the next cover. Out of the corner of his eye to his left, Charles saw John take a bullet. It hit him hard, lifting him off his feet and throwing him onto his back. He didn't move! Charles was stunned.

"Charles, Charles!" He could hear a voice that sounded miles off. "Charles! Damn it, Charles, let's go!" yelled Samuel. The others had been watching two Canadians, prone behind a stump. They took turns firing at them as they charged one at a time, consecutively toward the stump. Charles, George, Woodbury and the sergeant reached the stump just as the last ball threw splinters in the Frenchman's face. They jumped on them. The sergeant in one swipe of his belt ax split the head of one, dispatching him instantly. Woodbury jumped on the second as Charles struck him in the head with the butt of his musket. Charles kept smashing his head in a blind rage. Reynolds thrust his knife into the man's side and he quit moving. "Charles, he's dead, stop!"

Shots began to rain in on them. They had not noticed the other well-hidden groups of the enemy. They were everywhere, yelling, dashing about, firing! From the right Charles saw the colonel, another officer and several soldiers pinned down behind several trees and brush. They were firing frantically, even the colonel, loading and firing his musket just like a common soldier! Suddenly, the colonel flew backward, blood squirted from his chest. He was dead!

The men of the sally party continued to return fire, but alas, they could not move forward and now the Indians had flanked them and cut off their retreat to the breastwork. They grouped together as they could, loading and firing as quickly as possible, desperate, with no other choice.

Mortar bombs began to burst all around them, throwing metal and sparks into the enemy. General Lyman and Captain Eyre had seen the predicament. As the shells continued bursting the Indians began to flee into the woods! Charles and his fellow provincials who had been pinned down rose up and fired into the retreating enemy. Suddenly Charles felt a sharp pain in the back of his head, and warm wetness and then darkness.

Seeing the commotion on the right flank, the French commander moved his regulars in closer, thinking the provincials had shifted men away from the center. Lyman's men pounded volley after volley into the French at close range. The enemy commander, the Baron Dieskau and his second, Monteuil, stepped to the front into the open before their men, hoping if they were seen by the Canadians and Indians they would be inspired to join his frontal attack with his regulars. Dieskau was immediately struck down, a musket ball to the leg. Monteuil staggered as he, too, was hit in the arm by the same volley. Monteuil opened his coat, removed a pewter flask and poured brandy on the Baron's wound. Seeing the two were officers, Whiting had his men train their next volley on them, striking Dieskau twice more in the same leg. Monteuil ordered two Canadians to hurry and carry the Baron out of range. The first Canadian knelt down to help and was shot dead, falling directly on Dieskau. The second pulled the other from Dieskau then tried to move the Baron, but he would not allow the man to remove him from the field. Instead he ordered the Canadian and Monteuil to sit him against a tree where he could observe the battle. He directed Monteuil to rally the regulars and lead a final assault on the breastwork.

The provincial volleys were so devastating at that point Monteuil could not rally the regulars. Feeling the gravity of the situation, he ordered a retreat. Seeing the French and Indians beginning to fall back, hundreds of provincials and Indians leaped the breastwork and began chasing the enemy from the clearing. Those of the enemy who could not leave the field quickly enough felt the wrath of axes, musket butts, and hand-to-hand fighting. During this melee one of the Massachusetts men ran across Dieskau. He approached to about ten or twelve paces and took aim. Dieskau drew his sword to present it to him. Then he reached into his pocket to remove his watch to present it to him in a gesture of surrender. He shot, striking Dieskau in the hip, then ran and leaped on him ordering him in French to surrender. "You rascal, why did you fire at me?" cried Dieskau in a broken German accent. "You see a man lying on the ground bathed in his own blood and you fire, eh?" aspirated Dieskau in extreme pain.

"How did I know you did not have a pistol? I prefer to kill the devil than the devil kill me!" yelled the soldier.

"You are a Frenchman, then?" asked the Baron.

"Yes, it is more than ten years since I left Canada!" replied the man.

Then several Indians, seeing the wounded Frenchman, ran up and jumped Dieskau. They ripped the hat from his head and his coat from his back.

"I order you to take me to your general. Do you not realize I am an officer! I am wounded. I am the Baron Ludwig Dieskau, commander of all French troops in North America! I demand you unhand me!" ordered the Baron in desperation. At that moment Colonel Pomeroy came up and with great difficulty protected the Baron and accepted his sword.

The firing diminished as suddenly as it had started. There were too many provincials on the field before the breastworks to continue volley fire. Soon men from the final charge began to return, reporting the enemy had retreated. The provincials were too exhausted; they were not chasing the French beyond the clearing. All along the breastwork the men shouted, "Huzzah, Huzzah, Huzzah, we got the day!" They had succeeded in defending their camp and had driven the enemy back. They were jubilant. But almost immediately the adrenaline wore off and many men slumped down where they stood. They were exhausted after seven straight hours of fighting. No attempt was made to follow the French retreat. General Lyman placed half the men on guard and saw to the immediate casualties.

Eight men carried Dieskau off the field in a blanket to General Johnson's tent. They carried him into the tent. Johnson was lying on his cot face down. Several surgeons were treating his wound. Johnson pushed one of the surgeons away and rolled onto his side. The Baron was obviously in great pain from the strained look on his face and the shaking of his voice as he introduced himself to the general. "Sir, please excuse me. I am the Baron Ludwig Dieskau, commander of the French forces."

Johnson rose slowly, "Place him here on my cot. See to this officer's wounds immediately. I can wait," ordered the general as he limped to a chair and slowly lowered himself.

The surgeons cut away the Frenchman's clothes, exposing his wounds. The three bullet wounds in his leg had broken the leg in several places and the wound in his hip had passed completely through both hips and loins. The surgeons poured brandy over the wounds and carefully daubed them with fresh gauze to examine them. Without saying a word the surgeons looked at each other and shook their heads at the severity of his wounds.

The surgeons worked quickly on the two officers. Another cot was brought in for Dieskau and then the men were left to rest. Dieskau fell into a deep feverish sleep, but Johnson attempted to see to some of the business of command from his tent. Men were sent into the field to retrieve only the close wounded. There were hundreds of wounds for the doctors to treat.

After a short time several Mohawks entered Johnson's tent and confronted him about his prisoner. They wanted him to give them Dieskau in exchange for their grave losses of the day. An argument ensued and Johnson encouraged them to leave; then he refused to grant their wishes and he ordered Wraxall to issue them extra rations for appeasement. The Baron awoke and saw the Indians leaving and could feel something was amiss. Sensing Johnson's anxiety Dieskau asked, "What did your Indians want, General?"

Johnson turned his head slowly toward the Baron, looked him in the eyes and stated in a clear direct tone, "They wish to burn you, by God, eat you, and smoke you in their pipes." The Baron's eyes widened in terror. Then Johnson called to one of his captains, Daniel Claus and gave him orders, "Have General Lyman send me a captain and fifty men immediately to act as a guard for the prisoner. We must shelter him from our natives." The guard arrived shortly.

"Captain, I want you to have the Baron moved from tent to tent often enough to keep his whereabouts from the Indians. Under no circumstances are you to leave his side. Guard him as if you were guarding me." Now safely the two men again relaxed.

Near dusk the camp was alarmed by distant gunfire. Was it the French? Had they started killing survivors of Williams' party? The guard was increased and those who could, continued to try and recover from the day's horrors.

Late in the evening the guard on the road sounded, "Officer of the guard! Officer of the guard!" The men in camp shuddered! The officer and his supporting guard scurried out to the road. Then in a few moments they returned, followed by a detachment of provincials. It was a party of New Hampshire men and Yorkers. Many of the men lined the breastworks yelling, "Huzzah, Huzzah, Huzzah!" It was a relief column sent from Fort Edward!

General Lyman met them at the breastwork, "Welcome, gentlemen," offered Lyman. "Who is in charge? Is this all of you?" asked the general.

A captain from New York stepped forward and saluted, "I am, Sir, Captain Folsom. Captain MaGinnis was placed in charge by Colonel Blanchard, but he was bad wounded in our engagement. He is coming up with the other wounded. Can we get them medical help, Sir?"

"Right away, captain," said Lyman. He turned to one of his subordinates and ordered, "Have Captain MaGinnis and the other wounded taken immediately to the surgeon's tents." Then turning back he said, "Captain, would you accompany me to the general's tent while your men get some hot food and relax?"

"Yes, Sir. Lieutenant Cook, would you see to the detachment. Dismissed." replied Folsom.

"Sergeants, tell your men to stow their packs near that storehouse and see that they get something to eat. Dismissed," ordered Cook.

The detachment quickly placed their equipment together near the rear of the camp and crowded around the mess fires to prepare food. As they began to relax and eat, many of the soldiers started to tell their stories of the day's battle to the men who had fought from within the breastworks. William Smith, one of the Yorkers, told his day's events to a group of Rhode Islanders.

"Blanchard 'erd yer cannons an sent fer the captain. We marched out ta scout the road to the lake, 120 Hamsher boys and us. We marched long the road till we'd come on a small French guard. They run like rabbits to the woods.

"We could tell by their baggage it were a good size party after you. We kept moven and by a small crick the men in front sawed a horrible sight! There, in front of us were a group of heathen and Canadians hacken, scalpen, and strippen bodies that were throwed all over the place! Be'en so busy in their dirty business we were not seen. We quietly snuck in close like sneaken in on a deer and sprung up shooten and yellen!

"We jumped em so fast they fought only a couple of minutes and the survivors runned inta the woods. God we killed a lot of em! The captain was shot, bad, really bleeden, but he didn't stop until the fighten was done. Then he passed out. Ten more were hurt but only two was killed. Five of us never comed back after chasen em into the woods. We must of killed near fifty of em!

"We had to order some of our men back inta ranks. They thought ta scalp some of the enemy, ta repay em. I can't blame em. That must of been near four o'clock. Been on the move ever since. We did set and refresh ourselves with some French brandy and we done some looten of the enemy packs. Then we marched an comed here. We seen bodies all long the road, had to move slow, didn't hear any more shooten, and couldn't tell which ones was dead or alive still until we was right up by em. A hell of a day."

Johnson's camp slumped into an exhausted sleep with the troops still at the breastworks, too tired and too afraid to go to their tents. Some men were mentally devastated; most had never experienced such violence. Guards remained on duty as total silence befell the camp on this, one of the most devastating days in the history of New England.

Charles lay in a surgeon's tent. He had been struck in the head by an Indian's ax!

HELL

Several hours passed and Charles could feel an aching in his head. He could hear moaning, crying and praying but he could not see. The moaning was pitiful, as if someone were sick. He heard a man gasping for air, like a deer that had been shot. He also heard the crying sounds of men being tortured, and the praying of desperate men, and the same verses spoken by Reverend Wells when Charles' grandfather passed away. Charles could not awaken and open his eyes to find out where he lay, but he could smell a mustiness around him like that when he had opened up a deer on a successful hunt. The air about him was also stagnant with smoke, wax and alcohol. Suddenly he felt a wetness upon his brow and his eyes jerked open to a sharp light like the flash of a flintlock in the dark. He was in a surgeon's tent and a surgeon's mate, Benjamin Gavitt, had just dabbed his head with a damp rag. "Are you awake?" asked Gavitt.

Charles sighed, "I think so." He sat up ever so slowly.

"Oh, my head." He reached for the back of his head and rubbed his scalp.

"You'll be alright. Do you remember? You were struck in the head and your friend carried you here," explained Gavitt.

"I remember the pain and falling, but nothing since. Have we won?" asked Charles.

"Yes, the French have run away. Can you stand?"

Charles slowly rose to his feet and stood holding the mate's shoulder a moment until he gained his balance. "I'll be alright now, I think."

"Let me get someone to help you to your tent. After a rest, other than a headache you should be in good shape by tomorrow," said Gavitt.

When Charles awoke the next day, his head felt like it was filled with a thick dense fog. He rolled out of his tent and sat holding his bandage-wrapped skull for a few moments. The sun had just risen and the warmth bathing him felt refreshing.

"How are you feeling?" asked Jacob Morrill.

Jacob was setting in front of his tent finishing some cold meal, water and sugar. "Heard you took a good clubbing to the head," he said, as he slurped some food from his trencher.

"Where is everyone?" asked Charles.

"Some are still a-guardin' at the barricade and some have gone out lootin' for French supplies left when they took off runnin'. That's where I'm headed," said Jacob.

"Got any hot water left?" asked Charles.

"Yep, there's some left here in the kettle. Help yourself. I'm goin' out before there's nothin' left to find. You want'a go?" asked Jacob.

"No, I'm going to find me a spot and sit and let my head clear for a while," replied Charles.

Jacob slipped on his coat and grabbed his musket and cartridge box and walked off, joining several others on his way out of camp.

Charles rummaged in his haversack and pulled out a tin mug, his folding knife and a chunk of chocolate. His head was still pounding and he moved very slowly. He carefully shaved some slivers of the chocolate into the cup and then filled it with hot water from the camp kettle. Then he painfully stood to his feet and walked slowly down the tent street. Many of the tents were empty and there was little movement in the camps. The few men he passed were just sitting or lying in a forlorned state. As he rounded the edge of the street he could see to his left plenty of movement at the surgeon's tents. He began to feel the need to sit down again and walked to the base of a tree near the center of camp. Slowly he lowered himself to the ground and sipped the warm chocolate.

Just a short distance from the tree Charles rested against was General Johnson's marquee and canvas fly. Wraxall was directing several soldiers as they carried Johnson out of his tent and settled him on a cot under the fly. The general's military family was also congregated there for a council of war. From his vantage point Charles could hear most of their conversation.

"Gentlemen, we must strengthen our camp. I feel we may expect a more formidable attack by the enemy. I want half of our garrison continually on guard duty. I need all regiments to supply a list of carpenters so details can be formed from them to construct a battlement around the camp. This log structure must be high enough for the men to stand behind. It must as well have our cannon properly mounted along the wall. We must employ all our time securing ourselves here in the best possible manner. We must as well appeal immediately to all our colonies for more troops for fear of another attack with cannon!" ordered the general.

"General," addressed Lyman. "I think we must advance at all haste! It is imperative that we take advantage of the enemy's route. If we march we can take their camp between the lakes and then crush St. Frederic!" urged Lyman.

Wraxall interrupted, "We are apprehensive that the French will make a more formidable attack upon us and bring artillery up the lake!"

"Mr. Lyman, we cannot jump into another battle so quickly, for we are not prepared to meet the enemy," retorted Johnson. "We do not have enough stores to feed our army on a march and if they could be fed there are not enough batteaus to carry them up the lake. We must prepare our defenses and acquire our supplies before marching north."

"I have to agree with Mr. Johnson. We are not ready to move forward. With the low morale of the troops I cannot see a victory at hand until giving this army some time," supported Colonel Ruggles.

"I am disappointed the men aren't invigorated; instead the resolute and obstinate attack made upon our breastwork in the face of our cannon seems to have given our troops a dread of the enemy," said Johnson in a discouraged tone.

"Mr. Eyre and I have had discussions about a fort that should be built here on the lake. We are of the opinion that a strong fortress with earthen bastions should be constructed," stated Johnson.

A heated discussion ensued with most of the provincial officers insisting only a picketed fort be built! They did not feel their governments should fund a disproportionate fort and garrison to protect New York! The New Englanders won out and orders were given to start a small picketed fort. Their soldiers' aversion to digging a fort led them to denying an earthen structure. Daily 500 men were to be working on the new fort but no extra pay was to be given for this duty and the workers were to take their turns on guard, escort and scouting duties. The officers agreed but warned Johnson of the possible problems he might be creating.

Charles saw several of his company moving through camp and rose to join them. His head was beginning to clear. As the men passed near the surgeon's tents they had to make way for a small procession. Lieutenant Colonel Bagley and many of the regiment's captains were marching in a group following six men carrying a bloodied corpse blanketed on a stretcher. Mr. Bagley halted the men and was addressing the surgeon outside while the body was taken inside. When the officers started to walk away Charles and the others went over to ask Captain Burk who it was. "Was it the colonel?" asked Colby.

"I'm afraid so. This is such a hideous time. So many killed, so many wounded. Mr. Bagley says we lost near 30 men! Did you see our wounded last night?" the sergeant asked Charles.

"Wounded? I was in such a daze when I woke up that I had no idea who else was around me!" said Charles.

"There were a couple dozen brought in after you woke up and I hear a couple hundred are to march out for a burial detail early this afternoon," offered Samuel Foot.

"I heared from those out a lootin' that there's bodies all over the place!" said Abram Young.

"I was sickened at the Indians! When we were out near the pond this morning; they were digging up graves and scalping the bodies! I think most of them I saw them digging up were enemy Indians!" told Thom Greenleaf.

"I saw them coming in and out of camp all morning with scalps. I thought they were from yesterday or some enemy hiding in the woods," shuttered Charles.

"I saw them take John and the Major in late yesterday. Has anyone seen how they're doing?" asked Thom.

"John, John Benjamin! Lord Jehovah! I must check now!" yelled Charles. He immediately left the men and hurried to the surgeon's tent. Inside there were about six cots and in the back was a raised table. All the cots had men lying upon them moaning and crying. Several of the men were silent. There were several men scurrying about trying to help the wounded. At the large table in the back stood Amos Putnam, the regiment's surgeon and Benjamin Gavitt. They stood at the table with their shirt sleeves rolled up; a bloodied apron buttoned to their chests and tied around their waists. On the table lay Major Nicholes. He had been brought in yesterday afternoon. From behind Charles stepped Bagley and John Wood, the regimental chaplain. Putnam stepped back away from the table and dipped his hands in a bucket of pink-stained water and wiped them on his apron.

"How is the major?" asked Bagley.

"He will live. But he will require a long time to recover," answered the doctor.

"Thank God! If we had lost him and the colonel..." He paused. "A hell of a day," said Bagley. "A hell of a day."

"Thank Jehovah for sparing Mr. Nicholes," prayed the reverend. He looked skyward and placed his hands together in front of him, taking special care to have their shape resemble the steeple on a church. Then looking back at the surgeon he asked, "Amos, would you get the colonel's body ready for burial this afternoon? We think it best for us all if we not postpone it any longer."

"I will see to it right away," acknowledged Putnam.

Charles asked one of the nurses helping the wounded, "Have you seen John Benjamin? I heard he was brought in late yesterday."

"I ain't sure. Too many to know. There's more out back. Good luck," replied the nurse as he treated a man and turned away from Charles.

Charles walked back out of the tent and went around the side. He could see several men lying on the ground, but he was not ready for what he saw when he rounded the back of the hospital tent. The ground was strewn with bodies! He stopped and stood stunned, scanning the scores of soldiers. His heart began to race and his stomach tightened with nausea. Men were lying on blankets, many soaked with blood. Interspersed among them, others sat, and here and there men were wandering aimlessly. Charles took a few steps into the moaning crowd. A soldier lay at his feet with an outstretched arm begging for water. Charles just cringed. Another sat with his head in his hands; a bloody bandage about his head soaked through where an eye had been. Charles turned left; he scanned deeper into the mass of men, looking for John. Coming up near the back of the tent he almost tripped over a wooden bucket. Looking down abruptly, Charles shuddered! It was filled overflowing with amputated limbs and blood! Charles became instantly sick and choked trying to keep from vomiting. He sidestepped the limbs and continued his search. Then he spotted him! John was not moving; he just lay there. His face was almost as white as his blanket that he lay on. His breath was extremely slow and shallow. Charles's eyes caught a blood-soaked stain on the blanket that half covered John. Charles pulled back the blanket revealing John's bloody bandaged arm. John stirred and jerked as the movement shot pain through his body.

"John, it's Charles. I'm so glad to find you alive. I just heard you were brought in," whispered Charles.

"Charles, oh, oh my good friend. I guess we gave it to 'em." John's voice was lethargic. He spoke very quietly, wincing in great pain. "I saw the whole thing. After I was shot I propped myself up and watched. It looked like you were being surrounded and then bombs started landing among the Indians and Frenchmen. They ran and I knew we had the day. Then I can't remember. I must have passed out."

"Is there a lot of pain?" asked Charles.

"Ya, they said I might loose the arm." John lifted his other arm and held it over his face. His emotions were too much! His voice shook, "How can I be a blacksmith with one damned arm?" cried John.

Charles put his hand on John's arm, "I'm sure you'll keep it. You're too tough to let them take it. I'll sit here with you while you sleep. You've got to sleep for a while and let your arm heal." Charles sat quietly, periodically sponging John's brow. John slipped into a deep sleep.

After a few hours Charles left John and joined the others of his regiment. It was late in the afternoon and they were forming to bury the colonel. About 200 of the men were drawn up into ranks two deep and faced in toward each other forming an avenue for the detail to carry the colonel's coffin to the burial site just beyond the right of the lines and over the swamp. A carpenter nailed his crude coffin shut. He had been laid out in his best uniform adorned with his badges of rank, a Bible in one hand, his sword in the other. Leading the procession were the Lieutenant Colonel, Mr. Pomeroy and Mr. Ruggles. Following these officers were two colour men carrying the colonel's flags. Behind them was a lone drummer playing a slow march. Eight soldiers carried the coffin by ropes passed under the wooden box and draped over the men's shoulders. Marching in the rear were most of the officers of the regiment. What a melancholy sight! After the procession passed, the men who had lined the route were formed into ranks six deep, facing the burial ground. There were about 40-50 fresh graves. The bearers placed the coffin on the ground near the newly dug hole. The Reverend Wood stepped forward to the head of the grave and Mr. Bagley gave the order, "Uncover!" The men removed their tricorn hats and assumed a reverent stance. The Reverend then began a most solemn service. Here they stood, still exhausted and in fear of another attack, with the commander of their unit before them, dead. They had served their colony in great honor, repulsing an enemy army, hoping this to be the final war ridding New England of the French and their heathen. Many Sabbath services had talked of God, the devil and of heaven and hell. They had now experienced hell first hand!

As the service finished a captain stepped forward, marched three ranks of seven men from his company to the north of the grave and ordered three volleys in the colonel's honor. The service was complete. As the regiment returned to camp a burial party was returning from yesterday's battle ground. Surprisingly, they had very few dead with them. The officers reported their men had been spooked by their own advanced party. By the time the officers had suppressed the retreat most of their time had been wasted and they returned to camp.

As had been established for days now, half of the army was put on guard and the remainder tried to relax. Many were not able to sleep; many were still lying on their arms.

A MOST MELANCHOLY DAY

Upon the next morn a call went out for volunteers to follow Colonel Pomeroy out to the spot where Colonel Williams' regiment had been attacked. Pomeroy was to command 400 men in the collection of the dead and wounded. Charles and several of his friends volunteered. No longer could they sit in camp idle; they needed to put the battle behind them.

It was a hot, humid day and the men were ordered to wear small clothes or work smocks. Several wagons were taken to carry plunder and 40 biers were fashioned to carry the dead and wounded. The men were divided into detachments. Each detachment was to carry canvas and thread to wrap the bodies and, Bibles and crosses to say words over the dead. They were issued tools for digging graves. For those officers suspected of being dead, some personal belongings were taken to be buried with them.

Pomeroy's unit was not out far when they came across the first group of bodies near the pond where Whiting fought a heavy action. The previous day's party had not reached farther into the forest than this point before scurrying back to camp. The dead soldiers found here were interred on the spot.

As the unit pushed farther down the road, Pomeroy ordered smaller detachments to separate and march deeper toward the engagement site of the morning of September 8. Lieutenant Taylor was ordered to take Thomas Greenleaf, Gideon Woodwell, Joseph Nicholes, Charles and twenty others and march straight for the ambush spot. Lieutenant Daniel Pomeroy with twenty-five men was to lead the way; he had been there with Williams' regiment that terrible morning. Billy Williams, surgeon's mate assistant, was to accompany them for medical support. John Butler, one of Johnson's Indian Department officers, also accompanied the detachment.

All along their march the detachment found and buried groups of fallen bodies. Pomeroy told them most of these were spots where Whiting had halted and attempted to slow the retreat or rally his men and the rest of Williams' regiment. After about an hour the detachment was halted. They were near the ambush spot. Orders were given to proceed slowly. As they moved closer they began to see signs of ambush; blankets, axes, haversacks, and knapsacks were everywhere. As the victims had fled, they discarded all their extra weight. Then about 140 rods farther, bodies began to be found more frequently. The detachment halted on a small rise; before them lay heaps of bodies! The lieutenant immediately gave orders for one command, Pomeroy's, to stand fast, ready to engage while Taylor's detachment was to quickly survey the area in case the enemy was lurking in another ambush.

Taylor's 25 men climbed the rising ground to their left and proceeded along it, skirting the road. They now had the same vantage as the Canadians and Indians who had destroyed Williams' unit during their final attempts. Below them they saw no movement. After about 40-50 rods there were no more bodies; they had reached the front of the ambush area. Feeling the area safe, Taylor signaled to Pomeroy. A small guard was placed covering all four approaches and the others began the grim task of rooting through the bodies.

As Taylor's men descended the slope they were sickened. The heat of the past several days had begun to decompose the bodies, and the smells hung in the humid air. Several of the men untied their cravats and held them over their mouth and nose. Stunned, they surveyed the corpses. Here and there were uniformed men, but the majority of the bodies lay naked, scalped and mutilated beyond recognition. Blackened, thick, dried blood was everywhere! In several areas at the edge of the tree line groups of men were lying dead, bound together as prisoners who had hastily been executed. Bloodied heads revealed their fate; probably prisoners who were killed when MaGinnis' men surprised the enemy late in the afternoon. The men were ordered to work quickly. They finished their descent and began to check first for signs of life; there was total silence. The biers were brought forward and bodies were carefully placed on them and then carried to a central area where the corpses were searched for anything to identify them. The two detachments had combined again and a group was ordered to start digging graves, not for individuals, but for several mass burials. By eleven o'clock another detachment had arrived with Colonel Pomeroy and several wagons.

In spite of the eerie silence, several survivors were found. Captain Hawley was lying in a heap of his men. He had been shot in the shoulder; the ball had made a huge wound but had not exited his body. He was so weak from the blood loss he could barely speak once he had been brought to consciousness. Ensign Joseph Williams called out shortly after the parties began their labor. He had been assured it was not the enemy. He had feigned death as he had when the enemy had returned the afternoon of the battle, thus escaping capture. His wounds did not appear to be fatal, but he was unable to drag himself from the battlefield. Billy Williams cheerfully dressed his wounds, happy to see Joseph's survival, but leery about the fate of his other relations.

A third man was found alive, leaning against a tree. His wound was a hideous sight! The back of his skull was gone! His naked brains showing, he was an obvious victim of an ax assault to the head! The only thing that could be done was to wrap his head hoping to hold in his brains. About 25 others were found alive and loaded into the wagons.

As the afternoon progressed, the heat of the day and the smell of the dead made the already terrible duty even more sickening. The dead were wrapped and sewn up into canvas shrouds. Identifying items, if found, were taken to return to camp. One of the dead was Colonel Williams; his body had not been touched. He lay on his back as he fell, with his eyes staring toward the heavens; his sword still in his right hand. Mr. Pomeroy, Billy Williams and several others of his regiment prepared him for burial. They took from his pockets his watch, an ivory memorandum book and several other trinkets to take to his family. Then, in his dress uniform adorned with his sash and gorget, they sewed him into a shroud. His sword was placed with his other belongings to be taken home. The majority of the bodies were placed in group burials. The men congregated around the graves and words were said over them; tears were shed, and the graves were closed. Colonel Williams was taken to a spot at the edge of the battlefield. There a large pine tree was to be his marker. His grave was dug under it and a service was held and he was interred.

After the burials had been completed all the gear, equipment and stores left on the battlefield by the dead and retreating provincial, native and French troops was collected and loaded into the wagons. The loads contained quantities of food, clothes, blankets, hatchets and muskets. Some of the muskets were stolen "Brown Bess" muskets used by Dieskau's army that had been liberated at General Braddock's defeat.

The detachment then marched back to camp; it had been a most melancholy day. They had buried about 140 men this day, many unidentifiable! Hell had shown itself as the face of death and misery at Lake George; 143 dead, 92 wounded, 65 missing—presumed dead!

WE CAN ONLY WAIT

In the morning Charles was summoned to record events at an Indian council. General Johnson was in too much pain to leave his tent so General Lyman was to preside. The natives felt that this one great battle was enough for one season and insisted on returning to their castles. Many of the provincial officers also felt another fierce battle was not deemed necessary. In order to appease his natives and in hope of insuring their future support, Johnson sent them several French prisoners out of the 21 he had taken. The French prisoners were to be "adopted" by the Indians, and would assume the names and tribal ranking of the dead warriors they replaced. The one stipulation was that Shirley was not to be told of this! Many New England officers complained of the overabundance of plunder taken by the Indians. They stated many of the items were belongings of their colonial troops such as blankets discarded in the battle.

After a short council the Indians reassured Lyman that they would again return to help their brother Johnson, but they pleaded that they should not make a sudden peace with the French as was done last year which left them disappointed and unable to vent their resentments and anger upon their enemies.

As the council was dissolved Lyman issued orders to the commanders, and work parties were to be resumed. The hope was to take some of the memories of the past few days off the minds of the men as well as prepare for a defensive or offensive movement. One of these orders was to Captain Webster of Titcomb's regiment. He was to select 36 carpenters and finish the radeaux. Charles was one of those selected. Very little work had been done to prepare these floating batteries so Webster's detachment was sent out to the west to cut wood for the construction. A detachment of twelve Connecticut men was sent as a guard for Webster's carpenters. They selected the appropriate trees for the different parts of the boats, felled them and cut them into lengths, which would be dragged back to the lake tomorrow by teamsters. It was about four o'clock when they returned to camp.

After eating, Charles went to visit John. He had been moved into one of the surgeon's tents. Charles entered, scanned the cots and saw John. Gavitt, the surgeon's mate, had just left John's side. He stopped Charles as he approached. "We had to take the arm."

"God, no!" Charles groaned.

"He would not have lived if Dr. Putnam had not cut it. The veins in his shoulder were changing dark blue and the arm was dying. That musket ball nearly tore the arm off, and it shattered the upper bone into too many pieces to grow back into one. The doctor also believes the bullet may have been poisoned! There was a groove cut in it and a piece of leather was wedged into the groove. It was probably soaked in poison. It was the only chance he may have," reassured Gavitt.

"He'll not live without it either. He will wither and die like an over-pruned apple tree. His only skill was the swinging of his hammer." Charles wiped his forehead and sighed deeply. "Can I talk to him?"

"He's not awake. The doctor gave him a tincture of laudanum for the pain. He'll probably sleep very deeply for hours. We can only wait now and see how it heals. You can sit with him, but don't try and wake him," said Gavitt.

Charles walked slowly to John's cot. He quietly slid a chair to the edge of the cot and sat. John lay motionless except for the raising and lowering of his chest. After a few moments Charles put his head in his hands and prayed silently. Several hours passed and Charles rose and walked to his tent. It was difficult for him to sleep. What would happen now? Would John survive? Would he be able to work? What would Sarah and Mary do? What about the French? Would they come and attack again? What would become of them all? Amesbury seemed so far away!

For several days the men of Johnson's army worked in and around the camp. They were busy building boats, the two radeaux, storehouses and the battlement to surround the camp. Scouting parties tried to reach into the wilderness but most were driven back by their own fears. The weather had been kind to them but some, having lost their blankets in the battle, were chilled in the early fall nights. Some of the wounded were starting to improve; John was not one of them. He had only awakened for short periods and was beginning to weaken. Very few more dead were found from the battle.

The camp awoke to a pleasant day on Tuesday, the 16th of September. The sun shone brightly and there was a light breeze. It was a very comfortable day early in the morning as groups of wagons arrived from Fort Edward and a unit of about 200 men headed up the lake to scout for the enemy. The men had been working hard and had finished a fine battlement that totally encircled the encampment. It was fortified high enough for the men to stand behind in case of another attack.

In the middle of the morning most of the field officers were called to General Johnson's marquee. Charles had been ordered to attend Mr. Bagley in case notes must be taken. The general had been moved out under the fly and was sitting uncomfortably in a camp chair. The Baron Dieskau was lying on a cot propped up by several bolsters and pillows. As the officers crowded around, Johnson and Dieskau were cordially saying their farewells, "I hope your wounds are not too painful on your trip to Albany. I have made arrangements for your reception at my house there. I have arranged for a sizable guard to escort you unharmed. I must honor you, Sir, it was a valiant assault you made on our army. You have honored your King well," stated Johnson.

"General Johnson, it is you that must be commended, Sir. I assumed from the very beginning that my regulars would make quick time of your militia, but, alas, as the day progressed and my Canadians and natives became uninterested, your men's spirits progressed. In observation of your provincials during this honorable day, in the morning they fought like good boys, around noon like men, but in the afternoon like devils!" honored the Baron. "I must give sincere thanks to your hospitality now and for it at your home in Albany in the future, Sir."

Four soldiers advanced and carefully lifted the Baron and his cot into an awaiting wagon. Lyman stepped forward and gave orders to a captain who was to command the guard, then turned to the French general and saluted him. The Baron returned his salute and the procession of wagons, the Baron and the French prisoners, all under heavy guard, marched off.

Before the officers were dismissed, Johnson gave orders of promotion to fill some of the vacancies caused by the battle. Lieutenant Colonel Gilbert was to act as colonel of Williams' regiment and Captain Godfrey was to act as its major. Lieutenant Colonel Bagley was to be colonel of Titcomb's regiment and Bensley Glazier was to be acting major. When dismissed, Bagley ordered Glazier to form the regiment without arms.

The men were formed in three ranks, sergeants on the right of each company, corporals in the rear and officers in ranks before their companies; Bagley stood before all with John Whiting his adjutant, Glazier, William Taylor the commissary, and John Kingsbury the overseer.

"Gentlemen of the regiment," sounded Bagley's voice. "I have called you together to hear a reading of this document I have just received from General Johnson. Mr. Whiting, would you read this to the troops please."

"Sir," replied Whiting as he took the paper. "By virtue of the power and authority in and by His Majesty's royal commission to me granted to be General over His Majesty's Forces and the Province of Massachusetts-Bay aforesaid—I do by these presents (reposing especial trust and confidence in your loyalty, courage and good conduct) constitute and appoint you the said Jonathan Bagley Esq. to be colonel of the said 3rd Regiment of Foot. Raised to be employed in His Majesty's service this campaign. Given under hand and seal at Lake George this 16th day of September, 1755."

Whiting handed the paper back to Bagley. "It was with great sorrow at the loss of Colonel Titcomb that I accepted this commission. Under authorization of General Johnson, Massachusetts-Bay and my command as colonel of this regiment, I now offer the following promotions as well. I raise Benjamin Glazier to major of our regiment." The two men shook hands and saluted. "Mr. Woodwell, Mr. Colby and Mr. George, step forward. Mr. Woodwell and Mr. Colby, I commission you lieutenants of this 3rd Massachusetts regiment. Mr. George, I commission you ensign." The three men snapped a salute. "Eliezer Hudson, Jacob Smith."

"Sir," responded the two men almost simultaneously.

"Mr. Hudson, you are given a sergeant's billet, and Mr. Smith, you are to be a corporal." Hudson and Smith quickly saluted.

"Gentlemen of the regiment, I know this has been a very trying time for all of us. We have all come here expecting war, but many of us truly did not know what that meant. Now, after the latest engagement we have all seen what type of hell it brings to most who engage in it. But gentlemen, you have done myself, Colonel Titcomb, your King and yourselves a great honor by the courage and determination you showed here at Lake George! Gentlemen, we must protect our colony and continue our vigilance from this site, or if we are so ordered to advance to the French territories in the north, we must go! I expect your continued efforts and ask you to support, respect and welcome these men in their new positions!" Bagley removed his tricorn and lifted it as he yelled, inciting the entire regiment to chime in on the cheers in union, "Three cheers men! Hip, hip, Huzzah! Hip, hip, Huzzah! Hip, hip, Huzzah! Gentlemen, dismiss the regiment!"

After being dismissed Charles was summoned to the colonel's tent. "Mr. Nurse, I am placing you on the regimental roster as a clerk. You have been doing the duty diligently for some time now and you will be receiving the pay for it as well. You are too valuable to be taken from your normal duties so I will try and restrict your usage whenever possible so as not to take advantage of you."

"Thank you, Sir, I would be glad to help you and the regiment." Charles saluted the colonel.

"You are dismissed, Mr. Nurse."

Charles exited the marquee and went as he had the past three days to visit John. He walked in the surgeon's tent and walked to John's cot. Dr. Putnam was re-bandaging John's shoulder. Charles stood and waited. A pan on the floor next to the cot was filled with greenish-red soiled bandages that reeked of infection.

When Putnam finished he assured John he would check on him later and that he would have some food brought directly. Putnam took Charles by the arm and pulled him aside as he walked away from John. "Charles, he's not healing very well. I'm afraid the amputation has become terribly infected. If it continues to gangrene it will control his body and he'll die. We'll do what we can. Sit with him and make him comfortable, but don't stay long," whispered the doctor.

Charles was speechless. He walked over and sat by John, who was already asleep. The fresh bandages were already visibly soiled by a red-green-pungent smelling fluid oozing from John's arm. After a few minutes an orderly brought a wooden bowl of broth. Charles took it and gently shook John awake, "John, John, it's Charles. I have some food for you." John's eyes fluttered and in a few seconds opened.

"Oh, Charles, I'm too tired."

"John you must eat. Just a little. You need some strength." Charles put a hand under John's head and lifted it slightly as he spooned some broth into his mouth. John slowly licked his lips and swallowed. It took Charles near five minutes to feed John about a half cup of the broth. Then John insisted they stop.

"I am so tired," said John. "At least it don't hurt much any more. I need to get some fresh air. That'll do it, if I can get enough rest so I can get outside in a few days I'll be much better."

"Just relax, John. I'll come every day. As soon as Dr. Putnam says it's time for you to sit outside, I'll take you out under a big shade tree and sit with you," reassured Charles.

John's eyelids slowly began to close. They looked heavy and swollen. They opened and closed several times and then closed and John began to snore. "Good night, John, I'll be back tomorrow."

WHAT WILL WE DO?

For several days the men of the provincial army went through their normal routines of building boats and standing guard. Daily scouts would return with reports of an enemy sighting. The camp would be alarmed, guards increased and more scouting parties sent north. Every day Charles found time to visit John. He had become progressively worse and was not expected to live.

On Friday Charles was working on the radeau. It was becoming depressing work, not because of the labor of boat building, but because Captain Webster's detachment was also expected to mount guard. They were not exempt from other details, either. It was a fair day, a good time of year for manual labor—not too hot, not too cold. At about three o'clock Webster's men were dismissed for the day. Charles, Thomas Greenleaf and Abram Young were sprawled near their tents, relaxing. In front of them they had half of a mess kettle filled with beer they had just purchased from their sutler.

"I'm sick of working on that boat and then going on guard duty!" said Abram.

"At least at home when you're done at the wharf, you're done," complained Thomas. The three men had combined their rum ration and Thomas leaned forward, poured it into the beer and stirred it.

"Well, we are off tonight. Drink hearty, I hear this is the last of the rum for a while," yawned Charles.

"Pour me some of that brew," said Abram.

Thomas took their tin mugs and dipped them one at a time into the kettle. Each took his and started drinking. Abram lifted his glass and toasted, "Here's to heading home soon."

"Here, here," chimed Thomas.

For about a half an hour they just relaxed in camp, draining the kettle. In the distance where the road exited the wood line they could hear the sounds of cattle. Charles and the men stood and saw eight wagons of supplies and about fifty head of cattle being pushed by drovers through the clearing toward camp. It was now nearing four o'clock so Charles joined his messmates to eat. When Samuel and

Gideon received their promotions, Ebenezer Davis and Theodore Hoyt were assigned Charles' mess. Charles retrieved his wooden terrene and spoon from the tent and knelt over the kettle that had been brought from the mess fires. He scooped onto his terrene several heaps of rice and peas moistened with butter.

"There's no meat tonight," blurted out Hoyt.

"That's nothin' new since we've been up here at the lake," said Ebenezer sarcastically.

"We'll have some tomorrow. Just saw about 50 beef coming into camp when I was coming over here," said Charles. He sat down cross-legged on a slab of wood. After several mouthfuls Joseph Nicholes added, "It's a good thing we had a little butter left in our rations. It's the only thing makes these vittles eatable."

"Ya, I guess John ain't really missed much," replied Thomas.

The five men finished their meal in a few minutes. Charles looked up from his terrene and saw two women walking down the company street. It didn't hit home. Then suddenly Charles raised his eyes again. Women? It had been weeks since any had been at their camp. Was it? Yes! It was Sarah and Mary!

As the women stepped into their camp the men stood and greeted them.

"Sarah, Mary, it's good to see you," greeted Thomas.

"Thanks, Thomas," replied Sarah.

"Mrs. Benjamin, Mary, welcome. There's a little rice left, not much. Have you eaten?" asked Joseph.

"No, but we haven't much appetite," said Sarah.

"I thought you had probably gotten home by now," said Charles.

"No, a few of us were kept in Albany in case we were needed. In fact we were about to set off for home when word came that John was bad. Where is he? Is he still alive?" asked Sarah in a very concerned voice.

Mary had been standing beside her mother quite silent, staring with watery eyes at Charles.

"He's not doing very well. I usually go to visit him right about now. Let me take you and Mary to see him," said Charles.

He took Sarah by the arm and started to lead her and Mary down the street toward the surgeon's tent. "I should tell you before we get there. They had to take his arm." The women gasped. "It's not good. Dr. Putnam thinks he won't make it," said Charles softly.

The three walked into the surgeon's tent and were approaching John's cot when Dr. Putnam stopped them.

"All of you can't go back there," said Putnam.

Mary's body stiffened and her breathing began to shake.

"Mrs. Benjamin, you'd better come over. I don't expect him to live through the night. The infection is destroying him. Charles, take Mary outside," said the doctor.

Sarah and the doctor walked over to John. Charles put his arm around Mary's shoulder and walked her outside the tent. She immediately buried her head in his shoulder.

"Charles!" she cried. "What will we do?" her voice quivered. "His arm!" Then only her whimpering was heard.

"I know, Mary. I've come every day and sat with him. He has not been in much pain for some days now," said Charles.

He put one arm around her and the other around her neck and pulled her close to him.

"It's alright, Mary. I'll be with you."

Charles held her for several minutes.

"You need to try and not look sad. If he wakes up he's going to want to see you. You don't want him to see you giving up."

Benjamin Gavitt came out.

"Mary you'd better come in. The Dr. said he's going. Charles, you come too. He asked for you," said Gavitt.

Mary walked slowly across the surgeon's tent, holding Charles' hand as he walked behind her. Sarah was seated beside John. Dr. Putnam looked up from examining him and shook his head. John had already said his good-byes to Sarah.

"Mary, dear," John coughed.

"Come closer. I..." he sighed. His eyes blinked very slowly and rolled up into his head. "I hoped you would come. I need you to help your mother." John reached out for her. Mary fell to her knees and put her cheek against her father's chest, trying to hide her tears.

"You're a fine woman now. It will take you both to survive. Remember, dear." John could barely catch his breath. It was shallow, short and rapid. "Tell your babies that we drove the French away. You teach 'em to be good Christians." John's eyes closed and his body went limp.

Mary raised her head and everyone froze and stared at John. Then he took a long, gasping breath. His body jerked. John reached his arm out without opening his eyes and called, "Charles!"

Charles reached around Mary and took John's hand saying, "I'm here John. We're all here beside you."

"Charles, I've known you since you were a young boy. You've been a good friend to me here." John's voice was slower and his speech slurred. "Your family is one that can always be counted on. So…so I ask you. It is my last wish for you to promise. Promise me, Charles, that you will look after 'em! They have no man, no family. See that Sarah and Mary get home and watch over 'em. Swear it!"

The only sounds heard were Sarah and Mary crying. Charles' eyes filled with tears and he swallowed heavily.

"I'll watch over them. Don't worry," choked Charles.

John's eyes jerked open; he smiled, and then closed his eyes. He went limp and exhaled the remaining air in his chest.

He was gone!

Dr. Putnam pulled the blanket over John's head. Charles, Sarah and Mary slowly left the tent and walked down the company streets to Charles' mess tent. Half of his mess was on guard duty. The others had lit several candles and were sitting around the tent. The men offered the women some bread, but they couldn't eat. They talked kindly of John and tried to console Sarah and Mary. It was a great shock for them, having just arrived. What were they to do? They were not allowed in the camps. They had no means of support. No husband, no father. They wouldn't even have a house to live in now! What were they to do? Where were they to live? Sarah and Mary could do no more than weep most of the evening. Eventually sleep overpowered them.

The next morning was devastating for Mary and Sarah. Their sorrow was endless as they went through the day preparing John for burial. Charles did his best to console and help them but he was ordered to stand guard with the other half of his mess. That afternoon John was buried next to the others lost in battle.

The next day, Sabbath day, it was cool and rainy. Charles was able to go to service and took Mary and her mother, hoping the words of the chaplain would help them. A good number of men were ill, deemed unfit for duty. They were sent home via the wagons that had come on Friday. Charles spent the afternoon on guard duty. He slept under arms with the rest of his picket guard.

I WILL BE THERE

On Monday the camp awoke to a cool, drizzly fog. Charles had a severe headache. He often felt like this during the fall. Scouts were sent to the east and the west of the lake early. Shortly after daylight several companies of recruits marched in, along with a dozen wagons of stores for the camp. Captain Nathaniel Dwight of Belchertown led his company. As soon as the stores were unloaded, many sick and wounded were loaded in the wagons and they immediately returned south. The rest of the camp was either ordered to guard duty or fatigue details, as had been the routine for weeks.

Captain Webster ordered his group of carpenters to report to the waterfront where they were working on the radeau. It was a long hard job; laying in the keel, planking the sides, caulking the joints, building gun platforms and rigging the mast. Charles, Edmund Davis, Ebenezer's brother, and Thomas reported from Burk's company. As others arrived, they started grumbling about the cold and how the rain was going to make the day's work miserable. Then a heated argument began, about having to continue with normal camp duties. Most had read the day's duty roster posted at their sergeant's tents. Not only were they to work on the radeau, but many also had to go out on woodcutting parties, scouts, guard duty or other camp duties.

"Extree duty deserves extree pay! At sea we'd not settle for such treatment. Strike the bloody sails would we! If we'd done our work we'd be done! Can't expect men to pull extree duty!" roared a merchant sailor from Ruggles' regiment.

"I totally agree! If they expect us to finish this cursed floating fort for them, then they need to give us time off duty!" spouted a Connecticut man.

"I have no problem working damned hard but I'll be damned if I'm going to do two men's work everyday!" cursed a Yorker. "I agree, let's quit work!"

"What about the food? Can't the bloody generals and governors at least keep us in food up here? Can't expect us to win a war on empty stomachs!" responded a Rhode Islander angrily. "If they refused to feed us and not stop our extra duties then let's refuse to do duty!"

"I'm fed up with this army! I'm wet as hell and damned tired! I vote not to work!" yelled Thomas.

Many of the men in Webster's detachment chimed in with their disgust at their situation and after several minutes of loud expression of this opinion they turned around and walked back to their camps, refusing to do their duty, leaving Captain Webster standing at the waterfront alone! He immediately went to Johnson, who directed Lyman to handle the problem and his councils till he could heal more. They decided the men's grievances were just, so a council was called of the field commanders. They ordered that they were exempt from other work details while working on the radeau.

Meanwhile, Charles had returned to his tent. His headache had intensified. His clothing had been soaked for the second day in a row and now he was chilled. He boiled some water and mixed in some rum and sat down before his tent and sipped it. Still feeling chilled he reached into the tent and pulled a blanket out and wrapped it around him. He quickly fell asleep.

At midday Mary came back to camp. She had been with some of the other women who had come up with them. They were being sent back this evening. Seeing Charles lying in front of the tent asleep, she knew something was wrong. She knelt down beside him and tried to wake him. He only moaned! Placing her palm on his forehead she instantly felt he was feverish. She tried to rouse him again and he responded very lethargically. He sat up and she helped him to his feet. She could feel his wet clothes.

"Charles, we have to get you in your tent and out of these wet things!" Mary ordered.

"Alright, let me lean on you," whispered Charles.

She held the tent flap open and guided him inside. Charles dropped the blanket from his shoulders and he slipped off his coat. He swayed a little. Then he unbuttoned his waistcoat and Mary pulled it off.

"Now your shirt, Charles."

"No."

"You must. Do you have another in your knapsack?" asked Mary. She reached into the knapsack and pulled out a clean shirt. Charles removed the wet one and she helped him put on the dry one. He sat down quickly.

"Charles pull your breeches off and I'll cover you with this blanket." She grabbed a dry blanket and put it over him and he removed his breeches.

"I'm freezing!" chattered Charles.

Mary reached under the blankets and pulled his wet hose off and looked around, found another blanket and put it over him. She took her kerchief from around her neck and dampened it with water from a canteen and gave Charles a drink.

"Take a swallow. You're burning up."

After he drank, he lay down and shivered. Mary dabbed his forehead and sponged his face with the moist kerchief.

Charles' fever raged all afternoon. Sarah came back to camp and saw Charles' situation. She was concerned. They did not want to leave him. He had cared for John. Mary and her mother agreed that they needed to stay with him. Sarah sat with Charles and Mary went to General Lyman to beg for them to stay.

Mary explained about Charles' illness and that she and her mother owed him a great deal because of her father. Lyman insisted they leave.

"But General, Sir, you must understand!" pleaded Mary.

"I do. The man is ill and you and your families are very close. Many here have families very close. I counseled the officers all summer to have all you women removed. You and your mother must not be an exception. All the bad women will think they can come back and whore this camp!" preached Lyman.

"Sir, we are not that sort! Will you allow me to stay and care for him if my mother leaves? I promise, Sir, I will not be any bother to you or your men. I must nurse him. He must live!" cried Mary.

The general paused and rubbed his chin.

"If you stay and if you bother one man I'll have you flogged from this camp! You must leave the moment he is out of danger. I warn you, woman!" ordered Lyman.

"Sir, thank you, thank you, I'll be in your debt, Sir," said Mary as she burst down the tent row toward Charles' tent.

Mary explained to her mother that the general would only allow her to stay. Sarah was not happy with the idea, but she was at his mercy. She had no man in the army anymore. She agreed she would wait in Albany for Mary and that Mary would make haste as soon as Charles was better. They figured only a few days at the most.

Sarah left on a wagon headed for Fort Edward late that afternoon. Mary brought some broth to Charles and spoon-fed him several sips. He was still very feverish and was shaking from his chills. Charles had also developed a raspy cough. Mary realized she had to break his fever or he would develop pneumonia. There were no more blankets! She had to get him warmer. Mary slid off her bodice, hose and shoes, and crawled under the blankets pulling Charles close to her body. She knew how improper her actions were, but she was left with no choice! Gradually they both fell soundly asleep.

"Charles, Charles, sip some of this tea." Charles felt a warm hand reach behind his head and gently lift it forward. He opened his eyes and saw Mary kneeling beside him with a steaming mug. "Drink some of this, it will warm you and help your cough," coaxed Mary.

Charles took a couple of sips and Mary lowered his head. She rang out her kerchief in a bucket of warm water and washed his face, brushing the hair from his forehead. He was not fully awake; his brain felt as if it were in a fog. His muscles were limp. His head ached. As he sipped more of the tea he had a strange feeling for some reason about last night. He could not drink much of the tea and would only take a small nibble of a crust of bread Mary had brought him. Mary sat down and laid Charles' head in her lap and gently massaged his head with the warm kerchief. Charles became very relaxed, almost falling asleep again.

"What time is it?" he asked.

"It's afternoon. Rest, Charles. Close your eyes," whispered Mary.

"Where is your mother?"

"She's gone down to Albany. The general gave me permission to stay and take care of you for a couple of days."

"Mary, you really shouldn't be here like this," said Charles.

"Charles Nurse! Close your mouth and let me decide if I should be here like this or not. You relax and get better so I can get to Albany to meet my mother," said Mary in a half ordering fashion.

They sat in the tent, the flaps tied open. The fresh air felt good. After a few minutes, clouds rolled overhead and a mist began to fall. Mary reached back and closed the tent flaps.

"What is going on in camp?" asked Charles.

"Captain Hawley died of his wounds early this morning. He suffered a great deal. Many of the officers were at an auction this morning when I went to brew you some tea. They were selling plunder and items of the officers who died; things that were not being sent home to their relatives. Samuel George and Gideon Woodwell bought a few things; after all they're officers now. Some new companies also arrived when I was out. It's always funny to see the new recruits," chuckled Mary.

"Remember the captain of the New Hampshire regiment, Captain Rogers? He was the big news. When I was at the mess kitchens everyone was telling how he and two men had just returned from a scout. The captain was really raising a commotion. They said he and four men had gone up the lake and they had hidden their boat. The captain left two of his men to guard it and he and the other two marched to see Crown Point. They said he snuck in close to the fort at dark and watched the French, but couldn't find a good opportunity to take a captive, so they headed back. When they got to where they left the boat the guards had deserted and taken the boat! Rogers and the others walked all the way back! The men at the kitchens said he was as angry as a nest of hornets after being knocked from a tree! They said he marched directly to Johnson and demanded the two men! Everyone's talking about it," said Mary with excitement.

Mary held Charles' head up and gave him another sip of the lukewarm tea. Charles' eyes caught a glimpse of Mary's stockings, bodice and shoes lying beside his bedding. Again that strange feeling came over him as he wondered about the night before. Why had she taken them off? What had happened? Why couldn't he remember? Slowly Charles slipped into another deep sleep.

For nearly a week Mary nursed Charles back to health. His fever and headaches lasted for almost four more days. His body had become very weak. There were many ill men in the camp by this time, and wagons returning south carried more and more men being sent home unfit. At the same time recruits and stores arrived almost daily. Mary kept Charles abreast of the goings-on around the camp. The many scouting parties intrigued him, especially Captain Rogers of New Hampshire.

Toward the end of September, Charles was beginning to move about. He had started by just sitting outside the tent for an hour, then several hours, and then short strolls around the camp when the weather allowed it. The season was changing: Most days were cool and rainy. The woods were beginning to change as the leaves became colorful.

An extra fondness had grown between Charles and Mary. Not only had she helped him through his illness, but also she had helped him relax his mind after the mental torment of battle. As Charles had watched her about the camp he had begun to realize her maturity. He had consoled himself in the idea that she was not a child any longer, but a vibrant woman whom he cared for deeply. They had known that the day would come when Mary would have to leave and join her mother. It was September 28, the Sabbath day. Mary's departure had come.

Charles had been thinking of Mary and Sarah's predicament. He rose early and composed two lengthy letters. The first was to his parents.

"Mother and Father,

There has been more bad news since I wrote you last. John Benjamin's arm began to suffer from a terrible infection. The surgeon had to cut it off and it would not heal properly. Reverend Wood saw the urgency and sent for Mrs. Benjamin and Mary to come back to our camp, as he was not expected to live. Alas, the same day of their arrival he passed away. The poor women are devastated. They have no home, father, nor husband and they are being sent back home with our regiment's ill.

Mother, I know that you will be against what I am going to ask of you, but I am hoping that with your support our community will not look down at my help for these dear friends but rather understand my willingness. I have offered them to stay in my cottage during my absence. They would be able to keep up the house. Once I come home or they get on their feet, whichever comes first, we can see to a more proper residence. I am also writing to Goodwife Greenleaf to see if she could use the assistance of Mrs. Benjamin or Mary. First hand I know of Mary's nursing qualities. I have been ill now over a week and she has attended me with great skill. If you or father have any other suggestions for their employ in the community please make arrangements for them.

I implore you, take them in and see to their needs until I may again arrive home. I promised John on his deathbed I would watch over them! I remain your loving son,

Charles."

Charles penned a letter of recommendation to Goodwife Greenleaf, and Thomas, her husband, also wrote to her, asking her to take one of them on as a helper.

Charles had obtained permission from Captain Burk to leave camp for a short time this morning. It was a cool morning with a light frost. Charles wrapped a blanket around Mary's shoulders and asked her to take a walk with him. They went along a small trail to the west about a half-mile. Charles knew the trail well from guard duties and woodcutting. They crested a small knoll and in the small valley below them ran a quaint little creek. They sat here on a large boulder, which was softened by a thick layer of dark green moss. Charles pulled a handkerchief from his uniform pocket and unfolded it, revealing some cheese, bread and sugar. He broke the cheese in two and handed half to Mary, then sprinkled part of the sugar on half the bread and gave that to her as well. They sat quietly and enjoyed the small treat.

After a few minutes Charles spoke up and told Mary how he appreciated her help in his recovery. She did not respond. He went on and explained that he had written home requesting his parents to help her and her mother along till he returned. She still sat in silence. Then he went on, "I have also told them that you and your mother are to stay at my cottage."

Mary jerked her head up and stared into his face.

"I want you to stay there until I can return to Amesbury and help you," he offered again.

"But what will everyone think, two women staying in an unmarried man's home!" said Mary, concerned. "They will talk. I will not have gossip destroy your family. We cannot!" insisted Mary.

"Damn them all Mary! I will not have you on the streets! You have no place to stay, no job and no man to see to you. You must stay there. My mother will see to the gossips and I will be home soon. Please, I insist that you and your mother stay for the time being!" begged Charles.

Mary shook her head. There was silence again. After a few minutes Mary spoke. "I believe we have little other choice. We have no money. Father's pay will not come until all the troops are dismissed for the campaign. If you're sure, then we will stay there; on one condition."

"What's that?" he asked.

"That we pay you some rent, as meager as it may be and until we can afford it you let me make you new window covers and a coverlet," insisted Mary.

"I agree."

Mary reached beside her and grasped Charles' hand. She put her head on his shoulder as he put his arm around her. They sat there quietly for several minutes, neither one able to say their inevitable good-byes. Then they rose and walked slowly back to camp.

While they were gone some recruits and wagons of stores had arrived. They had been unloaded and ill men unfit for duty were being loaded on the empty wagons. Going back to the tent, Charles and Mary retrieved her haversack and rucksack she had made from an old bolster. With her belongings they walked to the wagons for Mary's departure.

"Charles, you must keep warm and stay dry or you'll get sick all over again!" ordered Mary. Her eyes had filled with tears.

The officer in charge of the escort walked over. "Ma'am, are you going with us? You'd better climb on so we can get going. We've got to get to Fort Edward by dark."

Charles had to touch her one last time. Trying to be inconspicuous he reached around her waist and picked her up as if to lift her onto the wagon wheel hub. Mary placed her arms around his neck. The embrace lasted for only a second. They could hold back no longer as they both unleashed a smothering string of passionate kisses! Totally forgetting themselves and those around them they devoured each other's emotions. Then Charles gently lifted her the rest of the way onto the wagon, their hands still locked. The teamster's whip cracked and the wagons began to move forward. Charles walked beside the wagon, their hands and eyes still embracing. Then at the last moment Charles remembered the letters in his breast pocket. He pulled them out and handed them to her, stating, "Mary, my dearest, wait for me. I will be there!"

His legs stopped, his arm still outstretched as the wagon swung down the road into the forest. What had he just done? How could he have shared his feelings in front of the camp! Then as if being slapped to consciousness he fully realized these were his true feelings toward her!

No work was done this day. It was the Sabbath and the field officers had started improving conditions for their soldiers, rather than lose them to desertion. As God had ordered it, a day of rest.

SCOUTEN FOR THIS ARMY

Late Monday morning the field officers were called together into a council of war. Several of Johnson's military family had been touring the encampment and fort site earlier that day. They were appalled when they found only about a half-dozen men working instead of the 500 that were ordered. Charles was ordered to keep a record of the meeting for the colonel.

"Gentlemen, I was shocked by the report by several officers of the lack of work performed on the fort!" Johnson's voice echoed with stern severity. "I gave specific orders, damn it, to have 500 men at work on it daily! Why haven't they?" he demanded, pounding his fist on the table. His Irish temper was ignited. There was no response. Johnson waited until his breathing slowed before he continued.

"Gentlemen, upon reviewing the need of this area for the defense against a possible artillery attack, it has become evident things must change. It is becoming imperative, from reports of the enemy build-up, that we must have a fort with bombproof walls. A picketed fort will do us no good! I have ordered Captain Eyre to engineer this project. These are my orders, Captain."

The captain stood and addressed the provincial officers. "A fort on this spot must be designed to protect our boats and, more importantly, to protect the new road and to prevent the enemy from establishing a direct route to Albany and east to the other colonies! It must as well provide a supply base for an advancing army or a defensible point for an army to retreat. Gentlemen, General, let us step over to the area I am recommending for this new fortress."

The officers followed Eyre to a sandy hill about twenty feet in elevation. Here, just west of the encampment near the lake's edge, Captain Eyre explained his plans. "I recommend building the walls as a 30 foot wide crib of pine logs." Eyre drew the layout in the air with his arms as he animated his fort plans. "The men will dig a 30 foot ditch, utilizing the dirt to fill the crib 10 feet high. In some places the wall will narrow to 18 and 12 feet in thickness. There must be embrasures cut into the parapets to mount our guns. The fort must be large enough to house a 500-man garrison with four regular protruding bastions, firing platforms, and a palisaded ditch on three sides. The lake side of the hill is steep enough that a ditch there will not be needed."

Johnson could not silence oppositions from Lyman and some of the other officers. They not only stressed their earlier objections to digging a fort but also that Johnson was going forth without General Shirley's approval. After a heated discussion, Johnson commanded the moment and issued these orders:

"Seven hundred men daily are to work on this new fort. These men are to be exempt from all other duty. All commanders must see to it that these assigned workers are to be at work daily! That especially the Massachusetts carpenters are to be at work on this fort rather than building huts and houses for their own troops." The three Bay Colony colonels flinched and stared at Johnson. "Starting immediately all work on the boats is to cease, the stockaded fort is to be pulled down, and work is to commence on the new fort." There were some grumblings, but Johnson was the general in command. "Any questions or comments, gentlemen?" None spoke up. "Then you are dismissed. Mr. Eyre, you will see to the details tomorrow. Gentlemen, give orders to your details. We begin at sunrise."

For almost a week, work was continual on the new fort. As ordered, 700 men, mostly from Massachusetts, worked on cutting timber, erecting a crib and digging a ditch. Part of the reason the men were not as opposed to the work must have been that some of them were nearing the end of their enlistments, particularly the men of New Hampshire.

On Saturday, part of the Hampshire men were to be sent home, for their times were finished the next day. While part of Blanchard's men were preparing for their departure, 25 wagons of supplies came into camp. The guard was comprised of part of Colonel Willard's regiment from Massachusetts. An officer attached to the party was Captain Gage. As soon as Captain Eyre heard he was in the camp he invited him to dinner. Gage was an officer in a British regiment, as was Eyre.

The next morning, the remainder of the New Hampshire men was formed ready to march home. Several of the field officers, including Johnson, addressed them, trying to get volunteers to stay on. Charles and several of his mess, having some time before reporting for work detail on the fort, walked over and watched the Hampshire men's departure.

"Gentlemen," stated Johnson. "I fully understand that your enlistments have run out and I blame you not for wanting to return to your homes, but as commander of this army I must ask you to consider remaining here. My Mohawks have left our army and this has left us blind for information. Daily, as many of you know, we have sent scouting parties forth, but to very little avail. It is also of the utmost importance that we conclude this new fortress here on the lake to rebuff any possible attackers."

"General," said Captain Rogers as he stepped forward. He spoke with a slight Scotch-Irish brogue. "I have been talking to several of my men, and there is a group of us that are of a mind that we could stay and do some scouten for this army." He was a tall muscular man, over six foot. He was only twenty-four, but already a veteran woodsman. His weathered complexion, large nose, pronounced features and his size made him a commanding figure. Rogers had been captain commanding the ranging company of Colonel Blanchard's Hampshire regiment. "I am willen to stay the winter here and bring in information, prisoners and scalps; so are my men. There are about six of us."

"Very well Mr. Rogers. We can use your expertise in the woods. Have your men quartered in one of the huts your regiment was using," ordered Johnson.

Toward dusk the next day, which was the Sabbath, Rogers, Lieutenant Woodwell of Massachusetts, Lieutenant Fonda of New York, Lieutenant Richard Rogers and Captain Israel Putnam of Connecticut reported to Generals Johnson and Lyman to go up to the narrows with 20 Massachusetts men, 10 Yorkers, 5 Hampshire men, and 5 Connecticut men. Charles was one of the men from Massachusetts. The detachment marched onto the general parade and Rogers ordered the unit to report to the beach, check their boats, load and prepare to depart. Rogers reported to the generals, received his orders and joined his detachment at the water's edge.

"Mr. Woodwell, Mr. Fonda, Mr. Putnam, load your men into the eight batteaus," ordered Rogers as he un-slung his knapsack and gently tossed it into a bark Indian canoe and handed his musket to a man waiting there. Then he marched down the line of batteaus inspecting each as he passed. Woodwell, Fonda and Putnam followed close behind him. "Mr. Woodwell, have one of your men who can scribe for me ride in my canoe."

"Nurse, ride in the captain's canoe," called out Woodwell.

"Yes, Sir," replied Charles as he hurried over to the canoe. A man was bent over the canoe, arranging several packs and muskets. He stood and peered at Charles.

"You should sit in the middle, the captain will take the bow and I the stern." The man had a proud, leathery appearance with a fair complexion and fair hair. He held his rough hand out to Charles, "Richard Rogers, from New Hampshire," he said and they shook hands.

"Charles Nurse, from Massachusetts. Glad to meet you."

"Crawl in, Nurse. The captain will want you to have writing materials handy. Are you prepared?" asked Richard.

As he was crawling over the packs, Charles answered, "I have my journal book and quill right here," he said as he patted his haversack.

"Push off, men," ordered Rogers in a quiet but commanding voice. He climbed into the bow of the canoe, and then Richard shoved off from the shore and hopped into the stern. The three men took up paddles and maneuvered the canoe quickly into the bay in lead of the eight batteaus as their passengers took up oars and the small fleet began to head across the bay.

As the darkness fell, fingers of lightning began to ripple sporadically through the distant sky. A light rain began to spatter the flotilla. Each man attempted to shield himself from the rain with blankets, canvas, or pieces of oilcloth. Charles unrolled an oilskin from around his blanket, draped it over his shoulders and pinned it around his neck with a touchhole pick. Rogers carefully stood in the canoe and motioned the fleet to keep close together. The boats traversed directly across the bay but when they reached the main body of the lake they skirted the western shoreline. In the final remnants of sunset the western mountains silhouetted the landscape. The conifer forest covering the mountains gave the appearance of a rough felted beaver hat. By the time they reached some of the larger islands where the army's advanced guard was, the wind had picked up and a full-blown storm with rain and hail was pelting the boats. In the darkness of the storm one of the batteaus became lost, but Rogers kept the remainder pushing forward. At several spots along the shore small fires were spotted, but no stops were made.

All night they rowed and paddled, forcing their way up the lake, fighting nature's fury. The rain and wind continually pelted them. They took no time to stop, but relentlessly pushed forward all night.

Then just before daybreak Rogers motioned the boats to fall into the east shore. The boats were cautiously dragged on shore and concealed. The captain ordered the detachment to lay in watch for any enemy movement on the lake. It was a long cold day revealing nothing. They could not build fires to cook, warm themselves or dry their muskets, at the risk of giving away their position. Most stayed awake, alert to all movement around them.

Then, late in the afternoon, the boats were launched and the detachment rowed up the lake and crossed, landing on the west shore. At a small point of ground the flotilla landed. The detachment carried their boats into the forest edge and concealed them. Rogers issued orders to five men to stand guard over the boats, insuring the detachment's transportation back to camp. With the detachment ready to march, Rogers issued his orders in a soft authoritative voice. "Woodwell, take two men as the right flank. Captain Putnam, take two as the left. Richard, take three as the rear guard. I'll take two and Nurse with me as point, and Fonda, you have the rest in the main column." Rogers shouldered his knapsack and pointedly ordered, "McCurdy, Stevens, come with me! Nurse, you too. Keep your paper where it is ready if you need to write messages for me. Any questions?" Rogers opened the pan of his musket lock, checked it for powder, closed it and ordered, "Make sure your muskets are ready! Let's move out."

Rogers, Charles and the two Hampshire men marched into the woods. The fog was thick by this time. The wind had subsided but a steady rain continued to fall. The onset of fall had been painting the foliage for near a week, and the rain from last night and this morn was causing ample leaves to cover the forest floor with a lush carpet of crimson, ocher, green, brown, and orange. The cushion of wet leaves and the rhythmic splatting of raindrops made it easy for the men to advance quickly without noticeable noise.

Nearing a small pond in a rocky outcrop close to the lake's beginnings, Rogers halted the detachment and motioned Lieutenant Fonda forward. The surrounding area was strewn with boulders and heavy foliage. The pristine water of the small thirty-foot pond was being fed by waters careening down the mountainside. "Hold the column here," whispered Rogers. "We are in French territory. I am going down to the lake's edge to reconnoiter. Have everyone lay low, no talking. I'll only be gone shortly."

The four men melted into the darkening woods of early evening and made their way to the lake. Crouching, they advanced, darting from tree to tree trunk, making sure to stay concealed. At the bank of Lake George the four scanned the water and opposite shoreline. With squinted eyes Charles peered through the rain and mist-filled fog. The fog hung very low in the air, resembling freshly carded wool. The visible sky and water had a green cast and the water churned continually but with no uniformity. At this point the mountains towered above those they had traversed through, mostly being tree-covered. To the north and slightly east on the same shore stood an imposing mountain with a nearly treeless face of rock and clefts stretching from the water's edge to the very sky.

Charles' eyes caught a motion by Rogers. He pointed cautiously up the lake toward some islands near its northern end. They could see several spirals of smoke drifting from the interior of one of the islands. With intense effort, Charles peered deeper at the edges of the island. Then his eyes caught the movement of a squad of white-coated Frenchmen moving out of the cover of the trees. Then he watched as they stopped and replaced concealed guards from the squad in key positions. Rogers sent a runner back to order three men to retrieve the canoe and paddle out toward the island and see what was there. The men in the canoe lay waiting a short distance from the island, but soon the fires were put out and no more movement was observed. Just before dawn, Rogers' men concealed the canoe again and they all returned to the pond. They presumed what they had seen was the French army's advanced guard.

Lieutenant Fonda placed the column on the forest floor, under cover of trees and boulders. Rogers and the four men came into the detachment and squatted down near the lieutenant. Rogers motioned for Woodwell, Putnam, and his brother Richard to join them. He addressed these men softly in his mild Scotch-Irish brogue.

"Just to the north we saw the advanced guard. I'm guessing about a hundred to two hundred. We'd best keep away from the lake until we are far past their guard. Are your men ready? I want extreme caution from here forward. Captain Putnam, Captain Heart, take four of the Connecticut men and advance, and find us a point of observation. Ensign Putnam, you have our left. The other guards are the same. Fonda, have your men march single file, not too close together. No noise. If you spot the enemy, send a runner to halt the whole and alert me. I'll take the advance. Wait about five minutes before you move out. Questions?" Rogers hesitated for about fifteen seconds, and then with his three men disappeared into the woods, following Captain Putnam's men.

After advancing about 600 rods, the four men arrived at a creek. Here they waited for the remainder of the detachment to catch up. Following the creek, Rogers and his party meandered through the valley between two majestic groups of mountains. About a league and a half into the valley, Rogers halted the column. Calling together the officers, he ordered Lieutenant Fonda to stay under cover with his Yorkers and most of the Massachusetts men. The remainder, about ten including Charles, along with Woodwell, Putnam, Rogers and his brother, slowly and silently moved off to the northeast.

Following the base of a hill, they continued about 300 rods and ran into one of Putnam's men who had been sent back to lead Rogers in. They began a slow climb up the mountain with Rogers leading. Charles was impressed how Rogers, in the lead, found his way up the mountain, breaking his own trail. At about noon they halted. Woodwell and three of his men were placed as guards over the area they had just traversed. The rest of the men lay low and crawled to the ridge. Being careful to conceal themselves, they stared down to a peninsula, Carillon, lying below them.

By this time the fog had burned off and only a cold drizzle fell. The water closest to the observers was a deep green-blue and as their eyes followed it beyond the peninsula it became a cold blue, matching that of the sky.

"Captain Rogers," whispered Charles. Charles pointed carefully. "Near the end of the peninsula."

"Frenchmen," replied Rogers in an icy tone. "Look close and above all, don't move! Lie still like waiting for a deer," he whispered.

As Charles scanned more of the tree-covered outcrop of the peninsula, he noticed many figures moving. From this distance it was almost like watching the fleas crawling in a dog's fur. Toward the end of the peninsula an area had been cleared and a hundred men were swarming the area, building a structure of some sort. He could see about a hundred rods to the west, where men were cutting timber. Close to the cleared area, Charles noticed rows of white tents. Putnam nudged Charles' shoulder. He looked at Putnam, who handed him a field glass. Taking the glass, Charles peered carefully, trying to count the tents, estimating about a score, by four score deep. With six men per tent, there must be near 2000 Frenchman in the area!

Shortly after midday more clouds began to move in; large, gray clouds, like a woolen blanket covering the heavens. The cool drizzle became a bone-chilling wash of continuous rain. The observers tried their best to cover themselves from the elements and remain vigilant till evening. At dusk Captain Putnam was left with four men to continue watching, while the rest returned to Woodwell's men. Ensign Putnam and two Connecticut men were ordered to take the canoe and lay off shore of Carillon over the evening and to return before daybreak. Fires could not be risked so the men tucked the locks of their muskets under their arms and huddled in small groups, sharing blankets, oil cloths, and body heat. Rogers ordered them to congregate in groups of 5 to 6. Two out of each group were to remain awake at all times. Charles sat on a stump, resting his back against a tree. Four others from his colony encircled the same tree and settled in. He buttoned the breast of his regimental coat closed, pulled the cuffs over his hands and wrapped his blanket around his shoulders. Then taking his oilcloth, he placed it over his head and bundled it around him, forming a waterproof tent. Quieting his hunger, Charles ate a cold meal consisting of bread, a mouth full of boiled beef, carrots and an apple. Sleep came with difficulty.

Just before dawn the canoe returned and the entire group was awakened. Ensign Putnam reported canoes on the water. Rogers immediately moved the entire detachment to the coastline. He placed guards on the land side so no enemy would fire in their backs, and sent Captain Putnam out to the north to scout for the enemy. Three canoes were spotted about 70 rods off. There appeared to be two dozen Frenchmen. They were sitting still in the water.

"Richard, take two men in the canoe, paddle out and try to draw them into our ambush," ordered Rogers. His eyes never left the enemy. Then he ordered, "Woodwell, Fonda, have the men lie perfectly still, no movement, no sounds; lay ambush!" The canoe was paddled out to about 30 rods then turned about and paddled back. Rather than following, the enemy paddled about a half-mile down the lake and landed.

Then Captain Putnam came rushing into Rogers' party. "Captain Rogers, Indians, coming fast!" Putnam was breathing hard; he had just sprinted back to warn Rogers. "Indians, about 50, and some Frenchmen farther in the distance. They are coming at our backs from the north!"

"Alright, three columns, I'll take the left with the Hampshire and Connecticut men; Fonda you have the right, and Woodwell, take the rest in the center. Indian files! We're moving now! Head for the boats! If you get cut off, make your way as best as you can to the island I designated on our way up the lake. Let's go!" sternly ordered Rogers.

After arriving at the appointed island, Lieutenant Rogers was left in charge of the main body and Fonda's detachment from the previous day went to observe with Captain Rogers, Woodwell and Putnam and Fonda took the Connecticut men and went to scout the area to the north of the peninsula.

Charles remained with the main body. For the next day and a half he stayed undercover. During the time he was not on watch duty that night and the next day, he penned a letter home.

Mother and Father,

Since my last letter to you I have embarked on a most memorable experience. On 7 October a detachment of about forty of us volunteered for scouting duty. I have been away from our encampment for two days. We have a very skilled woodsman as our captain. He is a Hampshire man but was raised partially in our colony, in Methuen, not far from home. His name is Robert Rogers. We traveled on the lake from its southernmost end to its northern. It is some of the most beautiful land which I have seen since leaving home. The mountains, so colorful, their tree leaves are all the colors of the earth. They look as if a marvelous painter planned their pallet for his most noble of masterpieces. After a day and a half we reached a place the natives call Ticonderoga. Here the enemy are preparing a fort. We lay and reconnoitered them for two days before heading back to our army.

The men I was with are a different lot. The captain is a skilled woodsman; a veteran of numerous scouts. He is normally a quiet man, speaking only after he has completely thought things out. He traverses the mountains with the confidence and cunning of an Indian. The men and officers alike, respect him and his expertise.

Two of the officers with us, his brother Richard and Captain Putnam do good justice to our scout as well. Richard Rogers, though lacking some of his brother's experience, has obviously been schooled in the art of the woodlands. He at times gives the air of being very aloof. Despite this fault he seems to be one of the most observant men I have known. Even when he is at rest, he lets nothing pass him unnoticed.

Captain Putnam is from Connecticut. He, as well, has learned from those who have ventured into the wilderness. Not only does he observe our enemy but he seems to watch our party as well. He, like Captain Rogers, easily finds his way in this foreign land. There is almost a rivalry between them at times, why I am not sure, maybe just that of all great men?

I pray Mary and Sarah have arrived safely back home. I hope you were able to help them in their endeavors to seek work and deal with their tragic loss. I will try to return soon. Our enlistments are coming to a close quickly. Please reassure Mary I will be with you shortly.

We have just been ordered to return up the lake. It is so very cold this eve, as a heavy frost is falling over this valley. It will feel warmer to be on the move tonight. Your Son,

Charles

Arriving safely back at the encampment, Rogers reported to General Johnson. Then the general called a council of war. Charles and several of the others who had been with Rogers listened from a short distance.

"Gentlemen, we have news of the enemy at the top of the lake. Captain Rogers has just returned. I will let him enlighten you." The general relinquished the floor to Rogers.

"We reconnoitered the enemy at the Carrying Place, Ticonderoga. A short distance south we observed their advanced guard, and then going closer, we watched them building a fort on the point there. I figure they have about 2,000 men. If we act quickly I believe we could take them by surprise," said Rogers enthusiastically.

The general shivered and pulled a woolen shawl closer around his neck. He took a sip of wine, then spoke again. "Mr. Rogers' bravery and veracity stand very clear in my opinion and of all who know him. His regiment is gone, yet he remains here as a volunteer and is the most active man in our army. It is my opinion that we need many men such as he, in order to scout and eventually defeat our enemy. I want as many volunteers as possible; men who will venture toward our enemies and bring me information, prisoners, scalps, and the knowledge we need to attack!" said Johnson, pointedly and sincerely.

For the next several days, different scouting parties went out. Charles, and the others who had just returned, rested and took turns working on the new fort. This time, large parties of men were continually working and quite a lot of progress was made. Then, on the 15th, Charles got a chance to go out again with Rogers; this time it was a small scout, including Rogers, Captain Putnam, Captain Butterfield, Captain Burk, and John Alexander.

The party left the southern end of the lake in the early darkness of the 15th and paddled their canoe all night, then landed, concealed the boat and lay hidden till dark on the 16th. Again they pushed off and traveled to near the site where they had landed about a week earlier. Here they concealed the canoe and marched around the back of the mountains. This time they continued farther, crossing a little creek and continuing northeast onto the point where they had seen the French before. The tension mounted as they took each closer step, being ever so careful of the placement of their feet, breaking no sticks, rustling no leaves, slipping on no rocks. Just before the first golden rays of the sun appeared, they took up a position in some thick willows only about 300 yards from the French fort!

As the sun rose at Charles' back he became very cautious of making sure he was still concealed. He quietly adjusted himself and made sure there were no sticks about him that would snap if he moved. Before him the majority of the trees had been felled and many had been taken to use on the new enemy fort. To his right was a steep slope falling to the lake, and beyond it was the mountain he had observed on the first scout. To his left, beyond the clearing was a forest, and past it loomed the silent mountains. The rising sun slowly revealed the fort before him in stages. First he saw the distant mountains across the water off the point, the snow-covered tops in a golden glow. Shortly after, the cribbed walls of the fort appeared, now nearly ten feet high. And when the sun had fully risen he noticed the ditch surrounding the wall, several redoubts and a multitude of tents arranged close to the fort.

Rogers motioned for the men to stay put, and he and Captain Putnam methodically crawled forward, inching their way around stumps, over logs and through bushes. Sneaking very close, they hid themselves in a hole behind a log and held bushes before their faces.

Throughout the morning different parties of the enemy came out of the fort area and from the tents. None of the English strayed. Rogers and Putnam were waiting for a group small enough to overpower. Several French guard parties marched close to Rogers and Putnam but none saw them. A woodcutting detail left the tent camp and marched down the road. There were about 25 of them with a covering party of a dozen. Near Charles' position, one left the road and walked toward him and the others. Charles froze; he felt as if he even quit breathing! Then near a tree about 15 yards from them the Frenchman stopped and relieved himself. When finished he hurried to catch up with the others. It was a close call, but Charles and his group had been unnoticed!

Suddenly, early in the afternoon around two o'clock, a single Frenchman came out of the fort area and walked right down the road toward Rogers and Putnam. From their vantage Charles and the others saw Rogers jump up like a wildcat and lunge at the man! The Frenchman immediately drew a knife, which flashed in the sun as he slashed toward Rogers' gut! Then Rogers thrust his fuzee into the man's chest! They stood there in the open for a few seconds, the man still pushing himself on Rogers. Then there was a muffled thud and the smoke from Rogers' musket covered the Frenchman as he flew backwards, sprawling motionless on the ground!

Instantly, a commotion was heard from the fort and camp, and drums began to beat. Rogers jumped on the fallen enemy as Putnam leaped from cover. Rogers leaned forward, drew his knife from his side and, grabbing a handful of the man's hair, sliced a large, bloody piece of his scalp! The captain stuffed it into his coat and he and Putnam sprinted toward Charles just as Indians began to pour from the camp!

Rogers motioned for the rest of his men to retreat, and Charles and the others took to their heels! Their orders had been to make their best way to the boat and await the others for no more than two hours before taking the boat back down the lake.

When Charles and the other two men made it to the boat they slid it into the water and one lay in it while one lay on shore and Charles climbed a tree to watch for Rogers and Putnam. Within minutes they came jogging in.

"Why did you shoot him?" asked Captain Butterfield. Rogers was out of breath, huffing and puffing.

Hyperventilating, he answered, "I offered him quarter—and he pulled his dirk—and tried to gut me—like a deer." He swallowed and took a long breath, "then I knocked the dirk from his hand with the butt of my musket—and shoved the barrel in his chest—and ordered him to take quarter!" He began to catch his breath. "He kept on pushing, thinking he could overpower me. The toad refused to surrender or to quit so I shot him and took his scalp! It should make the Frenchmen leery of Rogers next time I come back to their fort!" Rogers looked about the area as if taking stock of something. "We must not stay any longer. Climb in, let's go!" he ordered.

That night they stopped on a point on the west shore, part way up the lake. At eight in the evening the next night they came within sight of their encampment. The camp guard noticed them at about 500 yards and they could hear the drums beat in the camp. At 100 yards a voice from shore yelled out, "Who goes there?"

Then after a few seconds in a hoarse voice Rogers answered, "Rogers!"

By the time the party had landed and gotten out of their canoe, a crowd of New Englanders filled the beach. "How did it go, see any Frenchies?" yelled out a Yorker sarcastically.

"How many Indians?" asked one of Lyman's men.

"Are they coming after us?" asked a Massachusetts man in great concern.

Rogers stopped, turned and nodded at his party then turned back to the crowd. He sat the butt of his fuzee on the ground and reached into his coat with his other hand and drew out the scalp, raising it above his head! He said in a reassuring yet slightly demented voice, "This one won't be causing any harm!" He stuffed it back in his coat and marched off to report to the general. This trophy created quite a sensation among the men at the beach and the word of it spread through the camp like wildfire. Some men began to cheer while others shrieked in appalled disgust! It was not that they had not seen scalps before, but this was the first taken since the battle, not by an Indian. It re-kindled visions many had started to forget.

A week later Charles received a letter from home. It was dated October 10.

Dearest son,

We have so prayed for your survival and quick return to our arms after you finish your part in God's great plan. We anxiously await your letters hoping only good news is within.

Your Father has been pleased with the harvest. He and your brothers have been working diligently to collect the vegetables before the fall rains get here. Mrs. Benjamin and Mary have been a big help as well, working with them in the fields and barn daily. Their arrival was very timely, not just to help your father, but to help to nurse some of your fellow soldiers who have been sent back to their homes. Mary works with Goody Greenleaf mornings with these men. Mrs. Benjamin has been employed by the selectmen to prepare winter clothing for some of our men who may be volunteering for winter garrisons. She makes a good supplemental wage during her long evening hours, toiling with needle and thread in your candlelit great room. They are staying as you requested at your house. It is as clean as I have ever seen it! The townspeople have accepted their return and sympathize in their loss. They seem to understand your generosity with the use of your home.

Time is dwindling on this cool evening. Everyone is wishing to see you soon.

Your loving mother

As he read the letter his mind wandered to the days he had spent with his father and brothers on the farm. He reminisced about the bounty of the crops and the crisp clean air of his home in New England and longed to be there with his family. He also wondered what it would be like to be home again with Mary; Would the townspeople then be so accepting of his kindness to her and Sarah?

Charles was preparing to leave on another scout to the north. His time was limited, but he wanted to write his parents before he left. Hurriedly he removed ink, quill and paper from his haversack and began a letter.

Mother and Father,

It was so good to hear from you today! I am so happy the harvest is a success. I truly realize the extra burden that my being here places on Father, William and Enoch. I was relieved to hear also that Mary and Mrs. Benjamin arrived safely. Thank you for helping them. I truly wish I was home.

For the past week I have been working on the fort. On Thursday we completed the barracks excepting the roof. With the colder weather it will be a pleasure for our garrison to leave our tents and huts for a proper building! The condition of our meager rations is also a wanting. We have no butter or meal and we are running low on molasses and rum! Monday thankfully forty packhorses laden with bread arrived, but this is no sustenance for men doing hard labor.

The weather here has been fair as I hope yours has. Monday evening and Tuesday morning we received about three inches of snow!

By the next morning it was gone but a sure sign of our weather to come.

Some of my only enjoyment of late has been learning more about scouting for this army. There seems to be a skilled group of men here of which our generals should be proud. Daily scouts go out but most come back either short of their objective or without gathering sufficient information. Captains Rogers, Putnam, Symes and Lieutenants Rogers, Putnam, Fonda and Woodwell seem to have the most skill. Alas I must leave you now to venture out tonight on another scout. Captain Rogers is leading twenty-five of us. We are traveling up the lake in four batteaus. Men are at the beach now mounting two wall pieces and two blunder busses per boat.

Love Charles

Charles pulled his work smock over his waistcoat and put on his gear. His coarse linen smock had become a medium golden brown blotched with stains of green, yellow and red from dirt, sweat and hard work. It had faded and softened over the past several months, and now provided a perfect camouflage in the late fall forest. A melancholy feeling came over him as he thought about his family and home. Although he was looking forward to this scout and getting away from the daily toil and labor, he privately dreamed of leaving for home.

Hurrying down to the beach, he slid into the second batteau. Here he joined six other hardy men: Captain Putnam, Lieutenant Durkee of Connecticut and James McNeil, Nathaniel Johnson, William Cunningham and James Mars, all of New Hampshire.

General Johnson and Captain Rogers were standing at the bow of Rogers' batteau. Johnson was giving him his orders. "Captain, you are to make your way to within six miles of the advanced guard of the enemy and make the best disposition which circumstances will permit to intercept any scouting parties of the French who may be sent on this lake for discovery and take as many prisoners as you possibly can. Any questions?"

"You can count on us, General," answered Rogers.

"I expect you in several days," replied Johnson.

Rogers motioned for the detachment to depart. As the four boats headed out from the beach, Rogers stood in boat number one and held aloft his left hand halting the boats. He ordered the boats to row single file, keeping close enough not to get separated in case of bad weather.

Then he motioned to advance and the boats lurched forward into the dusk.

As they cleared the bay and rowed along the west coast of the lake, Charles took note of the lack of color of the forest. The sky was a gray mist that blended with the dark hue of the water, which was highlighted by the whitecaps rolling across the lake to the east shore. Even the forest's floor was covered with a mat of wet leaves, appearing to coordinate in a rainbow of monochrome shades, and the colors of the tree trunks and limbs ranged from medium grays to charcoal and black. It gave a cold appearance and sensation to the journey. The moon never became visible and rain never fell on them, but everything seemed to have a silvery glow for several of the hours in the middle of the night.

Seeing several fires on a point of land ahead, the flotilla landed about a half-mile from where they thought the French advanced guard was. They pulled the boats on shore and concealed them with limbs and leaves. The next morning Captain Rogers sent Captain Fletcher, Captain Putnam, Lieutenant Durkee and Lieutenant Grant to spy on the guard while the rest of the party stayed hidden. "Try and get some sleep, men, I think you'll need it in the next day or two," ordered Rogers. Two others, an Indian scout and Sergeant McCurdy, were sent out to scout the land around where they were waiting.

At evening Captain Fletcher and Lieutenant Grant came in and reported to Rogers. "They lay entirely open to assault!" reported Fletcher. "The guard has no works around them. This is our chance. There are at least four tents and several guard fires."

Captain Rogers then ordered Fletcher, "Take word to the general that if he sends me a sizable force quickly, I will attack the French guard and defeat them with the element of surprise. Tell him they have no defenses and I believe we must strike tomorrow! Take the five invalids and one batteau. I want the Stockbridge Indians to go with you in order to lead the relief force back. Be quick, go to the general!" The men slid their boat quietly into the lake and sped off toward their fort.

Rogers was not sure of the information from Fletcher; they had not heard yet from Putnam. Rogers took five men and rowed to spy on the guard. They came in just before daybreak, reporting seeing a small fort with several log camps about a half-acre in size.

All the next day and evening the men lay waiting for Johnson's reinforcements. About their only movement was a roving scout that alternated every six hours. It was cold duty. The wind howled, the temperature dropped, but no snow fell.

About ten o'clock in the morning they heard musket fire. Suddenly the boat with Captain Putnam and Durkee swung into view! They landed and explained that the enemy was hotly pursuing them! Durkee had taken a ball in the thigh and Putnam had a bullet hole in his canteen.

"Who are you? Why are you here?" Came a shout from the hill top overlooking their camp! It was two Frenchmen! Everyone in camp froze; no one answered; then the two Frenchmen disappeared back into the trees.

From his vantage point Charles could see two bark canoes appear in the distance. "Captain Rogers, canoes," reported Charles as he pointed up the lake.

Rogers wasted no time issuing orders. "Lieutenant Grant, take McCurdy and five men in boat number three, I'll take Johnson and five more in number one. Take one wall piece per boat and leave the others on shore! Captain Putnam, I leave the rest of the detachment under your command."

The canoes stopped in the middle of the lake. Putnam ordered his six men to hide themselves, awaiting Rogers' next move. Charles and William Cunningham loaded the remaining wall piece and hid at the very water's edge behind some brush.

Rogers' two batteaus raced forward. It almost looked like they were going to race past the canoes and speed for the provincial camp. Rogers must have been trying to make the enemy believe this as well, because when they neared them the canoes tried to close on Rogers and Grant, which drew them within about 100 yards of the batteaus. Suddenly, the wall pieces belched fire, sparks, smoke and shot into the canoes! Charles could see several Indians and Frenchmen disappear inside the canoes. In a quick jerking motion the canoes swung about in total confusion; some were paddling with all their might while others bailed out water. They broke toward the west shore, trying to avoid the guns in the batteaus again.

Charles watched intently as the enemy canoes continued toward his shore. They were steering directly for Putnam's land party! Putnam whispered, "Hold your fire a little longer. When they're upon us, jump up and fire." Charles and Cunningham had rested the stock of the wall piece on a stump before them. It was larger than a musket; almost a foot longer and had a bore of almost an inch.

Charles placed the butt of the piece to his shoulder, rested the cheek of his face on the stock and watched the canoes closely as he took careful aim. Rogers and Grant were chasing the enemy right into Putnam's ambush! "FIRE!" yelled Putnam. Charles had a direct aim at the lead canoe. He instantly pulled the trigger and a cloud of smoke and sparks spewed forth, blocking sight of the canoe. The rest of Putnam's men began an independent fire at the canoes, placing them under a deadly crossfire! Charles held the butt of the piece toward the ground as Cunningham reloaded it from the muzzle. The smoke cleared and Charles saw that his shot had removed large chunks of bark from the canoe's bow.

Several more times, Charles discharged the wall piece. Then suddenly Rogers' voice pierced the din of the battle, "Putnam, behind you! French!"

Putnam's and his men's heads swiveled, catching a glimpse of a large enemy land force charging toward the water's edge! "To the boat!" shouted Putnam. He reached over and pulled Durkee to his feet, and putting Durkee's arm around his neck, hurried him to the batteau, which the other men had launched. They stowed Durkee in the boat while Charles, John Kidder and Richard Rogers took several shots trying to slow the French advance! Rogers and Grant had pulled their batteaus closer and were also firing on the enemy land force, trying to cover Putnam's retreat. Putnam, Charles and Lieutenant Rogers shoved the boat into the lake and climbed in. Just as Putnam leaped, the enemy force appeared at the water's edge and unleashed a spirited fire, punching holes through the blanket he had over his shoulder and splintering holes in the bow of the batteau! The men dug their oars into the water and strained to save their lives, pulling themselves out of range as quickly as possible!

After all three batteaus were clear of the enemy on land, Rogers ordered them to chase the two bark canoes. Rogers, Grant and Putnam positioned their boats and fired all the wall pieces into the canoes, which immediately paddled in desperation for the guard, with the three provincial batteaus in hot pursuit. As they closed in on the canoes the men could see about 100 French regulars forming on the beach! The canoes arrived at the beach just as Rogers' boats came within range of the regulars! They began volleying into Rogers' flotilla! Quickly Rogers order the boats swung broadside to the beach and the three boats fired everything they had into the regulars on shore, driving them into the cover of the trees!

Rogers flagged his men to follow him and the boats rowed out of sight of the French guard. Then they halted. Standing in his batteau, Rogers took stock of his detachment, "Sergeant Johnson, Captain Putnam, Lieutenant Grant how are your men? Make sure everyone is fit and check out your boats as well," ordered Rogers.

Each in turn sounded off to Rogers' inquiry, "Boat number one has no casualties and only minor damage," replied Johnson.

"I have one man, Lieutenant Durkee shot in the thigh," said Putnam. Rogers turned his head toward Putnam's boat inquisitively. "He's all right. The bleeding has almost stopped. The boat, though, is taking on water. Give me a few minutes to stop up some of the holes and we can continue," insured Putnam.

"Boat number four is in good shape and no one is injured," reported Grant.

"Alright, not bad then. Captain Putnam, get your boat seaworthy. We did a lot more damage to them. I think they will be a little more leery about attacking any of our scouts now! There must have been at least 150 of them, and we are very close to Carillon. There's no sign of a relief party. Let's head towards our encampment. Keep a watchful eye out!" The three batteaus made a leisurely retreat up the lake, resting that evening on a large point of land on the west shore.

The next morning, just before daybreak, the flotilla of three boats pushed off again. About half-way up the lake they spotted eight boats headed toward them. They immediately swung to shore. After only a few moments they recognized them to be other provincials; it was Johnson's relief column; Captain Billings with 80 men. After a consultation the officers decided it prudent to not attack the enemy but to return to camp and report to General Johnson.

Upon returning later that day the detachment was heralded on its success; the first battle since Dieskau had attacked the army. There were disputes between Rogers and some Mohawks about the true whereabouts of the French, but eventually General Johnson sided with Captain Rogers and ordered him out for more spying. Charles was to remain; his expertise in building and keeping records was needed in the garrison.

HONOR

On the eighth of November, almost a week had passed since the scout, and Charles was working with a party of carpenters, fitting timbers for firing platforms on the fort's walls. The regimental drums began beating to assemble and the garrison quickly formed on the parade. The walls of the fort were built to their optimum height, and with two completed barracks within, it was taking shape nicely.

As soon as the regiments were formed, the field officers marched out of Johnson's quarters on the ground floor of the eastern barracks. General Johnson led them into the middle of the parade and began a speech. "I would like to commend you, gentlemen, on the fine progress we have made here on Lake George. We are finishing a strong fortification here and are preparing to move forward and drive our King's enemies from North America. We have done ourselves honor in the great battle of this campaign and now I draw you together to honor our King. From today forth, this fortress, built on the southern shore of this lake named after our Sovereign, Lake George, shall be called Fort William Henry. I have chosen this name to honor Prince William and Prince Henry."

General Lyman stepped forward and commanded, "Three cheers for King George and the royal family, Hip, Hip, Huzzah! Hip, Hip, Huzzah! Hip, Hip, Huzzah!" raising his hat in salute as the men chanted the huzzahs in unison.

The garrison really needed this ceremony. Morale had started to deteriorate in the army during the month of November. The weather was wet and cold, rations low, work hard, illness rampant, and homesickness was the rule. On the 17th Charles wrote Mary a long letter.

Mary,

I hope this finds you still well and safe. A great deal has happened since I last wrote you. The officers have not accepted me for a volunteer on any scouts since coming back on the 2nd. They have utilized all of us with any building skills to continually work on our fort. The general has named it Fort William Henry. Four days ago we mounted the flagstaff on the northeast bastion. The red ensign waves boldly in contrast to the gray skies of late.

Our weather has been bleak. The temperatures are cold, the winds blow and it is very wet. It has rained most of the days; a cold rain. There have even been a few snow blasts already.

The work here is endless. Although I am very used to hard work, the frustration of being away from wives and sweethearts brings on severe melancholy to our garrison. We try to support each other, and most of our officers are not tyrants, but we have much on our minds from our experiences this season.

But even more devastating to our troops is the lack of provisions! For weeks now our meat rations have been reduced, and worse is the total lack of some of our promised victuals!

And to top it all we are on constant guard. For the past week we have had false alarms and have been mustered from our sleep almost daily! Now they are overworking us, trying to finish enough defenses to ward off an attack. So many sick: fevers, pains in the head, flux, pukes, and worst of all the pox! Men go home or die daily! There are too many here suffering in these poor conditions!

A week ago 600 of the Connecticut men decided to go off without orders! Their threat of mutiny stunned the officers, who promised to send them home in a few days. The very next day thirty of the Yorkers slung their packs, took up their muskets and deserted! Colonel Cockcraft and Captain Skuyler went out after them. The Yorkers thought their enlistments were up. They returned as well, promised an early dismissal.

Yesterday we carpenters working on the fort, feeling our contracts broken, refused to do duty! Without proper allowance we will not work! Now today we marched to the work and demanded our allowances due. None was given and we refused to work again until finally in the afternoon wagons came in with bread and rum! Additional allowances were given us with a promise of better treatment! We went back to work.

With all of the problems that have plagued this place of late it makes me all the more relieved that you and your mother are safe back home. You can only imagine the intolerable conditions we live in.

I was pleased that our neighbors in Amesbury have accepted your living at my cottage in my absence. With the fondness that grew between us in our short reunion before you left, I find myself wondering on lonely evenings if all is well with you and if you are remembering our friendship?

There is more talk of volunteers for winter here. I am undecided as to staying here any longer than my contract requires. But, I must struggle internally trying to understand if part of my destiny lies here in this army. I do hope to see you soon for I feel drawn to your kindness and friendship. Please let my family know I am all right, but try not to worry them with the sad conditions I have told you of in this letter.

Your Humble Friend,

Charles

That night Charles felt some relief after putting his frustrations on paper. Despite this he still had a problem falling asleep. Sometime after midnight he finally drifted off.

Suddenly Charles woke with a start! There was an uncontrolled shaking; the very ground was shaking; were they under a cannon fire? Charles and his messmates crawled from their tent quickly, struggled, and made it to their feet. Charles's eyes quickly scanned the camp. Was it some sort of storm, artillery, or God's fury? The tents around them shook; several fell. At the edge of camp the horses in the artillery park were rearing, bucking and neighing in terror. One horse had broken loose and was spinning about slashing with its hooves at everything around it. Then as quickly as it started the earth quaked no more.

The earthquake was just one of many distractions that the garrison would soon experience. In two days 1,000 men were added to the garrison, bringing its number to over 4,000. Supplies were not even adjusted to support them! The weather became colder and it was dark, wet and rainy every day! On the 20th the Connecticut men slung their packs and mutinied; marching off. General Lyman rushed to the breastworks and headed them off! He leaped up on the log wall and, raising his hands aloft, tried to harangue them into staying.

"New Englanders, I must ask your mercy and request that you deny yourselves the pleasure of returning to your homes so quickly! We are within days of discharging the entire army. The colonial commissioners and officers of the army feel that within the week we will be leaving! Think how much better we will be thought of if we do not desert, but rather hold on a few more days. Our Puritan ancestors came here with the idea of making this place what they wanted! They did not walk away and we should not either! What say ye, men? Let us return to our work and I promise you we will be leaving for home within the week!" Slowly in small groups the Connecticut Yankees began to return to camp.

That very afternoon 500 were sent down to Fort Edward and then the next day 200 more were sent home. Then on the 22nd the troops were again ready to mutiny, and sixty packhorses arrived loaded with bread! In the evening 150 wagons also arrived with bread, but no meat. That night again it rained. The garrison was becoming desperate—no butter or meat for a month, no molasses for a great while, no meat in camp, and no rum for a fortnight!

Charles, as many in camp, had standing water in his tent. Fires were kindled all over the camps and every man was trying to dry his belongings. Charles had fashioned several racks and hung his blankets and extra clothing to dry. Even in his disgust he could see through all the hell and understand the honor of his part in this army of God's glory. He had just received a letter from couriers who came up at daybreak from Fort Edward. He found a stump, one of the few dry spots in camp, and sat down to read the letter. It was from Mary.

My dearest Charles,

I do not know if you will receive this letter before you march home for the winter. I just received your last letter of the 17th and hurriedly penned you this note. I am so lucky a rider is leaving for Lake George with urgent dispatches late this morn. It was wonderful to hear from you.

It is always distressing to hear of poor conditions for our army. I remember how hard you worked and how dangerous it is being so close to the enemy. I continue daily to help care for the men who are sent back from the war. Every time I see a new face returning I pray that if you need help someone is caring for you. I continually worry about your well-being. With so many illnesses, low rations and cold damp weather, I hope you will not relapse into poor health.

I have given some thought into your dilemma of staying the winter. I dream every night of your safe return, but realize that if a garrison is not left to defend our western borders, the French and their heathen will raid despite the season. I believe your plight will change if you do decide to remain. There will be fewer of you, as most will be discharged, consequently the food will go much farther. With such good officers I also would believe that they would send for more proper clothing for winter garrisons. Our mothers, as have most of the ladies, have been preparing winter garments for just such a purpose.

I know that you must ultimately make up your mind, but if it is any reassurance I understand the importance of our men staying at Lake George. If you decide to be of the select few, I, and I am sure your family, would understand and honor your decision.

The rider is about to leave so I must hurry. Again thank you for allowing my mother and me to stay in your cottage. It is such a nice house. William comes over and helps and spends time often. He is a comfort to me. I feel he wishes he were with you in the army. Enoch makes a point of looking after your horse. He takes great pride in his responsibility. Even though everyone has been so nice to us since we returned I still feel a void in my heart. I became so fond of you in those final weeks and I hope that your comments about our friendship allude to a deeper feeling you have as well. I await your next letter or your arrival home soon.

Affectionately,
Mary

Charles folded the letter carefully and placed it in the pocket of his waistcoat. His heart raced as he went over the letter's content time and time again in his head; her concern, his family, Sarah's and Mary's acceptance in Amesbury, but above all Mary's closing lines. He felt the truth deep within; a much stronger feeling toward her than just friendship. But what was he to make of the comforting by William? What if he as well had feeling for her? His mind wandered and impressions of Mary and home sped through his head for hours, keeping him awake till long past midnight.

The next morning, the 25th, the men in the camp awoke to an inch of snow. General Johnson called together the field command for a council of war. Charles was ordered to take notes as one of the scribes for his regiment.

"Gentlemen," said Johnson in a tired, hoarse voice, "I believe this to be our final council of this campaign. There is to be an attack on our enemy to the north next spring and it is in our best interest to finalize our defenses, prepare this fort as a final staging area for next year and select our winter garrison.

"I have selected Colonel Bagley to command the garrisons here and at Fort Edward. Both garrisons are to act as a regiment under his orders. His second is to be Colonel Whiting. Colonel Bagley is to be commandant here at Fort William Henry, as well as regimental commander. Colonel Whiting is to be commandant of Fort Edward. Edward Mathews of New York is to be Major of the regiment. New Hampshire and Rhode Island are to furnish one captain each, at each fort.

"For a breakdown of the soldiers staying for these winter garrisons I am recommending 232 volunteers from Massachusetts, 193 from Connecticut, 154 from New York, 95 from New Hampshire, and 76 from Rhode Island. Of this 750 man regiment, 320 are to be quartered at Fort William Henry and 430 at Fort Edward.

"The Connecticut troops, after leaving the aforesaid quota, are to march homewards under the command of Major General Lyman.

"A commissioned officer and 18 men are to march immediately on a scout towards Wood Creek and South Bay, to stay out three days. Another scout of the same number is to march to the westward of this lake 10 to 12 miles and stay for three days. A batteau and five men are to go down the lake toward the enemy advanced guard."

After the council had concluded, recruiting commenced. Colonel Bagley, Whiting and Major Mathews were ordered to stay with several clerks to record orders. Johnson had Captain Eyre put together instructions in case of attack. General Johnson, Eyre, the three officers and the clerks sat around a table in the general's quarters. Charles was one of the clerks. He was anxious to hear what the officers had to say, hoping it would help him make up his mind about staying at Fort William Henry all winter. Before Eyre was a small stack of papers and a pair of silver-framed reading glasses. Putting on the glasses, he read the orders in a slow, well-pronounced, English-accented voice.

"Gentlemen,

"If you come under attack you must keep the enemy off the heights to the southwest with your cannon. If the lake is frozen cannon will be useless to hurt the fort. An enemy would be too exposed to attack from the heights over the site of the battle of September. Materials must be stored within the fort to repair gun carriages, ramparts and parapets. Have your powder divided and stored in two magazines, one each under the northeast and northwest bastions. Your off-duty garrison should be prepared to fight fires during an attack."

The captain laid down the papers and removed his glasses, and spoke directly to the three regimental officers. "If you fall under a traditional siege, gentlemen, have great resolution. You must continue your defense until the siege is broken off or the enemy cannon are close to the ditch and have battered a hole entirely through the wall. Then, and only then, should you consider an honorable surrender!"

Eyre put the glasses back on and continued reading again. "If surrender is imminent, demand the honors of war. You must be allowed colours flying, drums a-beating, with one or two pieces of cannon and match lighted and rounds, and provisions." Eyre then looked up over his glasses at Bagley and stated, "and the whole to march through the breach. These honors are only to be allowed armies who make an obstinate defense!

"The only possible attack without artillery would be with scaling ladders. Have your flank guns loaded with grapeshot; sharpened brushwood and gabions should be ready to strengthen your parapets. Keep half your garrisons on duty under attack, maintaining mortar and musket fire day and night. Fire your cannon only at night. I recommend placing a party with a light cannon outside the fort, providing there is a quick retreat."

General Johnson then stood up and spoke. "Sirs, these recommendations are sound and of good military thought. It is my hope that if an attack occurs this winter or spring before reinforcements arrive, you are prepared and steadfast in your vigilance to defend these fortresses left to your command. You are to finish building as much of the forts as possible and make preparations for the next campaign. Have your scribes furnish you with our orders. We will be marching off tomorrow. Dismissed."

That morning the newly appointed officers of the winter garrison had each regiment formed before them individually and asked for volunteers. The drums were beat, promises made and speeches presented. Charles was one of Massachusetts' volunteers. Mary's letter had consoled him enough to make his decision. It reaffirmed support from home. His entire mess had volunteered together to stay and support their beliefs.

The next morn Colonel Bagley called to his tent Charles, Jonathan Gulliver from Boston of Ruggles' regiment and Ebenezer Harthorne from Marlborough of Whitcomb's regiment. "I appreciate you men volunteering for duty here this winter," explained Bagley. "We must finish the fort and keep a constant watch on the enemy's progress. I have a job for you three. We received word that winter clothing has been accumulated in several towns back in the colony. I am sending the three of you to collect them and get them to us as quickly as possible. We have sent dispatches asking the winter clothing to be gathered in your hometowns for you to pick up. Transfer your belongings to the barracks and prepare for your departure on the morrow. Dismissed."

Charles was ecstatic! If only for a day, he was going home. He ran to his tent, opened his knapsack and began cramming all his belongings into it with such vigor he tore off one of the leather straps. He had so longed for the chance to see his parents, brothers and Mary. Thomas Greenleaf and Joseph Nicholes helped him get his meager belongings together and walked him to the barracks. All along the route Thomas was giving him a message to give to his wife back home.

Part way to the barracks, Charles, Thomas and Joseph saw a Yorker sprint past them. Right on his heels was a soldier of Colonel Pomeroy's regiment. Charles and his mates followed them. The Yorker made it to his camp and several dozen of his fellow Yorkers jumped the Massachusetts man just before he reached their camp! Meanwhile, Pomeroy's regiment had seen what had happened and they charged after their man. Hanging back a little, Charles and his mates observed an all-out brawl begin, and all of a sudden the rest of the Yorkers poured out of their camp yelling and swearing, and swinging clubs and cutlasses! They swarmed forth in a hellish manner like a bobcat tearing into a pack of dogs! Several men from each side were struck down. Charles could not believe what he was witnessing! Then, into the middle ran General Lyman, Captain Dwight and several Yorker officers. One of them fired a shot in the air and somehow stopped the fighting! General Johnson and some other officers arrived and could only appease them with a promise of dismissal tomorrow. Charles inquired later into the reason for the ruckus and was told the Yorker had bought a mug of beer from the Massachusetts man but refused to pay and attempted to run off. The morality of the army had met its lowest stage; fighting each other—and over a mug of beer!

Early, just before dawn, Charles, Gulliver and Harthorne were given their final orders. "The weather is bound to get real severe quickly now and the bulk of the regiments are marching off around noon today. It is imperative that you get a head start, for the roads will soon be blocked with thousands of men marching for home," ordered Colonel Bagley in a consoling voice. "You are to ride these horses and make haste." He pointed at three horses being led toward them by a wagoner. "You will have only enough time to collect the needed winter clothing and extra blankets you can and rent a cart or wagon to transport them back to us. Then I want you back here, for these items will allow some comfort to our men. Here are passes and papers for each of you, to get you through the lines and to rent and pay for what you need." He paused, then continued. "I know it will be tempting to take extra time with your families and neighbors, but the entire garrison is depending on your swiftness. One night at home, then back on the road. You are dismissed." The three men climbed onto the horses and galloped down the road toward Fort Edward.

WAR, HELL AND HONOR

For the next several days the three men pushed their horses forward, making only quick stops to water, feed and rest their mounts. At the end of the second day they rested in a stable in Springfield. Both horses and men were exhausted. After seeing to their mounts Charles and the others sat down to a quick meal at the local tavern. The keeper and wenches were very inquisitive, wanting to know the news from the war and how many would be following them. After supper Harthorne headed toward Marlborough and Charles and Gulliver lay down and slept several hours. The tavern keeper woke them shortly after midnight and they road off to the east.

On the outskirts of Boston, Gulliver and Charles separated, and Charles picked up his pace as he headed north toward home. Just past midday he neared the point where the road to the Amesbury ferry turned west. Here he slowed his horse. He wanted to absorb all the sights, everything that he had remembered. On his left the water of the Merrimac was a deep steel blue along the banks and sky blue ice had begun to form. The gray trunks of the trees lining the road stood out dramatically against the background of a bright white covering of a fresh inch of fallen snow. Here and there dormant grass and clods of earth stuck through. The road beneath his horse was muddy and rough from the traffic of a moist autumn. In the distance Charles saw his father's fields and the stone fence along the road. Finally he reached the opening leading down the trail to the family homestead! Charles stopped his horse and just gazed in serene comfort. Home at last, even if only for the night! It was all as he remembered: the majestic oaks, rail-fenced yard, garden, tool shed, and their house—built by his grandfather nearly sixty years ago. Home! He was home at last!

A few moments later the barn door opened and someone started walking toward the tool shed. Suddenly they froze and peered at Charles, then jumped and sprinted to the shed screaming, "He's home, Father, he's here, he's here, it's Charles!" It was Enoch. He reached the shed as Caleb opened the door and stepped out. Charles spurred his horse forward and galloped down the trail. Simultaneously, Caleb began running to meet him. Enoch sprinted past his father and reached Charles first.

Charles drew his horse to a halt and leaped to the ground just as Enoch met him. The two embraced and greeted each other. By then Caleb had hurried to them. Enoch and Charles let go of their embrace and Caleb reached out; father and son shook hands and then pulled each other together. Charles closed his eyes but Caleb's remained open; they reddened and began to tear with joy.

"Praise Jehovah," offered Caleb, "you're home, my son. I knew you would make it back to us." The two men stood in a comforting embrace for several moments of silence. Then letting each other go, Caleb wiped a tear from his eye and told Enoch to fetch his mother. He started to run toward the house but Charles stopped him, saying he would rather surprise her. Enoch tied the horse to a post and the three walked to the back of the house, Charles and Caleb with their arms upon each other's shoulders.

Reaching the fence gate, Caleb put a finger before his mouth, gesturing to his sons to be silent, and in a sarcastic voice yelled out, "Margaret, is that meal fit to eat yet? How long must Enoch and I wait?" The three could barely hold back their laughter.

From inside they heard the rattling of pots and the crack as one was slammed on the table. Then the latch on the back door lifted as Margaret yelled back, "If you are so unwilling to wait for a good meal then you and your son had better eat with the hogs!" Just as she was finishing her sentence she stepped from the door, wiping her hands on her apron. Looking up, her eyes widened, her body became stiff, and her hands dropped to her sides. "Charles!" They all stood silently, as the surprise sank in. Caleb patted Charles on the back. "Praise be," she whispered. "We've prayed for this moment!"

Charles stepped forward and lifted his mother from the step. They both held each other in a long, comforting hug. She sobbed, "You came back to us."

Charles reassured her, "I'm alright Mother; I'm alright."

"Mother, you take Charles into the house and warm him and give him some hot apple cider. Enoch and I will see to his horse and finish our chores before supper," said Caleb.

Margaret took Charles by the hand and led him into the kitchen. "Set yourself down there by the hearth," said his mother. Charles stood and looked all around the room. Everything was in its place; the trestle table, chairs and bench, the stone hearth with the black iron pots,

Margaret's blue hutch with her cream and earthen ware, the tin lined dry sink and behind him over the back door, his father's fowler.

Charles smiled contently and walked to the hearth, warmed his hands, and removed his hat and coat. Laying his clothing on the bench, he settled into the large armchair close to the fire. His mother brought over a mug and ladled some cider into it from an iron pot and handed it to him. He cupped it between his hands, blew gently into it and sipped.

"That's real good mother, real good!" She had spiced it with sugar and cinnamon. She reached over and pulled off his shoes and slid an old rush-topped stool under his feet. "Stop, Mother, no need pampering me like this. I feel uncomfortable, you waiting on me," said Charles.

"I'm going to finish supper then, and make a special treat. You sit here and tell me all you've been doing." Margaret turned around and continued her work and Charles gave her a condensed, sterile version of his experiences.

About 45 minutes later Charles slipped on his shoes, stood up and told his mother, "Looks like you're about ready. Why don't I go and see if father is about finished?" He walked out the back door and stood on the step. Charles raised his hands above his head and stretched. He gazed across the field, scanning from west to east. From around the front of the house Charles heard the plodding of hoofs of a horse and the creaking of a wagon. He stepped out of the garden fence and looked out front, seeing a small wagon being drawn by his own horse. In the seat of the wagon was William, and beside him was Mary!

Charles stepped over to the horse as William stopped the wagon. He grabbed the halter and pulled the horse's head down and reached up and patted him on the side of the neck and whispered, "Hey old boy, its me, Charles. You look good." The horse raised his head, jerking slightly. "Easy, boy, easy. It looks like Enoch has been taking good care of you."

By this time William had tied off the reins and jumped off the wagon. He reached out and shook Charles' hand. "Welcome home, Charles! It's so good to see you finally here!" William said enthusiastically. "We've all been praying for your safe return."

"Brother, it's great to see you! You're a man now! Going to need your own place pretty soon," said Charles. Before Charles could move William had leaped to Mary's side of the wagon and was lifting her down to the ground.

Charles felt uneasy, almost jealous. He had yearned for weeks, anticipating the day he would arrive home and see Mary again. Why was she with William; why had he rushed to help her from the wagon? What type of relationship had fostered since Mary had returned home?

"Charles, you're finally home!" uttered Mary in excitement.

"I am only here on orders from the colonel to pick up winter clothing. I must leave tomorrow."

"Yes, many of the town's women have worked hard collecting items for our men, if they remained in the army all winter. I thought you might volunteer," said Mary in a questioning tone.

"Part of me said I had served my time and part said I had a duty to continue to protect our families and colony from the French. I figured I've probably seen the worst of it," offered Charles.

"Your brother was just taking me from town to your house. I was working with Goody Greenleaf today. Where will you be staying?" She asked.

"With my parents."

"Will you come and visit this eve? You must see your house and talk to mother and me," urged Mary.

"Yes, I shall come after supper, around an hour?" asked Charles.

"That would be wonderful," replied Mary. She could tell something was bothering Charles.

Mary and William climbed back into the wagon and sped down the lane. Just as Charles turned around, his father and Enoch came out of the barn heading toward the house. Enoch took off on a dead run. Charles and his father met about half-way to the back door. They stopped at the well, drew a bucket of water and washed for dinner.

"Its good to see you, son," said Caleb with a relaxed sigh. "The men that have come back said you would make it home. They said you are a pretty good soldier. Are you home for good?"

"Colonel Bagley is in charge of the winter garrisons at Fort William Henry and Fort Edward. I have volunteered to stay with him. He has ordered me to pick up the winter clothing and blankets the women have been collecting. I have only till after services tomorrow."

"We must talk tonight before you leave," said Caleb.

"I promised Mary I would come and visit her and her mother after dinner, but then I will return and stay here tonight. Will you wait up?" asked Charles.

"Of course," reassured his father. "Let's eat."

William returned from dropping Mary off at Charles' house. He drove the wagon to the barn, unhitched the horse and followed them in. "Tonight I will feast with all three of my sons again!" said Caleb proudly.

The three went in through the back door and were drenched in the aroma of their supper; roast beef, vegetables, fresh bread and butter, corn bread and above everything else was the sweet smell of pumpkin pie! The family quickly took their seats around the trestle table; Caleb at the table's head, Margaret at the foot, Enoch on the bench on the table's left, and William started to sit in the chair across from him. He stopped, looked up at Charles and stood again.

"Sit William, sit, I'm going to sit here by Enoch," said Charles. The two smiled and sat.

"Let us pray," said Caleb. They bowed their heads. Caleb closed his eyes; Margaret clasped her hands before her face and smiled.

"Lord Jehovah, we thank You for this wonderful meal we have here before us. It is truly a blessing how You provide for us. Our bounty has been plentiful this season and our harvest has been duly stowed away for winter." Caleb opened his eyes and looked skyward. "Jehovah, You know I am a plain talking man. I must raise our family's praises, Lord, to You for Your thoughtfulness in watching over Charles and bringing him back safe to us! We have laid ourselves at Your feet allowing You to use us in Your Holy War against the French and their heathen. Our son is safe and we feel so very blessed." Caleb paused and lowered his head again. "Oh Lord Jehovah, we thank You for our bounty, our family and our very pursuit of life's happiness. A-men." With smiles beaming they all filled their terrenes and mugs and feasted with joyous conversation. A complete relaxed state had fallen over the household as the family enjoyed each other's company, and the delicious meal.

After their meal, Charles excused himself, and he and Enoch went to the barn. Enoch told him how he had been taking care of his horse. Charles admired the care of the horse and thanked Enoch. They saddled him and Charles rode out the fence gate toward his cottage. His mind darted anxiously with vivid remembrances of when he last saw Mary. His stomach churned, upset; worrying about what he had perceived from their last parting. Had he read more into her good-bye and her letters, or was she actually smitten?

Charles quickly reached the stone fence perimeter of his farm. As he rode up to his weathered cottage he became very relaxed again.

Everything looked familiar, with the exception of a soft colored glow emitting from the windows. He tied his horse to the hitching post and quickly walked to the front door. He almost automatically lifted the latch: after all it was his home. Taking a step back he adjusted his cravat, brushed off the shoulders of his uniform and removed his tricorn. He ran his hand through his hair; then reached forward and nervously knocked on the door.

The door swung open and Mary's soft voice welcomed Charles, "Charles, come in, we have been waiting for you!" Mary's voice was full of excitement. She reached out and took Charles' hand, leading him into the great room. Her touch sent warmth through his body and every muscle seemed to become weightless. Mrs. Benjamin sat close to the fire, winding wool onto a knitty-knotty.

"Hello, Charles," greeted Mrs. Benjamin as she rose from her seat.

"Hello, Mrs. Benjamin. I'm so glad to be home, if only for one day," answered Charles. He stood in the center of the room and just gazed about him, taking everything in; his chairs, table, the hearth, shelves with his books. Everything was in its place and immaculate. Charles' eyes were drawn to the red checked curtains. "I like what you did to the windows. The red really brightens it up. Much better than the old pieces of wool I had up there.

"We are so in debt to you, Charles," said Mrs. Benjamin in a sincere thanking tone. "If it were not for your generosity we would have been homeless on our return."

"It was nothing, nothing any good Christian friend wouldn't do for another," said Charles.

"The least we could do was drape your windows and keep the place up for you. Is it as you remember?" asked Sarah.

"It is as it was, but much cleaner. I thank you ladies," said Charles.

"Will you sit and take some bread pudding and cider with us, Charles?" asked Sarah.

"Oh, yes! It's been months. I'm not sure if I remember what it tastes like," answered Charles.

Mary served Charles, her mother and herself the pudding. The three sat, relaxed, and discussed the local and camp gossip since last they had been together. Charles' mind fogged as he stared intently at Mary. He heard her words as if in a tunnel, yards away. Periodically they would ask him a question and he automatically answered, but he truly was continually wondering if he and Mary would be alone.

The eve was dwindling and Mary suggested she show Charles how they had kept up his farm. Sarah agreed but added, "It is getting late. Do not be long, for Charles must rest for his journey on the morrow."

Charles followed Mary out the back door as they slowly walked to the barn. She again took him by the hand and led him through the yard. He could just make out the outline of the wood-line behind his fields. They opened the barn door and stepped inside. Charles reached to take the lantern from the wall and light it from the hurricane lantern they had brought from the house. Mary put her hand on his and pushed it to the small of her back, wrapped her arms around his neck and pulled them together until their lips met. Without hesitation Charles drew Mary even closer, embracing, kissing, panting. Time seemed to stand still and Charles moved from her lips and began to turn his passionate attentions to her neck.

"Oh, Charles!" she sighed. "I have prayed for your return, for our lives to be brought together again."

"Mary," whispered Charles over and over as he drenched the nape of her neck with wet kisses. "I have so needed you."

As the moments progressed their passions became more intense, as their hands caressed each other's bodies and their mouths glided over one another. He could no longer hold himself back as his impatient hugs began to suffocate them both.

"No, Charles, we must not."

Slowly he slid his mouth down her neck. She could feel his hot breath bathing her shoulders and he began to softly kiss her breasts as he pulled her even tighter.

Then Mary slid an arm between them, and with another soft protest separated their passion, momentarily satisfied.

"You are right, my dearest. Only the Devil would allow us to continue such passions, but I find you so hard to resist," whispered Charles as he gave her one final kiss.

Mary sighed, and then asked, "Will you be coming home in the spring?"

"I know not what the future will bring. If the enemy begins a large build-up of troops early in the spring, I foresee our officers recruiting heavily here at home and at our forts," answered Charles.

"But my dear, I don't know if I can wait that long to see you again. I would have to see you before the end of another campaign. My heart would not survive such a long separation," said Mary as she put her arms around him again.

"But, if we do not drive the French out of our colonies they will return. What kind of a life can we expect with the constant threat of attack? I must do what is needed to insure our future." Charles put his head on her shoulder and continued. "If that means staying in the army till this war is over, then so let it be. I must think of the safety of my loved ones and my honor that I have sworn to my colony."

"I understand, Charles, but I will find a way to see you," answered Mary.

"You must not worry. I will return to you. Don't do anything rash; stay here in Amesbury."

"But what of William?" Mary asked. "He talks nothing but of joining you in the army. He thinks it is so glorious."

"He is a young man now and nothing that I, my parents or you say to him can prevent him from joining any longer. If God so wants it, then he will enlist. My hope is that we can finish this war before that happens."

Charles gently ran his hand over her silken auburn hair. "We must go back inside now, it's getting late and your mother will be wondering."

Then the couple quickly returned to the house, Charles said good night, and he rode to his father's.

Entering the back door, Charles followed the soft glow of candlelight from the great room. His father sat in his chair before the hearth, his head resting on the back of the chair, his pipe gently clenched in his teeth.

"Come and sit, Charles," offered his father without stirring.

Charles sat in his mother's rocker. Both sat for a moment in silence.

"Your mother wishes you to stay. She feels you have given enough. I have consoled her and explained your duty lies back at the forts. Her selfish mothering compels her to keep you safe," explained Caleb.

His father sat forward in his chair and laid his pipe on the table and talked. "War as I experienced, and as you now have, has no reasoning. It is the useless slaughter of men for money, land, or greater men's wishes. Within each of us we must find our own reasons for participation. Those who survive must live through the hell of war. This was something I really couldn't explain to you when you left. I could not find the words to explain the tragedy which surrounded our triumph in '45."

"I understand," said Charles in a soft voice. His eyes were fixed in a glassy stare at the fire. "I have seen Hell; men dying, the pain and suffering. I will always remember the smell of the smoke, sweat, dirt and blood. The men crying and screams of pain." They both again sat in silence.

Charles broke the pause. "I also saw men fight for the honor of God, their colony, the regiment and themselves. Men who, when all others were ready to give up, charged forth and inspired others. Now I, too, must earn my honor. I must continue with this army and return with its supplies and protect our frontier until New England has time to prepare for another campaign. This is my duty, to keep us secure. I can not come home until that security is achieved."

"Go forth on the morrow, son, your mother and I understand and relish the fact that you honor your family with your commitments. We only pray that the Lord will continue to guard you and bring you home safe. We must rest now, for your journey tomorrow will be long." Caleb climbed the stairs to his bedchamber and Charles lay on a feather-tick his family had placed on the floor near the right of the hearth. He slept very little. His mind was consumed with visions of his family, home and Mary. He was concerned about what the winter would bring at Lake George.

In the morning Charles arose and headed out to the Greenleaf farm to rent another horse and to drive to the meetinghouse. He needed to arrive early for services, for the ladies of the community were to bring blankets and warm clothes to load in a wagon for him to take to the colonel's men. When he arrived the wagon was already there and the loading was being supervised by old John Davis, a veteran of '45, who saw this as his service to this war. You would have thought him a general. Davis wore his old, brown uniform coat and soldier's hat and directed and ordered all with his cane; probably the only time in ten years it had not been firmly planted on the ground.

The wagon filled quickly as the congregation stowed their contributions before entering the meetinghouse. All praised Charles and asked questions about the war. Inside, the service was started on time as praises were lifted to God by the Reverend Wells. His Congregationalist sermon was long. It was not only filled with the normal preaching and ceremony but also included praises to the group of local men who had extended their enlistments, and to whom Charles was taking supplies. Charles sat in the pew next to his parents. He paid little attention to the service. His tired mind was engrossed with thoughts of the day when he would return here for good. He could see Mary and Mrs. Benjamin to his left and several pews back. Every time he got the chance he stole a glance at her.

After the service, all adjourned to the yard, where last-minute packages and belongings were placed in the wagon and messages were given to Charles. His family was gathered close to him and they were trying to say their good-byes amongst the crowd. Charles' eyes strained, searching the crowd. He had caught glimpses of Mary, but had not been able to talk to her. An oilcloth was draped over the loaded wagon and the horses were being hitched as Charles gave his final reassurances and affections to his parents and brothers. "I hope to be back in the spring. Do not worry, our worst enemy now will be the weather, but the fine folks have given us plenty of woolens to head the cold off," reassured Charles. He shook William's and Enoch's hands and told Enoch to take care of his animals. He knew it would be a touchy subject, but tried to tell William that he should wait as long as he deemed possible before enlisting. Then Charles turned and said his farewells to his parents. His mother pulled his collar up around him and embraced him warmly. Caleb and Charles gave each other one last hug.

Then he again quickly scanned the crowd; Where could she be? He could not fathom Mary not coming to say good-bye. Charles could wait no longer. He climbed the wagon and reined the team forward. His heart was pounding inside his chest like the thunder of siege guns. He had promised the colonel he would make haste. Charles snapped the reins and the crowd of townspeople cheered, cried and yelled as the wagon lurched forward. Then in the corner of his eye he caught Mary making her way through the crowd. His face began to beam and his heart nearly leaped from his chest as he reined in the team and leaned down and took Mary's uplifted hand. "I looked for you, but could not find you!" cried Charles earnestly.

"I forgot this scarf I had made for you." Charles bent as low as he could and Mary slipped it over his head, folding it around his neck. "If I can not be there to keep you warm and comfort you, this will in my stead. "You must come back this spring!" protested Mary as she held his head between her hands.

"I will return! I will come back to you!"

The crowd began to catch up again with the wagon, and the horses started to step forward. Charles and Mary continued to hold onto each other's hands as the wagon slowly advanced.

"I must go, my duty awaits! I . . . I . . . I," stuttered Charles.

"I will wait for you," whispered Mary. Their grip on each other slipped as the wagon started to move more quickly. Charles snapped the reins and sped forward, his head continually turning to watch his parents, brothers and Mary wave to him.

Mary stood wiping away tears as they streamed down her face. Caleb held Margaret close as she began to weep on his shoulder. Enoch rubbed his eyes as he waved and William snapped a quick salute to honor his brother. The gentle wind blew Mary's scarf over Charles' nose and mouth releasing the sweet smell of her perfume. He touched his hand to the left pocket of his coat feeling the outline of his father's timepiece; its case, which also held the lock of Mary's hair. A tear ran down his face, but he could not turn back.

It had been a campaign of change for Charles and the rest of the army, trying their beliefs, ambitions and their fundamental ways of life. As his wagon swayed and plodded down the road he knew so well, the crispness of the late fall was nearly being overrun by the dead of winter. Every turn of the wagon wheels crunched in the frozen mud and only the whistle of the wet chilling breeze could be heard. As he rounded the turn in the road to head south toward Boston a light mist of snow began to fall like feathers from the sky. What course would Charles' life take next? What more hell would this war take him through, before truly achieving his honor?

Brenton C. Kemmer was born in West Branch, Michigan, in 1954. He graduated from Central Michigan University in 1994 with an M.A. specializing in Colonial America. From 1991 to the present he has had many articles published in national magazines and has published six non-fiction works dealing with the Salem Witch Trials, the French and Indian War, and the War of 1812. Mr. Kemmer is a professional educator.